Fear Has Long Fingers

River View Series, Book Three

Jeanette Taylor Ford

Cover by Dave Slaney

PUBLICATIONS

ISBN: 978-1-9993107-0-7

SaMona Fiction
Copyright © Jeanette Taylor Ford 2019.

This is a work of fiction. The characters came from my imagination and any similarity to anyone, living or dead, is entirely accidental, (mostly!)

As always, my sincere thanks to my wonderful editor, Angela. I appreciate her hard work making my book presentable.
Also to Adam Rigby for his advice on police procedures and order of the police hierarchy, and to Lofty Wiseman, author of SAS Survival Guide, and author extraordinaire, Seumas Gallacher for their advice regarding SAS policies.

Once again, thank you to my awesome cover designer, Dave Slaney

When you look into my eyes,
Can you see the real me?
Can you probe through my disguise?
Please tell me what you see.

Who knew those tendrils of fear
Would find me from the past?
Will you wipe away my tear,
And your love hold me fast?

Cold fingers, long and creeping,
Squeeze around my heart,
To ruin my life they're seeking,
They aim to break us apart.

When once before I escaped my fate,
Now it's found me again,
Will your love be able to expel the hate,
And free me from my pain?

J.T.F. 2018

Fear Has Long Fingers

Chapter 1

Harry's heart beat rapidly when he caught sight of the foam in the river that announced he was in for a bumpy ride. His dad had given in to Rowena's pleadings: he insisted that Harry would enjoy canoeing down the River Wye.

"It's a great river for canoeing, lad, and I'll be right with you." His dad had slapped the boy on his back

"Oh, George! Are you sure you're doing the right thing? You know Harry doesn't like water. Ever since he got swept off his feet by the sea when he was little, the lad has been afraid of water, except in the shower

"Time he got over it, Netta! A river is different to the sea; there's no tides, no waves. He'll be fine. I'll be with him.

The family were holidaying in Hay on Wye, staying in a house that belonged to a 'friend of a friend' of theirs who had let them have it for a week while the owners were away on their own holiday. Part of the bargain was they would look after the two cats, a canary and the pony that belonged to the family. It wasn't really the kind of holiday that Netta and George wanted but since George had been made redundant they could not afford their usual trip abroad. This was a cheap holiday and they had to make the best of it. Harry's sister, Rowena, was quite happy; she loved Hay-on-Wye with its dusty book shops and all its history. Not only did she get excited about reading, she also loved water sports and had been begging her dad to take them canoeing. Harry was happy with all kinds of other sports but not anything involving water

. He panicked as his canoe bumped and twisted and he tried in vain to control it. As he tipped over the edge of a four-foot waterfall, he could barely breathe; his heart seemed to rise up to his throat and he felt the downward rush of his canoe.

The canoe toppled over and even though he was wearing a life jacket, his head went under the water. He tried in vain to remember how to turn his boat as it was swept along by the force of the river. The rains that had fallen over the past couple of days had swollen the river as it rushed down from the mountains; it was not a good environment for a young man's first canoeing trip. Harry totally lost control in the rapids, and suddenly, he knew he was going to die. The canoe fell again on its side. There was a grating sound and Harry felt a crunch, a severe pain in his neck and he lost consciousness.

****

Clarry raced ahead of Lucy as she walked along the river path to the house where her mother-in-law lived. The little dog suddenly stopped, pricked up her ears and then rushed off, barking.

"Clarry! Clarry, come here!" Lucy shouted. The dog raced backwards and forwards, barking non-stop.

"What's up girl? Show me."

Lucy followed the little white bundle down the path to the weeping willow and the seat where Kenny had proposed to her. Clarry bounced up and down as she barked on the river bank. Something in the water, in the roots of the tree, caught her eye. She hurriedly opened her mobile.

"Kenny! Quick! There's someone in the river, caught up under the willow. Bring help!"She knew her husband would be there in moments. Then she dialled 999 and gave rapid instructions for an ambulance. As she stopped speaking to them, two men joined her, out of breath. It was her husband Kenny and Joe from the nurseries.

Quickly, Kenny tied one end of a rope around the tree and the other end around his waist, and stepped into the water. He reached the object, a canoe, lying on its side, and the unconscious lad. It might be dangerous to move the boy, but it was worse to leave him in the water, so he grabbed the lad's torso and pulled but he didn't move. Joe, seeing his predicament, tried to get hold of the canoe from the end stuck in the bank but he had no luck either.

"Phone the nursery for more help!" shouted Ken as he held the boy's head above the water. "Tell them to bring more ropes. Be quick!"

It seemed an eternity but was actually only just over five minutes when Roger and Patrick appeared, both carrying ropes. Joe rapidly wrapped a rope around the tree and his waist and stepped into the river. Roger followed suit. Between them the three men managed to haul the canoe and the boy out of the water and up the bank. They laid him on the grass and Kenny proceeded to give him mouth to mouth resuscitation.

Paramedics appeared; Lucy had run to the end of the path to show them where to go. Just as Kenny was in despair that the boy would not revive, he coughed, spluttered and took a big breath. Everyone heaved a sigh of relief.

Lucy became aware that two more figures were on the river in a canoe, a man and a girl. They were struggling to control their canoe to watch the proceedings but obviously were helpless to land, the current being so strong.

"Idiots," remarked Patrick. "Fancy being out in the river in this condition. If that's their dad, he wants his head looking at."

Although everyone agreed, Lucy felt she had to do something. She cupped her hands around her mouth and shouted with all her might:

"We've got him. He's alright. They're taking him to Hereford hospital."

The man waved and nodded and stopped trying to keep the canoe still, but allowed the current to sweep them on.

Two ambulance men arrived with a stretcher on a trolley. The paramedics had examined the boy and he'd managed to tell them his name,

'Harry'.

"Well, Harry, you're going to be alright, son. We're going to take you to hospital and get you checked over properly. Your dad knows, okay?"

"Yes."

With his neck immobilised, they laid him on the stretcher and carried him up the steps to the upper path and along to the ambulance parked on the road in front of River View farmhouse, the closest road point they could reach. Moments later, the siren sounded, getting fainter as the ambulance sped through the village. The group dispersed; the paramedics to their car and the three men who had gone into the river came to River View to dry off. Patrick returned to the nursery.

Lucy brewed a pot of tea while they showered. Ken gave his men some of his own dry clothes and they sat at the kitchen table, grateful for the drink and a moment to relax after their heroics.

Clarry was petted and made a fuss of.

"She was a hero once before and now she is again," laughed Lucy. "If it hadn't been for her, Harry might not be alive now."

Chapter 2

Rowena's mum, Netta, was furious.

"I told you Harry shouldn't go canoeing! And to take him on the river when it was so swollen with rain – of course it would be bad. What were you thinking of, George?"

"I thought he'd enjoy it once he got going."

"Enjoy it! Couldn't you see the boy was terrified? But you won't listen, will you? Well, one thing for sure, he won't do it again! You've just made his phobia worse, haven't you?"

"Well, I wasn't to know, was I?"

"You didn't know? How can you say you didn't know? You must have known the river was dangerous after so much rain. My poor boy – you could have killed him!"

"But he isn't dead is he?"

"No thanks to you!"

"Mu-um…" Rowena began.

"No! Don't you 'Mum' me! You're as bad as your father; you knew your brother was afraid. But you didn't care, did you? You had to have what you wanted, never mind what he felt."

Rowena hung her head. It was true, she did go on and on about canoeing and, like her dad, she thought Harry would like it once he got started. She loved it; loved the drama and the speed. He was a boy, how could he not like it?

Rowena was a tomboy; she should have been a boy. Her dad would have been much happier to have had her as the boy. Instead, there was Harry. A gentle lad, who was kind to his mother and his sister, who was artistic and talented; fairly good at sport but hated water sports. Come to think of it, what was wrong with that? The one thing he had a phobia about and Dad thought it was a weakness, that it stopped Harry from 'being a man'. Rowena had a moment of enlightenment; she suddenly understood her brother. It was okay to not like doing something – it didn't make him less than anyone else.

She got up and went over to her mother. She put her hand on her mum's arm.

"Mum, I'm really sorry. Please don't hate me."

Her mother looked at her and all the anger went out of her.

"I don't hate you, my love. I'm just upset about your brother, that's all."

Mother and daughter put their arms around each other and hugged. George watched, looking defeated and left out.

****

Harry lay in the hospital bed. His head hurt and he was so tired. His neck was immobilised in the collar and he couldn't feel comfortable enough to sleep. However, he didn't want to sleep, he found that his mind just kept playing over and over the terrifying ordeal he had just been through. Except that he couldn't remember anything from going over the four-foot drop until he came to under the willow tree. Even after that he floated in and out of consciousness.

What a way to end his holiday! Because it was nearly over; there were only two days before they had to return home. School started again next week. It would be his last year and he had to decide what he was going to do with his life. He sighed, for he knew that whatever he thought he might do, his dad would disapprove. It seemed that whatever he did these days wasn't good enough for his father. His mates all said that their parents got on their nerves but Harry wasn't like that. He'd always had a good relationship with both his parents but a few months ago his dad had seemed to change. Now he had time to think about it, Harry realised it must be the strain of being out of work was telling on his father.

He had become moody and seemed to pick on Harry when it wasn't necessary. Harry couldn't work out why it upset his father so much to know that his son couldn't stand water.

It had actually been his fault that as a small boy he had found himself being swept away by the large wave that had crashed on the beach in Devon. He had been afraid of going in too far and his dad had pulled him further in, saying, 'It's fun, it won't hurt you. I've got you.' But his father had stumbled on a hidden rock under the water at the same time a huge wave broke over them. George had slipped and let go of his little son, who had been rapidly swept up and pulled backwards into the sea.

Harry had tried to catch his breath but every time he opened his mouth the seawater came in and no sound came out. Terrified, he'd thought he was going to be swept away into the huge expanse of water and never be seen again.

His father had recovered and swam out strongly and caught him, by then as lifeless as he'd been yesterday in the river.

His dad had revived him, having done first aid training with St. John's Ambulance and he had recovered quickly. But ever since then, he'd been terrified of large expanses of water. Even the school swimming pool filled him with dread but he'd been made to get in and learn to swim, bullied by the teacher. The only time he swam was in school, and now he was in sixth form he didn't have to do it any longer and that suited him just fine.

A nurse came to his bed, interrupting his train of thought.

"Hello there, young man, how are you feeling?"

Harry managed to give her a weak smile.

"I'm getting there. Got a massive headache though."

"That's natural after such an accident. Good thing you were wearing a helmet."

"We have to, health and safety and all that."

"I should think so! I'll give you something for the pain and something to help you sleep."

He smiled again. He did want to sleep; he needed to sleep. If only the bad dreams would stay away. He also contained a niggling worry about something he hadn't yet mentioned to anyone.

****

"What do you mean, his legs are paralyzed?" Netta's eyes widened in fear, as she gazed at the white-coated doctor.

"Try not to concern yourself too much, Mrs Thompson. It could be temporary. Your lad had a nasty accident, you know, and his spine took a lot of the strain. His nervous system has been seriously jarred. This can cause temporary paralysis. It can last a day or a month or more, depending on how bad the damage is. We will know more when we've done some tests."

"Oh, George, what shall we do?" She turned to her husband, who put his arm around her.

"We will deal with it, dear. The doctor says it's likely Harry will recover."

Netta laid her head on his shoulder for a moment, and then she straightened up.

"Get your arm off me! This is all your fault, I'll never forgive you for this, never!"

She hurried out of the room, allowing the door to slam shut behind her. George looked at the doctor, who appeared embarrassed and concerned at the same time.

"Sorry, doctor, she's a bit overwrought at the moment."

"I can understand that, Mr. Thompson, don't worry. I'm sorry, but I need to get on now. We will of course keep you informed."

"Thank you."

The doctor left the room.

Rowena, standing in one corner, observing the scene, wondered what to do. She was upset for her mother but also for her father. He hadn't meant Harry to get hurt, she knew. She stepped forward and took his hand.

"Come on, Dad, let's go and see Harry. Mum will get over it; she's just worried about him."

George looked down and gave her a distracted half-smile.

"Of course. Let's go to Harry."

Chapter 3

"Any idea how that kid is that we pulled out of the water?" Kenny asked Lucy the following day.

"I haven't heard anything. I expect he's okay, he just swallowed too much river," Lucy replied as she put a plate of food in front of him.

"Well, he's very lucky you and Clarry happened to be there, or he'd be a dead lad."

"Well, it's really thanks to you and the guys that he survived. I'd like to know, but I don't think they will tell us anything. We only know his name is Harry."

"Oh well, if I know anything about you, you'll try. This pie is gorgeous, my love."

"Glad you like it. Now, John, you eat your dinner, not put it on your head." Lucy turned to their little boy who was sitting in a high chair.

"I think I'm going to call the hospital this afternoon, see if I can find out anything." She turned back to her husband after sorting out the toddler.

Kenny stood up.

"Well, love, I must be going. Good luck with the hospital."

He kissed the top of the child's head then kissed Lucy tenderly.

"Wave to Daddy, John," said Lucy and the little one obediently waggled his fingers.

"Bye bye," Kenny waved and was gone.

Later, while John was contentedly playing with his bricks on the sitting room floor, Lucy called the hospital in Hereford. She explained about the boy who had been rescued and asked if anyone could tell her how he was as she only knew that his name was Harry.

The telephonist stopped speaking and Lucy heard the tapping of computer keys and she was put through to a ward. She explained again who she was to the person on the other end and asked after the boy called Harry.

"Just a moment," the other voice said and all went quiet. After a while another voice said, 'Sister Wilson speaking. How may I help you?"

"I am just enquiring after the boy you had brought in yesterday after a canoeing accident, Harry."

"Are you a relative?"

Lucy sighed tiredly and then explained yet again who she was.

"Oh, I see. Well, as you're not a relative I can only say that he is comfortable. But the visiting hours are two until four and six until eight-thirty." And with that, the phone went dead.

Lucy looked at the phone in her hand.

"Well, thank you very much," she said, and put it back on the cradle.

****

"I'm going to visit him," Lucy informed Kenny when he came home from work that evening.

"I'll come with you. I'll call Mum and ask her if she can pop over and sit with John while we go."

Lucy put her hand on his arm.

"Thank you, my darling. I love you."

He kissed her briefly.

"In fact, I'll call Mum now before we have dinner."

An hour later they set off for Hereford, leaving John in the safe hands of Sheila. It took less that twenty-five minutes to reach the city and ten minutes after that, Kenny and Lucy were walking briskly through the hospital corridors.

When they found Harry, he had a man and woman with him, obviously his parents. A girl of about thirteen hovered in a corner.

"Hello, excuse us trespassing on you like this," began Lucy. "We're two of the people who helped to rescue Harry. We wanted to see how he was because they wouldn't tell us anything."

George stood up and shook their hands.

"We can't thank you enough for rescuing our lad. There was nothing I could do to help him."

"Yes, we are very grateful," chipped in his wife. "Of course, he should never have been there in the first place. I did tell his father not to take him."

George laid a hand on his wife's shoulder. "Not now, please Netta. These good people don't want to hear us fighting."

"Nor do I," came a voice from the bed. "And they've come to see me, haven't you?"

"We have indeed, lad." Kenny strode over and smiled at Harry. "I'm Kenny Baxter and this is my wife, Lucy. It was Lucy who found you – or rather, our dog Clarry who brought her to you. I came with two of my workers and helped you out."

"I remember seeing your face, I think. Or perhaps I didn't, I'm not sure." Harry screwed up his face trying to recall what happened.

"It really doesn't matter. Don't worry about it. I'm just glad you're safe and alive."

Lucy and Kenny chatted with Harry and his family for a while. After about half an hour, Kenny said,

"Well, we'll leave you good folks in peace. We have to rescue my mum from our little son – or the other way round! We're glad to have met you. This is our address and phone number if you should want to contact us, or if you want to visit the area again, we can help you find a place to stay." Kenny handed George a card and the man tucked it away in his wallet.

George walked a little way with them.

"I didn't want to say this in front of the rest of the family, but we are very concerned about Harry," he told them in a low voice. "It seems that Harry has a form of paralysis, caused by the injury to his spine. The doctors say that he will probably recover but they don't know how long it will take. It could be a few days, or weeks, or months. In the meantime, we should be going home the day after tomorrow. We're staying in a friend's house while he and his family are holidaying abroad but they are coming back then and we'll have to leave."

"We're sorry to hear about Harry's complications," replied Kenny. "But you have our details on that card so if you need our help, just call. We will do what we can."

The man nodded his head and smiled, rather wanly.

"You probably gathered that my wife blames me entirely and I must say I agree with her. I should have realised it would be dangerous after so much rain and my son has a phobia about water anyway. I shouldn't have insisted that he come. Now, my boy is crippled." His eyes filled with tears and he wiped them away with his hand.

Kenny put his hand on George's shoulder. "We all make mistakes sometimes. You couldn't have known what would happen. No father would put his child in danger on purpose."

George bowed his head. "I'd better get back to them," he said and headed back to his family. Kenny and Lucy went through the outer doors of the ward and finally exited the hospital.

"Poor Harry," said Lucy, once they were in the car. "Paralysed. I do hope he recovers, he's so young to be left like that."

"Perhaps it would have been better if we hadn't rescued him in time," remarked Kenny.

"Oh, don't say that! I feel sorry for his poor parents too. They're obviously struggling financially and now they have to deal with this."

"I feel particularly bad for George. He feels so wretched because he'd made the boy go with them but Netta is right, he should have known better."

"That's true, but it's no good going on about it, is there? It's just making a difficult situation worse."

They said no more until they reached home and filled in Sheila on the boy's condition. She shook her head sadly.

"Poor lad, poor parents. Now, I must get off home. I'll see you tomorrow, Son."

"I'll see you home, Mum."

"I'll be alright going along the river path, dear."

"No, I insist. If anything happened to you, Tom would skin me alive! In any case, it's not far and I'll be easy in my mind knowing that you're home okay."

"Oh, alright then, son, if you insist. Goodbye then, Lucy, my dear."

The women kissed and Lucy waved to them as they set off towards the river path. Then she sank down thankfully on the sofa to await the return of her husband. John was a darling and not really any trouble but now she was pregnant, she tired more easily.

As she sat, eyes closed, she thought about the family they had just left at the hospital and in her mind she prayed for Harry's recovery so that the pain the parents were going through would be eased.

Chapter 4

Netta sat in the conservatory of the beautiful rented house and sighed deeply. She should be preparing for the family's return home but somehow she just couldn't get herself together. She wished with all her heart that they'd never come here. She hadn't wanted to but they had needed a holiday – that is, they needed to take the kids somewhere so at least they could say they'd had one – and it was kind of the Athertons to let them come to this house. The holiday had been good too, until the wretched accident.

They all loved Hay-on-Wye, which was so quaint and interesting and surrounded by history. By all accounts it had once been an important place and had once had a castle. The Wye Valley was beautiful and they had enjoyed visiting Hereford and Ross-on-Wye, exploring Goodrich Castle and the activities at Symonds Yat. Yes, for at least ten days they'd had a great time.

Now though, everything had changed and Netta felt that the life had been punched out of her. She loved both her children, of course she did, but she had always been so proud of her boy, her first baby, and it tore at her heart to see him lying helpless in his hospital bed.

Every time she thought about it, her anger against her husband rose to the surface; she felt like she never wanted to be near him again. How utterly stupid could a man get?

"Mum?" Netta looked up at the sound of Rowena's voice.

"Yes, love?"

"Are you alright?"

At the sight of her daughter's eyes, full of concern, gazing at her, Netta pulled herself together. She put her hand out to her daughter and Rowena pulled a wicker chair over so she could sit closer to her.

They sat next to each other, holding hands.

"Will Harry get better, Mum?" Rowena's voice was anxious.

"I wish I knew, Rowee."

"We have to go home, don't we? How can we be so far away from Harry, Mum? He needs us here."

"He does. But we have nowhere to stay. We can't afford to pay for Bed and Breakfast anywhere. And you have to go back to school."

"I don't want to go back to school! I want to stay here, with Harry."

"So do I, love."

"Why can't we stay here with the Athertons? This house is so big, we could easily fit in here."

"We can't impose upon them; they don't actually know us. They wouldn't want strangers living with them."

"Not even for Harry..?"

"No, absolutely not. Your father wouldn't stay either. It was touch and go that they let us stay here while they were away."

They fell silent, each to their own thoughts.

Netta felt thoroughly defeated; she just didn't know what to do.

"Dinner is on the table!"

Mother and daughter looked up at the sound of George's voice. Netta slumped down again.

"I'm not hungry."

"Come on, Mum, you have to keep your strength up. Somehow we have to work out what to do. Try to forgive Dad. He really didn't mean for Harry to get hurt and he's as cut up as you, you know."

Netta marvelled at the old head on the young shoulders of her daughter. What she would have done without Rowena since Harry's accident, she didn't know, for she wouldn't let George near her.

She let the girl take her by the hand and lead her through the sumptuous lounge to the kitchen, where they ate their meals round a square table just big enough to seat four people. There was an elegant dining room but they felt there was no need to use it. Now, they sat down to sausages, mash and baked beans. Probably not the kind of cuisine that would suit the Athertons, but it was good enough for them.

The kitchen was large, with modern cupboards and gleaming accessories. Netta felt they could probably get the whole of the ground floor of their house in the kitchen of this one! The Athertons were obviously well off.

Netta forced herself to eat but the food seemed tasteless. There was no conversation around the table. Only a few days ago, their meals were accompanied by banter and laughter but no longer. The holiday that had been so delightful and the accommodation so luxurious had turned into a nightmare.

****

Lucy was hanging out the washing when a car pulled up the drive of River View Farmhouse. It was an old, rather dull red Ford Mondeo. She put the peg bag down and went to see who had arrived. It was the Thompson family.

"We have to leave tomorrow and we couldn't go without thanking you again for saving Harry," said George.

"Come on in," Lucy invited them and they followed her through the kitchen door.

"This is a lovely place," offered Netta as they sat in the living room.

"It belonged to my Aunt Beatrice for many years. She was my dad's sister and she helped raise me when my mother died. Aunt Bea left it to me in her will and Kenny came to live here when we married because we love it."

"We've been staying in a big, posh house, belonging to a family called Atherton; we were put into contact with them through mutual friends. It's gorgeous, but it has no heart. This place has heart."

"You feel it? It's what I loved about it right from the time I first came here. Now, I've just baked some flapjacks, do you fancy some? And a drink – tea, coffee? Or maybe you would prefer a milkshake or some of my home-made lemonade?"

"That would be lovely, thank you," replied George. "I think I'd like to try the lemonade. What about you, dear, and Rowena?"

"I'd like lemonade too, please," said Rowena. "Mum? What would you like?"

"Oh, erm, anything, thank you."

Lucy noticed that Netta was pale and obviously ill at ease. She could understand that, with her son in hospital. She brought in the drinks and a plateful of flapjacks. She gave everyone a plate and told them to help themselves. Rowena took one and sat down to take her first bite.

"Mmm, this is gorgeous, Mrs Baxter. Wish mum could make these!"

"I'm not much of a cook, Mrs Baxter." Netta attempted a smile.

"We can't all do everything. And please do call me Lucy. Although I love being Mrs Baxter, I think Lucy is more friendly. So, how is Harry progressing?"

Tears welled up in Netta's eyes.

"There's no change as yet. How can we go home and leave him?"

"Won't the hospital transfer him to your local hospital?"

"They said they would once he starts to show progress, some sign of the nerves being repaired. But also, there's currently no bed available where we are. We would stay here if we could but, with George out of work, we can't afford it."

Lucy had a light-bulb moment.

"I've just thought of something. I have another house, here in the village, a bungalow actually, which has just been left to me by a friend who had no family. It is furnished; has everything you might need. I could let the three of you stay there, rent free, as long as Harry needs you here. How does that sound?"

Netta and George looked at each other incredulously.

"I – we – don't know what to say," finally responded George.

"Tell you what, I'll take you to see the bungalow, and then you can decide. My little boy is currently having a nap so when he gets up we can go."

"That's so kind of you. How can we ever thank you?"

"No need. Have a flapjack."

They each took one; Lucy encouraged Rowena to have another which she ate with relish.

"You're right, Rowee, these are very good," said her father and Netta nodded.

"As it's such a lovely day, would you like to come and see my garden?"

They followed Lucy outside, looking at the large natural pond and then through the gate into the walled garden.

"It's wonderful. What's that big house over there?" Lucy looked to where Netta was pointing.

"That's Sutton Court. It's a residential and nursing home. It's run by some lovely friends of mine, the Miltons. This walled garden used to be part of their estate but they sold it to my aunt some years ago because it was too much to look after and Aunt Bea needed more ground to grow her fruit. My husband owns the garden centre and nursery on the other side of my farmhouse and he and his workers help me to keep the garden in order, which they used to do when my aunt lived here."

They made their way back towards the house.

"What on earth do you do with all the fruit?"

"Oh, didn't I say? I have a business called 'Aunt Bea's Pantry' and I make jams and jellies, pickles and chutneys to sell in the local area. I also supply the village shop with bread and cakes every day."

"However do you manage all that with a small child? And another on the way, I see."

"Sometimes I wonder!" Lucy laughed. "My friend Mary Price helps me during my busiest times. She's very good. My mother-in-law, who also happens to be my stepmother, is brilliant and helps me with John a lot. The Milton's youngest daughter, Sophie, used to help me but she's working now – she became a chef after working with me."

"I'd love to help you!" exclaimed Rowena. "I would love to learn how to cook like you, Lucy!"

"Well, if your parents decide to stay in the bungalow, you will be welcome." Lucy smiled at the girl's beaming face. Even Netta smiled and hugged her daughter briefly. Although George was with them, he said little, and it seemed to Lucy that he was like an outsider in this family. Lucy's soft heart felt for him.

"Oh, I think I can hear John. Do sit here on these garden chairs if you'd like. I won't be long."

Lucy ran off towards the kitchen door and soon disappeared inside.

****

"It's lovely. So light and airy."

Netta was standing in the lounge of the bungalow left to Lucy by Sam Williams. She looked around at the green armchairs with embroidered head protectors and the Royal Dolton ladies, tastefully arranged on the mantle and on shelves in an arched alcove.

"Someone had good taste and those covers have been hand-made, haven't they? Who lived here?"

"It was a sweet couple called Emily and Samuel Williams. She died in March and he died only a few weeks ago. She had cancer and he looked after her devotedly. Then he died in his sleep. They had no children, sadly, so I kept watch over them, especially after Emily had gone and Sam was alone. There is a young woman next door, Sue, who used to pop in as well. Emily loved her home and she made those covers. In fact, you'll see her handiwork all over the house. Sam loved his garden and there is a greenhouse where he grew his seeds and tomato plants. I took all the plants away after he died – Kenny wouldn't be happy if I let plants die!"

Lucy chuckled delightfully.

"This, of course, is the main room and through there is a very adequate kitchen. There are two bedrooms through here."

She led them across the hallway and opened a door to a sizeable room with a double bed and an attractive wardrobe and chest of drawers set. The other bedroom held a single bed and a built-in wardrobe. There was also a bathroom with a shower.

They went out to the back garden, which was a fair size and had flowers still blooming in the beds surrounding a lawn that was neatly mowed.

"Kenny makes sure the garden is kept tidy," explained Lucy.

"If we came here, I'd do it," said George. "I love gardening."

"Oh well then, that's great. It would save Kenny a job. So, what do you think? Tell you what, I'll just pop next door to say hello to Susan while you have a chat about it."

Lucy took John's hand.

"Come on, darling, let's go and see Sue."

"Thee Thue," repeated John.

"That's right. I'll be back in a few minutes. Don't feel obliged. If it's not going to work for you, don't be afraid to say no."

****

When Lucy came back about ten minutes later, she knew straight away what their answer was going to be. Netta was already looking in the cupboards in the kitchen and George was pottering around the garden, pulling out the odd weed. Rowena was in the lounge, curled up on the sofa, eyes glued to her mobile phone. They looked at home.

When Netta came through from the kitchen, her eyes glowed.

"Mrs Baxter – Lucy – I can't thank you enough for this. I can't tell you what this means to me – to us. I promise we will look after your bungalow."

Lucy put her hand on Netta's shoulder.

"I know you will. I'm happy to help. You'll have good news to tell Harry when you visit him."

"Oh yes! He was really down because he knew we had to leave the house tomorrow. We need to go and fetch things. Is it alright if we move in right away?"

"Of course. Here are the keys. Move in whenever you're ready. I'll leave you to it now. Do give my good wishes to Harry when you see him."

"I will, of course I will."

"Good. Rowena, here's my number. If you want to come and help me on Saturdays or whatever, just give me a call."

"Oh thank you. I will. Can I come tomorrow?"

Lucy laughed.

"My word, you are keen! Yes, just let me know, okay?"

As Lucy drove away with John in his seat in the back of the car, she felt happy that she was able to help this family. She hoped that the obvious rift between the husband and wife would eventually be bridged.

"Thank you for leaving me your house, Sam," she murmured. "It's enabled me to help some people who desperately needed a fairy godmother."

Chapter 5

The Thompson family quickly settled into the bungalow in Dorothy Avenue. As soon as Lucy had left them, they piled back into their old Mondeo and went to collect their things from their holiday house and they stayed in Sam's home that very night.

"I don't know what it is about this house, but I feel more at home here than I did in that house, even though it is beautiful," commented Netta to Rowena.

"I think it's because, although their house is gorgeous, it's not homely like this is."

Netta nodded.

"Yes, you're right. It is homely. Sort of welcoming really. I would have liked to know the old couple who lived here, they sounded like lovely people."

"Yes. Dad likes it too, he is happy as Larry out in the garden."

"Humph! Long may he stay out there."

"Oh Mum! Please forgive Dad, he's really miserable."

"I'll think about it."

"You think too much, Mum!"

A knock came at the door.

"I wonder who that is?"

"I don't suppose it's anyone for us, probably a passing trader. Go answer it, will you Rowee, please?"

The girl went to open the door to Kenny.

"Hello there, Rowena. I've come to see your dad."

"He's in the back garden."

"Oh, ok, I'll go round."

Not long after, both Kenny and George appeared at the back door.

"Netta, love, Mr Baxter here has offered me work!"

Netta looked at her husband, who seemed much younger than he had earlier, and then at Kenny.

"What's this?"

"Well, Lucy told me that George here loves gardening and I know he has no work just now so I thought he could come and work for me while you're here. I'm sure you could do with some money coming in."

Netta sat down on a kitchen chair, her eyes brimming with tears.

"Oh, Mr Baxter, you don't know what this means to us. I can't thank you enough."

George went over to his wife and put his hand on her shoulder. She patted his hand, sniffed and offered a watery smile. He smiled too; it was the first time she'd allowed him to touch her since the accident. She'd even made him sleep in the small bedroom while Rowena slept with her mother in the double bed.

"We start work at eight and finish around five-thirty to six-ish. It's a long day, but you do get an hour for lunch and a break in the morning and afternoon. We keep the garden centre open until eight in the summer, six in the winter. We open longer hours because we don't open on Sundays. George, in your case, I'll make sure you are finished so you have time to visit Harry. If you need to go in the afternoon instead of the evenings, let me or Joe know. You do drive, don't you, Mrs Thompson?"

"Oh yes, I do. This means so much to us, Mr Baxter, especially as I'll have to leave my job because we don't know how long we'll need to be here."

"Please, do call me Kenny. Everyone does. What work did you do, Mrs Thompson?"

"I just served in a shop. Nothing special. It was all I could get. But they will need to get someone else now. Please call me Netta."

"Netta it is." Kenny smiled at her gently. "Don't worry, I'm sure things will work out. I'll see you in the morning, George."

"You certainly will."

Netta and Rowena smiled at each other while George went with Kenny to the door. Things were looking up. All they needed now was for Harry to get well.

****

Working at Baxter's Nurseries was a delight to George. He settled in quickly and was good at whatever he was asked to do. Everyone was friendly and welcoming. People, workers and customers alike, would say hello, whether they'd seen him before or not. What a lovely atmosphere to work in! His admiration for his boss, Kenny, grew, as he saw how he treated his staff and the customers.

Most of all, he loved the plants. It wasn't until he moved away from London that he realised how much he loved growing things. They rented a small terraced house on the outskirts of Manchester with only a back yard, but even so, he had flowers in a tub and tomato plants in a sheltered spot. He had a flair for hanging baskets and had provided his neighbours with them so that each house had a floral display. He hoped his next-door neighbours, Bill and Madge, were keeping his basket watered. They said they would but of course they should have been home by now. In fact, they really should go and take more of their things out of the house and notify their landlord. He might want to sublet the house while they were away as they really could do with not having to pay the rent. He decided to talk with Netta about it that evening.

"Hello there, George," Lucy's voice sang out as he worked on the front flower bed. He looked up to see her with little John in tow just coming in.

"Hello there, Lucy and John. What are you doing today then, little fellow?"

"We've come to say hello to Grandma, haven't we John-John? And to have a cake with my friend. She will be here in a while."

"That's nice. Have a good time."

George returned to his dead-heading and Lucy and John went inside. As he worked, he saw people coming and going and wondered with whom Lucy was having a cake. Not that it mattered; he was sure she was friendly with lots of people. The thought occurred to him that she was probably going to buy one of her own cakes! That amused him and made him smile as he continued with his cutting.

Rose bushes edged the garden centre and a grassy path that people could walk along to see them in mature form; Baxter's was a specialist rose growers. Even in the couple of days he'd worked there, George had already learned so much and each new piece of information was gold. Apart from the obvious worry of Harry's condition and Netta's coolness towards him – which thankfully seemed to be getting a bit warmer – he couldn't remember when he'd felt so content. He hoped nothing would happen to burst his bubble.

Chapter 6

"I hear a new family has moved into Sam's bungalow?" Lucy's friend Stephanie said, her head to one side, eyebrows crooked in a questioning expression.

"Yes. You heard about the boy that Kenny and Joe rescued from the river? He is still in hospital; the accident has caused paralysis that they hope is temporary. But obviously the family didn't want to go home and leave him here alone. So I've let the three of them stay in Sam's place. I thought they might as well; the place was empty and they needed somewhere."

Steph nodded.

"They aren'tt very well off. The father was out of work and they had been holidaying in a friend's house in Hay. But they couldn't stay there after the family came home. I've let them live rent free to help them out. And Kenny has given the dad a job here at the nursery – you might have seen him pruning the roses as you came in."

Stephanie frowned as she thought back to when she had come in.

"Oh yes, there was a man doing the roses but he wasn't near so I didn't really see him. You're very generous, Lucy. I hope they don't take advantage of your good nature."

"I really don't think they're that kind of people, Steph."

"Well, I hope you're right. So, what are you going to call this baby? Do you know if it's a boy or a girl?"

"No, we don't know. We decided that, as it doesn't matter, we'd like a surprise. I'm not really sure yet what we should call it. I feel that if it's a girl I'd like to call her Rosemary, after Joseph's sister."

"That's a nice thought. I wonder if Alex and I will ever have a baby," she sighed.

"Oh! I thought you and Alex didn't want children. You're so busy running your restaurant."

"Well, it's true that setting up the restaurant was a big thing but now it's all going nicely, I'd like to have a family before it's too late. The clock is ticking you know."

"You have plenty of time, Steph."

"Not as much as you'd think, Luce, I'm thirty five."

"Are you really? I'd no idea. You seem so young, only my age."

"Thanks." Steph gave a tinkly laugh. "I'm actually older than Alex."

"Does he want a family?"

"Of course he does! What man doesn't want a son to play football with?"

The two young women giggled.

"Mmm, this cake is gorgeous. Did you make it, Luce?"

"Of course I did! It's not often I get to eat my own cake but I agree with you, it is pretty good, even though I say it myself."

The two young women chatted about other things as they enjoyed each other's company and the cakes. After half an hour or so, they reluctantly parted company, Lucy to go in search of Sheila and John and Stephanie back to prepare for work.

As Stephanie passed through the garden centre's door, she caught sight of an unfamiliar figure working along the borders. Was that the new man? As she looked, he straightened to stretch his back and, although he had his back to her, there was something about him that snagged something in her memory. Jimmy! He reminded her of Jimmy. She didn't want to think of him or of her life years before. She turned and hurried away, as if she could put distance between herself and her memories by walking swiftly.

****

Netta loved the afternoons she spent visiting Harry on her own. George was at work and Rowena liked to stay at home. She often went with her father in the evenings, knowing her mother wanted time alone with Harry.

In spite of his situation, Harry always showed a positive attitude when his mother came. She brought something with her every visit, fruit or a magazine. He was grateful for her thoughtfulness. The two of them had always been close; something she tried very hard not to show to Rowena. It was just mothers and sons, she told herself; that was the way they were.

"How's Dad doing at his new job?" Harry asked.

"Oh, he's in his element, son! He's never late and he comes home and tells me all about what he's done and learnt, and the people. I've never seen him so happy, apart from the worry over you."

One day, the doctor took her to one side.

"The examinations, ex-rays and scans have revealed that the spinal cord is not broken but we need to operate. We will insert a metal pole on either side of the broken vertebrae to support the section of his back that was fractured and, providing Harry co-operates, there is no reason why he shouldn't eventually make a full recovery."

Netta thanked him gratefully and told Harry what the doctor had said, crying grateful tears..

Not long after, she went to the desk to sign the forms and left to impart the good news to Rowena and George. The operation was scheduled to take place two days later.

When she told her husband what the doctor said, his face lifted in a big smile and she allowed him to hug her in gratitude.

****

After his mother had gone, Harry was left to his own thoughts again. In spite of what his mother had just told him, he feared they were only jollying him along and he would never actually walk again. Bad dreams plagued his nights and, upon waking after another dark dream he tried hard to stay awake. It made his nights very long.

Harry made big efforts to keep the dark thoughts away but he just couldn't stop worrying and wondered what his life would be like in the future. He loved to run, in fact sprinting was his speciality and he'd fostered an ambition to become a professional sprinter. Now, he feared the worry was sapping his energy and dragging him down. Sometimes, he wished he'd never been rescued.

****

With some of the worry over Harry lifted, Netta had something else on her mind.

"George, I'm concerned about Rowena's schooling. She should be starting year nine and can't afford to miss. We should see if we can get her into a school here."

" Yes, you're right. We'll talk with her about it tomorrow evening. While I'm at work today I'll ask about the nearest secondary school. Someone will be able to tell me."

Rowena was happy with the idea.

"I didn't like my school much, it'd be good to start at a different place. I miss my mate Natalie, but that's all."

"Your dad says there's a school called Whitecross this side of Hereford city. I'll apply there for you. They may let us look around it."

Whitecross School was happy to take Rowena. She settled in quickly and found that she soon made friends. Harry's accident and rescue had been in the papers and in a strange way, Rowena found she was something of a celebrity to her fellow pupils, related as she was to the boy in the drama. Her form-mates often asked her how he was getting on and some even gave her cards for him. He was amazed at getting cards from complete strangers, but they helped to cheer him a little. It was nice to know that people cared.

Chapter 7

Two days after the operation, Linda Cooke walked briskly along the corridor towards the young accident victim's ward.

"Hello there, are you Harry? I'm Linda and I'm your physio-therapist. I've come to put you through your paces. Sharon has gone on holiday. How are you?"

"Difficult to say really."

The woman looked at the lad in the bed. She liked what she saw; he had a pleasant face, with brown eyes that really smiled along with his lips. However, she could see the fear that he valiantly tried to hide. Her heart softened, he was obviously a brave lad. However, she needed to be business-like.

"Well, young man, let's see what we need to do."

She worked his limbs, especially his legs, keeping a sharp look out for any signs that life might be coming back. However, it was obvious today was not the day. As she worked, they talked. She liked to learn as much as she could about her patients and, wisely, she also knew that talking was just as much of a therapy as her physical one. She admired him for his stoical attitude towards his condition. He would get well; he had to believe it. The possibility of not doing so was completely unthinkable. Linda would do everything in her power to help it happen.

****

That evening, over dinner with her husband, Linda told him about the boy.

"He's so plucky, Dan," she said. "I could see in his eyes that he's frightened but is determined to get well. I'm glad Sharon has gone on holiday and that I've picked up Harry to work with."

Dan held out his hand and gripped hers for a few moments. He was so proud of his lovely wife and her skills.

"You always get involved with your patients, my love. Try not to become too fond of him. It will break your heart if he doesn't recover properly."

She looked at him ruefully. "You know me so well. I can't help it. I became a physio-therapist because I wanted to help people – you know, make a real difference and help once the medical team can't do anything else. I've seen some tragic things but I've also seen miracles over the years. What happened to Harry should never have happened. His dad should never have taken him on the river when he hated water so much."

Dan raised his eyebrows.

"Was that the lad who had a canoeing accident at Sutton-on-Wye?"

"He had a canoeing accident, yes, but I don't know exactly where. He did say something about a lady letting his family stay in a bungalow in a village. He said her name was Lucy."

Lucy! Dan smiled; Lucy Baxter was helping someone else! She was always helping someone. He remembered how tenderly she had looked after Sam Williams. He wondered if it was Sam's bungalow that Harry's family was living in. It would be just like Lucy to let them live there to enable them to stay in the area.

"Lucy Baxter."

"You know her, darling?"

"Yes. I've had two cases out in Sutton-on-Wye, both involving Lucy. Well, that is, she was the victim in the first one and in the second one it was her family who lost the murdered girl."

"Ah, I see. Harry makes her sound like a really nice person."

"She is."

"Hmm."

"Don't worry, love. She is a lovely girl but she's young, only in her mid-twenties, and happily married to her Kenny. She's a great cook though, you should try some of her cakes!"

"Oh, should I? And what's wrong with my cakes?"

He got up and stood behind her, putting his arms around her and nuzzling her neck.

"Your cakes are amazing."

"Liar!" She laughed. "You know I'm hopeless at making them, they always sink."

"Well, they always taste fine, even if they are a bit gooey in the middle."

"Thanks."

"Anyway, Lucy's cakes have to be good because it's her business. She inherited it from her aunt, it's called 'Aunt Bea's Pantry.'

"You do know a lot about her."

"Well, having solved two cases around her, I've seen her a bit – and tasted her cakes. Wish you could meet her, I think you would get on well with her. She and her husband Kenny live in the loveliest old farmhouse, left to her by her aunt. It's a few hundred years old, I believe. She has a huge garden and they grow a lot of the fruit that she uses in her jams and jellies. It's really nice out there. Maybe I'll take you out to the village some time if you want."

"I'd like that."

Although he'd suggested it, Dan didn't think it likely that he would take her to meet Lucy. What reason could he give? But he was glad Linda was looking after Harry. She was good at what she did. He hoped the boy would recover. He agreed with Linda; the lad should never have been canoeing in those conditions. But it wasn't a police matter. In any case, he was a detective, they didn't need a detective to look into something like that.

Dan loaded the dishwasher while Linda tidied the table. Before long, they settled down on the sofa together to watch some television.

When Dan was busy with work, they often missed out on evenings like this. Linda sighed contentedly and rested her head against him and when his arm came around her, she snuggled into him. This was an evening to savour as all too often he had a call that made him rush away. Not tonight though.

While she was engrossed in Coronation Street, Dan let his mind wander. He didn't particularly like soaps but was indulgent to his wife's desire. The earlier conversation about Lucy and Samuel Williams made him remember the misgivings he'd felt when he'd had to arrest Samuel. He cast his mind back to the investigations he and Grant had entered into regarding that skeleton. He smiled as he recalled poor Farmer Price's disgust at finding not one but two skeletons during the course of his work. In spite of the outcome, it was one investigation he'd enjoyed. Not all of his work produced such good results, or took him to various places in the country. At least Lord Smethwick had reason to be happy, ensconced in his new home on Dave Blackwood's land, helping him with the vintage cars.

His thoughts then brought him round to his Sergeant, Graham Grant, who had met his future wife in North Wales and they were engaged. Dan wondered when he was going to lose Grant. He sighed heavily.

"What's the matter, my dear?" Linda looked up just as the closing music for Coronation Street sounded.

"Nothing really. I was just thinking of Grant. I fear he's going to leave us and I really don't want to lose him. We work so well together."

"You're a good boss, Dan. You will cope if you get a new sergeant. Jenny's a gorgeous girl and I don't blame Graham for not wanting to take her away from her family. Try to relax, whatever is meant to be, will be."

"You're right, as usual, my dear. Do you fancy a nightcap?"

"I fancy a cup of chocolate."

"Your wish is my command." Dan kissed her and rose from the sofa. Making hot chocolate was his speciality.

Chapter 8

While his family were settling down to a reasonably happy new life in the village, Harry was in a place he did not wish to be. As the days went by and there seemed to be little sign that he would recover the use of his legs, he could hardly quell the panic rising within him. It seemed that only Linda, his therapist, understood how he felt. Even his mother, who came every day to visit, now seemed to accept his situation and she sat and chattered away to him about life in the village, the new friends she was making, Rowena's new school and his father's new job at Baxter's Nursery. He barely listened to her. At first, he'd tried to be brave for her sake but as time went on, he sank deeper into depression and when she was there, he just wanted her to go. Not that he said so; he merely waited for the time to pass. With his neck still immobilised, he grew tired of his view of the ceiling. He knew all the little cracks and marks on it. As he watched a small insect making its way across, a small dark speck on the white, he sighed, envying the tiny creature its freedom of movement. Tears welled in his eyes and he felt one trickle down his face..

"Hello Harry."

He turned his eyes carefully to the side and tried to focus on the blurry face. He felt a soft tissue pat his cheek and closed his eyes so they could be wiped, hearing the same voice say gently "There now, Harry, there, there." The patting stopped and he opened his eyes, to see Lucy Baxter.

"Sorry," he muffled. Embarrassed, he felt his chin wobbling.

"Don't be sorry, my dear. You must be feeling pretty frightened and worried."

At the sound of the sympathy in her voice, the tears came again and this time he couldn't stop them and he sobbed helplessly, while Lucy soaked up his tears with her tissues and murmured softly to him.

-Gradually, the flow lessened and eventually stopped and he was able to open his eyes again. Lucy smiled as she wiped away the last of his tears. She stroked his hair as she sat on the arm of the chair at the side of the bed, so she was high enough for him to see her.

"I'm sorry, Lucy. You must think I'm a wimp."

"Of course I don't think that, silly lad. You're being so brave but it's good to have a cry – it helps, you know."

Harry was surprised to find he did feel a little better, having let his feeling go for the first time.

"I don't know what I'm going to do if I don't walk again. I'm afraid."

"That's natural. Anyone in your situation would be. You must remember that the doctors are hopeful. You've had an operation and you have to exercise those muscles and get them used to working again. We are praying for you. The Reverend Trevithick prays for you in church on Sundays too, and I'm sure he prays for you every day. Try to have some faith, Harry."

"I don't really know how to have faith. We've never gone to church or anything. I don't know God."

"Well, He knows you and I'm sure He will help you. But the nerves and whatever that were damaged in your accident need time to heal. I know it's hard to be patient and I'm sure the time passes very slowly in here."

"It's not too bad. There's always something going on. Nurses checking everything, doctors stopping by, the physiotherapist comes every day and the meals. The food's not too bad, I've had worse."

"Hello there."

Harry smiled at the sound of the other voice and Lucy turned to see an attractive, dark-haired woman in a track-suit and trainers.

"Hello, Linda. I've got a visitor."

"So I see." She turned towards Lucy and smiled.

"I'm Lucy Baxter. My husband pulled young Harry out of the river."

"Oh, I'm pleased to meet you. I'm Linda, Harry's physio-therapist. I've come to put him through his paces. I believe you know my husband."

"Do I? Who...?"

"DI Dan Cooke. I'm Linda Cooke."

"Oh! I'm very happy to meet you, Mrs Cooke. DI Cooke has helped me and my family a couple of times."

"He speaks very well of you and has told me about your lovely home."

"Has he? Well, I know he likes my cakes!" Lucy laughed. You must come and see my house. Get him to bring you."

"I'd like that."

"Right. I must go," said Lucy, getting up. "I just popped in to see Harry because I was in town without my son. They said I could see him for a few minutes and I've already been here too long. It was nice to meet you, Linda. Cheerio, Harry. I'll pop in again when I get the chance."

"Thank you for – you know."

She nodded, stroked his cheek gently in farewell, and walked swiftly away.

****

Lucy almost ran through the hospital corridors, hurrying to get out before she was completely blinded by the tears welling up. Not able to reach her car, she sat on a bench outside and allowed herself to give way. Crouching sideways in an effort to hide herself from curious eyes, she let her sorrow for the lad overcome her.

"Are you alright, Miss?" a sympathetic male voice sounded beside her. She nodded, half turning towards the voice.

"Lucy?" An arm went around her and she looked up through her reddened eyes at DI Dan Cooke.

"Oh! Oh, Mr Cooke. I...I'm sorry. I'm being silly. I've just been to see Harry – you know, the boy Ken pulled out of the river? Oh, it's so sad, the poor boy is so frightened he might not be able to walk again. He cried in my arms. I think he's been so brave in front of his mother and family and I think he's been sinking into depression. I didn't want him to see me cry so I hurried out here." She dabbed at her eyes. "You must think I'm very silly. I must look a sight."

"You look just fine. At least, you will very soon. And I don't think you're silly at all. You're a kind-hearted young woman. I understand you've allowed Harry's family to stay in a house that belongs to you. Is it Sam Williams' bungalow?"

"Yes it is. It seemed the best way to help them. How did you know about that? Oh, I just met your wife! I expect she told you?"

"She did. She's very taken with Harry and of course they talk a lot when she works with him."

"I'm glad he has someone to talk with. Your wife – Linda, was it? – seems very nice, very caring. I must go, I'm late already. Thank you, Inspector."

She rose to leave and he stood too.

"I just popped in to leave a message for my wife," Dan said. "I'm glad I did. Are you feeling better now?"

"Marginally. I suppose it doesn't help Harry for me to feel like this. But I couldn't help it."

He patted her arm. "You wouldn't be human if you could walk out without feeling anything. You're doing all you can to help the family."

They walked together towards her car.

"Well, the bungalow is fine for the three of them. But if Harry comes home and needs special facilities, I'm not sure what will happen then."

"I suggest you take things one step at a time. From what I've gathered from Linda, Harry is going to be in hospital for some while so there's no point in being concerned about that yet. There'll be time enough when it's known what condition he will end up in."

Lucy nodded. "You're right. I really must go. Poor John will think his mummy has abandoned him – or rather, his grandma will think I've left her holding the baby! Not that he's a baby now, he's a lively little lad. She'll be tired out!"

They laughed as they reached her car. She opened the door.

"Goodbye, Inspector. It's good to see you again, especially at a time when there's no crime involved."

He smiled. "I think you should call me Dan as there's no crime involved."

She climbed into the driving seat. He shut the door gently and she opened the window.

"If I were you, I wouldn't stand there, Dan, I might drive over your toes – you know what terrible drivers women are!" she joked and gave an infectious giggle. He saluted and moved out of the way. She could see him through her rear view mirror, watching her, as she carefully drove out of the car park.

Chapter 9

The months passed, and the Thompson family loved everything that went on in the village. Rowena joined in the Halloween Party with enthusiasm, dressing up as a witch and bringing a couple of her friends to join in the fun. George and Netta didn't go, they went to visit Harry. Their daughter came home from the party, bursting to tell her parents all about the Grand Wizard and his Lady and the amazing witch who performed a song on the stage and the 'witch's brew', handed out for everyone to drink, which was an interesting plum colour.

"It's a different colour every year," she told them excitedly, "and the witch on the stage pretends to send her goblins to catch the children and they giggle and run away. It was great fun."

"It sounds like a terrific party, Rowee," said her mother. "I'm glad you had a good time."

"Harry would love it. I hope he'll be well enough to come next year."

"But this is our home now! I love it, can't we stay? Harry would love it too – and Daddy has a job here, he doesn't have one in Manchester. And I like being at Whitecross School. What's to keep us in Manchester? Oh, do let us stay."

"We can't make plans for the future just yet. We have to wait and see what happens with Harry first."

Rowena went to bed, hoping against hope that somehow they would be able to remain in Sutton-on-Wye.

****

November arrived and with it came a cold snap that brought out winter coats, gloves, hats and scarves. Netta, George and Rowena loved the Bonfire Night celebrations that took place on Lucy's field, with the huge bonfire, the travelling fair and the remarkable firework display. They were really feeling part of the village now.

Some of Rowena's friends came up, brought by their parents to see the display, having been told it was going to be good. They agreed afterwards that it was.

George had joined Kenny's team preparing the field and the car park. Netta visited Harry in the afternoon and, when he heard about the coming bonfire display, he insisted that she go instead of visiting him.

The village firework display which Kenny did was excellent, every bit as good as the display put on in Hereford, if not better.

Later in the month, the Christmas lights were erected in Hereford although they had not yet been turned on. Even the little village of Sutton-on-Wye had colourful strings of lights and Kenny and his men erected a huge tree on the village green.

The Thomson family delightedly watched the Christmas preparations in the village and were determined to be involved in everything. They'd been told about the village Christmas Fayre which would be held on the village green later in December and were looking forward to it.

Baxter's Nurseries had long since decorated and were selling products for the festivities; everything the keen gardener might want as gifts and lots of other things besides. One could do all one's gift shopping at this place. To Netta, it was magical. She loved to wander around the large nursery shop, marvelling at all the wonderful things. As time went on, so the number of customers increased. One day, when Netta was once again wandering around the nursery, Sheila hailed her.

"Netta! Just the person I wanted to see! Can you spare me a minute?"

She hurried over to Sheila, who was behind her checkout as usual. "Hello Sheila, what's up?"

"I understand you are used to shop-work, Netta. Would you be interested in helping us out during the next few weeks leading up to Christmas and again afterwards for the January sales? We need some extra help."

Netta's eyes shone. "Oh yes, I would indeed! Thank you very much. I love this place, it's magical."

Sheila laughed. "Not so much magical as hard work! When can you start?"

"As soon as you like."

"Great. Hmm, it's Thursday today, can you start on Monday? Saturdays are really busy but if you start Monday, I'll have more time to show you the ropes."

"That's wonderful. Thank you very much. Won't Kenny mind you asking me?"

"No of course not. He suggested it. In any case, he leaves the shop to me."

Netta beamed. "Thank you, thank you. It will help a lot with Christmas coming on."

"That's what I thought. See you on Monday then?"

"You will indeed."

****

In her element working at the nursery, Netta was always willing to do extra – just the kind of employee that Sheila liked, especially at that time of year. She never tired of being there and gradually became acquainted with all the people who worked at Baxter's. Her admiration for Kenny grew just as her husband's had. Netta knew she would be sorry once the busy season was over and she'd have to leave. But she wouldn't think of that yet. 'Take a day at a time', she would tell herself. That was all they could do anyway, with Harry's condition. Everything rested on him.

So, Netta savoured every day and blossomed under the friendliness of those around her. She didn't know when she had been so happy. If it were not for poor Harry, life would be perfect.

Chapter 10

"That's it, Harry, you're doing very well."

Linda smiled as she watched Harry between the parallel bars, hanging onto each bar for dear life. His legs, strapped into callipers, were straight. Beads of sweat appeared on his forehead and his face reddened with the effort as he tried desperately to will a leg forward. Linda's male assistant stood behind the boy, his hand on Harry's back. Linda stood beside him on the other side of the bar.

"Okay, that's enough for today."

Simon helped Harry back into a wheelchair, which stood ready behind them. Harry sank into the chair and closed his eyes.

"I – I can't do it! I've tried and tried and I can't do it! It's no good, I'm useless, my legs are useless."

Although he struggled manfully to hide his distress, tears rolled down his cheeks. Simon silently handed him some tissues and he dabbed at his face. Linda bobbed down in front of the wheelchair and laid her hand over Harry's.

"I know you won't believe me right now, Harry, but you are doing brilliantly. We have made so much progress. You can sit up on your own, and stand with help. The repair operation you had has made a terrific difference. But you have to re-teach your body to walk again, to hold your weight. You will do it eventually."

Harry's shoulders slumped.

"It will be Christmas in a month and I wanted to surprise Mum and Dad by walking by then. It's the only gift I can give them. I want Dad to stop feeling bad about the accident and I want us to be a proper family again."

"You haven't even let your mum see you in a wheelchair, have you?"

"No. I'm always in bed when they come in the evenings. Mum hasn't been coming in the afternoons since she's been working at the nursery."

"Which is good, because it's given us the chance to have these sessions without her catching us out. Believe it or not, you will be walking by then – with crutches, but you will be on your feet."

Harry's eyebrows shot up.

"Really?"

Linda nodded firmly. "Really. You've made wonderful progress and we just need to make your legs a little stronger, get your muscles to do what your brain wants. You'll be home for Christmas."

"That would be wonderful. I don't see how I can though, they are only in a little bungalow."

"I'm sure that they would make some arrangements if they knew you are coming out. I'll have a word with the doctors and then we'll talk with your family. How about that?"

The lad smiled and Linda's heart lifted. She and Simon smiled at each other over the boy's head.

"Right," she said briskly. "Back to the ward with you, my lad. I have other people to help you know – you're not my only patient!"

Harry looked up and grinned.

"I know, but I'm your favourite."

Linda took a playful swipe at the top of his head, wafting a lock of his hair in the breeze it caused.

"Cheeky! Get off with you!"

Simon steered the wheelchair out of the room and Harry gave a salute as he left. Linda gazed thoughtfully at the door as it swung shut. She sat down at her computer in the corner of the room and updated Harry's progress as she had a few minutes before Simon would return with her next patient.

****

When Harry arrived on the ward, he had a visitor waiting. It was Lucy. She smiled widely when she saw him being pushed into his bed area by Simon.

"Lucy!" His young heart missed a beat. He hoped she'd never realise he had a crush on her.

"Hello there, young man. They told me you'd be back shortly, so I waited."

"I'm glad you did."

Seeing Lucy always made Harry feel happy. Beside his family, Linda and Lucy were the two people to whom he had become attached. Lucy had been to see him several times since the visit where he'd cried in her arms. He had confided in her that he wanted to surprise his parents by learning to walk by Christmas and he reported his progress on every visit.

"Simon, this is Lucy, my friend."

Simon nodded and smiled, then turned to Harry.

"Do you want to get back into bed, or stay in the wheelchair a while?"

"Oh, in the chair, I think. In fact, perhaps we could go into the day room?"

"Oh yes. About turn!"

Simon deftly manoeuvred the wheelchair around and headed out of the area again and Lucy followed. It only took a few minutes to reach the room set aside for patients and visitors. Seating herself comfortably in a chair, Lucy looked at Harry and grinned.

"This is a good time to visit you with your mum busy at the nursery. Dad and Granddad are watching John."

"I wish I could meet John, I'd love to see him."

Lucy fished her phone out of her pocket and brought up a photo of John that she'd taken a couple of days ago. She handed it to Harry, who looked at it carefully.

"He's a cute lad. Bet he's full of fun."

"He certainly is, he's become a 'terrible two'! He's on the go all the time. I'm always thankful if he takes a nap but he doesn't often do that now. Dad is good with him though, he'll keep him out of mischief until I get back. He doesn't mind. Usually, Sheila will look after him but the nursery is so busy now, with Christmas close, she has to be there all the time."

"I'm glad Mum has the nursery shop. She loves to be busy and it's so much easier for me to exercise without her coming in every afternoon. I won't be able to surprise them at Christmas by walking, though. I can still barely move my legs."

He looked down at his lap, the blackness closing in around him again. How could he live like this, being unable to walk, do his running? What point was there to life? He felt useless and wished he'd died in the river that day.

Then a hand crept into his, and he looked up to see Lucy sitting on the edge of her chair so she could reach him and see into his eyes.

"Harry, try not to despair. I'm certain you are going to do it."

"Not on my own though," he said, bitterly.

"Maybe not yet, but you will. And you will walk again, I know it, I feel it in here." She put her hand to her heart. He couldn't help smiling. He wanted so badly to believe her but really, how could she know? But somehow her words soothed him and, as he felt the pressure of her hand on his, it was almost as if power passed through her to him and he felt better. He couldn't explain how or why, he just did.

"Linda was talking about me going home for Christmas."

"Well, that's wonderful news. I'm sure your parents will be so happy."

"I don't see how I can though. There won't be room in the bungalow for me, we would never manage."

Lucy sat back in the chair, frowning. She leaned forward.

"Give me time to think about it. I'm sure something can be worked out." She looked at her watch. "Oh dear, I'm afraid I must go, I've already been gone longer than I told Dad."

She stood up, buttoned her coat and picked up her handbag. She touched Harry on the shoulder. "Don't worry, I'll take care of things my end. You just keep working. I'm sure by next Christmas you'll be able to look back on this and wonder that it ever happened."

"I'm not sure about that, Luce."

"My Aunt Bea used to say that everything happens for a reason and sometimes things happen in order to teach us something. There is always a point to life, whatever your situation and there are lots of people who don't let a disability put them off living life to the full."

Harry nodded; he knew she was right but it was so easy to be discouraged. He watched her walk out of the room and when she turned around and gave a little wave, he waggled his fingers at her. Once she's disappeared, he stayed where he was. He had a lot to think about.

Chapter 11

Naturally enough, Lucy told Kenny that evening about the plans to allow Harry to come home over the Christmas period.

"But I just can't see how. Another person won't fit into the bungalow. It's perfect for his parents and sister but no more than that. He'll need certain facilities which the bungalow doesn't have, even if there was a bedroom for him, which there isn't, as you know."

"You're quite right, of course. But if I know anything about you, you'll find a way. Why not sleep on it? You never know, perhaps Aunt Bea might give you the solution during the night."

Lucy nodded, thoughtfully. "That's a good suggestion, darling."

Aunt Bea was Lucy's aunt who had left her River View farmhouse in her will. Although she was dead, it was obvious she wasn't far away, for often she gave Lucy the solution to a problem or a hint as to something she should do. Kenny's suggestion was a good one, Lucy felt, and so she was happy to go to bed early. She needed it anyway because these days her pregnancy meant that she felt worn out by the evening.

Lucy didn't know what woke her at first. Then she realised that the curtains were not closed properly and the moon shone brightly through the opening. The moonlight gave the homely room a mysterious appearance, the furniture hints of dark shapes in the dim light. Kenny lay, sound asleep, beside her. There seemed to be a stirring in the air, in spite of the window being closed against the cold of the December night.

"Aunt Bea?" whispered Lucy. Although she stared intently into the barely-lit air, she saw nothing.

Into her mind came one word: *'Cessy'*.

Cessy? Lucy frowned. Had she heard right? Then, *'Talk to Cessy.'*

Lucy settled down again in her bed. As she did so, Kenny's arm came around her. She snuggled into him. Yes, Aunt Bea was right, she needed to talk to Cessy. With that thought, Lucy allowed sleep to claim her again.

****

"Hello, Lucy, hello there, young John."

The smiling face of Cecelia Milton appeared upon the opening of the impressive door of Sutton Court. Cecelia, known to everyone as Cessy, the matron and co-owner, along with her husband, Neil, of the Residential and nursing home in the village of Sutton-on-Wye, opened the door wider.

"Come on in, quickly. Let's keep the cold out."

Not long later, they were in Cessy and Neil's private sitting room, with John playing happily with toys Cessy kept for visiting children.

Tea and biscuits had been brought but John was busy with the toys and wasn't interested. The two women had a chance to chat for a while, bringing each other up to date with the doings of their respective families. Cessy and Neil had two daughters; Penny was a nurse and Sophie a chef and their parents, quite rightly, were proud of them but of course missed them.

Once they had exhausted all other news, Cessy said, "Now, Lucy, what did you want to talk with me about?"

Lucy didn't question how the older woman knew she wanted something.

"You remember the boy Kenny pulled out of the river back in August?"

"Yes of course - Harry."

"Well, I was wondering if you could help us with a problem," Lucy outlined what that was. Cessy caught on quickly.

"He can come here," she said. "It won't exactly be home with his family but they can spend as much time as they like here. My staff are all qualified to help someone like him and he can be wherever he likes, do what he likes. It'll be better than spending Christmas in hospital, and will give his parents time to decide what to do. I suspect they will have to find somewhere else to live, or return to Manchester. Perhaps we'd better ask them all what they think about it."

"Thank you, Cessy. I'm sure it will mean a lot to them to have him close. Much easier than trying to get to the hospital all the time and more comfortable too."

"His family always visits him in the evening, don't they? I'll pop along tonight and have a chat with them all."

"That's wonderful. You're wonderful. Are you sure you have room?"

"Oh yes, that's no problem. I have a lovely room that became available only a few days ago. It's a big room too, overlooking the front garden and river. He'll like it, I'm sure."

When Lucy left Sutton Court a while later, she felt happy that it looked like another problem might have been solved.

****

Cessy was as good as her word. When she arrived at Harry's ward, his family were surprised to see her come in. They had been discussing how to manage if Harry came home over Christmas but, no matter how they talked, they couldn't see how it could happen. Harry knew he was going to have to stay in hospital.

"Hello there, everyone. I'm Cecelia Milton. I've seen you at Baxter's, I believe, Mrs Thompson? And I've visited young Harry here before. Hello, Harry."

"Hi Cessy. You don't usually visit me in the evenings. The doctors say I can come home for Christmas but I'll have to stay here because there's no room for me."

"It sounds like I've come just at the right time then. I came this evening because I wanted to talk with all of you. I would like to invite Harry to stay at Sutton Court for the holiday period. It wouldn't be coming home, exactly, but you would at least be in the village, Harry, and your family can spend as much time as they like with you without being restricted to visiting hours."

She looked around at their faces and could see the expressions of wonder. She went on hurriedly,

"I have a beautiful, large room empty that you could have, Harry. It's a 'home from home,' a bed-sitting room with a settee and a television – and a gorgeous view over the river. Of course, you wouldn't have young people around you, except for some of the carers, which you might not like but many of my elderly residents are quite fun. And you wouldn't have to be with them if you don't want to. We have quite a good time over Christmas with a party and all sorts of other things going on if you want to join in."

Harry's face glowed and was about to speak when his mother said,

"Oh, but we couldn't! We can't afford for Harry to be in Sutton Court, it must be very expensive. Thank you, Mrs Milton, but Harry will stay here."

Harry's head went down. Cessy couldn't bear it. The poor lad had already been through so much.

"It won't cost anything, Mrs Thompson. Harry will be my guest. We've become friends, haven't we Harry? I'd like to give him this, as a gift. The room is free, I have staff who can provide all Harry's needs and he'll have the freedom to be wherever he wants. Too cold outside, of course, otherwise he could be out too. And you can be there for the meals or whenever you like. What do you say, Harry? Would you like to come?"

Cessy deliberately focussed on Harry, giving his mother no chance to butt in.

"Oh, yes please, Cessy, I'd love to come. Please say I can, Mum? Dad? It will be so good to be out of this hospital at last."

"What do you think, George?" Netta turned to her husband, who, up to then, had kept pretty much out of things.

"I think it's a wonderful idea. Thank you, Mrs Milton, thank you."

"Do call me Cessy, everyone does! Mrs Milton sounds so stuffy and we are all friends in the village."

"How did you know about the problem?" Rowena spoke for the first time.

It was Harry who answered: "It was Lucy, wasn't it, Cessy?"

"Got it in one, young man!"

Everyone laughed. Rowena and Harry immediately put their heads together and started talking excitedly.

"What if they won't let him?" asked Netta. "I can see he's set on coming to you."

"Don't worry about that. They know me here and I've had many patients come to Sutton Court for recuperation or rehabilitation. I'll deal with it, it'll be fine."

"How can we ever thank you?"

"No need. I'm very happy to be able to do something for Harry. I'll say goodnight now and let you get on with your visit. I'll see you in a couple of weeks, Harry. Goodbye all."

Chapter 12

Cessy arranged everything with the hospital and, two days before Christmas, Harry found himself in one of Sutton Court's special vehicles, heading out of the city of Hereford. He looked out of the windows with pleasure as the car made its way slowly out of the city and up the Whitecross Road, then Kings Acre Road (he took careful notice of the road names) The Kings Acre road was lined with trees, their branches bare but standing proudly like sentinels along the route. He remembered this road from their holiday. He recalled thinking how beautiful the trees were; he'd never seen a road like that before.

The road forked by a garage-like place that was called 'Kings Acre Halt' but they went straight on. Minutes later, they were in the country and before long they turned left at a junction where the signpost said 'Sutton-on-Wye' and he knew they were very near to their destination. Upon arriving in the village, he saw a village green with the conventional village duckpond on his left and on his right a building that said 'Sutton-on-Wye Village Hall'. Here, the road formed a T-junction and they turned right. He saw Baxter's Nurseries and a few yards beyond that was a lane and then they came upon a drive with large, wrought-iron gates, which swung open with barely a squeak. Shortly after, the car stopped and Harry was helped out by Peter. Inside the great, white mansion, Cessy was waiting to greet him and beside her stood a man.

"Harry, you're here at last. Welcome to Sutton Court. This is my husband, Neil."

"Hello there, Harry. Welcome," said Neil, smiling and shaking hands with the boy.

"Thank you, Sir."

"Now, we'll take you for a quick tour down here then take you up to see your room."

Harry wasn't able to walk that far, so they sat him in a wheelchair for the tour.

Harry was very impressed. He was shown into room after room which were all very grand. Elderly folk were playing board games, or listening to music or watching television. Some of them waved when they saw him and someone even called out 'Hello Harry'. Everyone seemed happy, contrary to what he'd heard about old people's homes. They didn't look like they were just 'waiting for God'.

Once he'd seen downstairs, they went up in a lift to his room. He was stunned, the room was gorgeous. He'd never stayed in such a place, it was like a five-star hotel. He got up from the wheelchair and, on his crutches, moved over to the large window and looked out. The view was beautiful, even in the starkness of winter. And there was the river where it had all happened.

Cessy suddenly realised what she had inadvertently done. She stepped forward.

"Oh Harry, I'm so sorry, I never thought. Let me put you in another room. I'm sure someone wouldn't mind moving for a few nights...."

"No. No, don't worry, Cessy." Harry turned from the window. "I don't have to look at it. I've never slept in such a lovely room. I'll be fine in here, honestly."

He looked earnestly at her.

"Are you sure? I don't want to make you feel bad."

"Honestly," he repeated. "I like it. There's lots of room for me and my family, much more comfortable than being in hospital. Anyway, I'll probably be downstairs a lot."

She put a hand on his shoulder.

"The days will pass quickly, especially with everything going on. I'm sure having you here will please our other residents, they love having young folk around. Now, I'll leave you with Peter to help you get sorted, then he can bring you down."

"Thank you, Cessy. I really am very grateful."

"I know," she smiled. He watched her go out of the room and then turned his attention to Peter.

Later, Peter brought Harry down, and took him into one of the lounges, where he was greeted by quite a few elderly people.

"Hey, young man! Can you play chess?" This was from a man who reminded Harry of a mad professor – he had a shock of white hair and round glasses perched on a nose that looked as if it had once been broken.

"Yes. I enjoy it."

"Would you like a game?"

"Very much – erm?"

"Harry, this is Jack," said Peter.

"Hello Jack, I'm Harry." He grinned at Jack the Mad Professor. "Where's this game then?"

Jack rubbed his hands with glee as Peter brought the chess set to a small table. The pair were soon engrossed in their game and Harry knew he was going to enjoy his sojourn at Sutton Court. When his family came to visit, after their evening meal, they looked at the place in wonder. Like Harry, they had neverseen such a grand house with its wide, sweeping staircase in the central hallway and the large, elegant rooms.

Rowena was positively envious of his room. She flung herself on his bed.

"Wow, this place is something else! Pity it's full of old biddies though. Bet you'll get really bored with no one to talk to."

"I tell you, Row, those 'old biddies' are fantastic! I've played chess with Jack the Mad Professor and played table-tennis with Simon the Pie Man _ "

"Jack the Mad Professor? Simon the Pie Man??"

"Yeah," grinned Harry. "I think Jack looks exactly like my idea of a mad professor and Simon used to work in a bakery! I decided I shouldn't call him Simple Simon 'cos he's really not, so Simon the Pie Man he is."

They laughed.

"These old folk are great, they are fun and very friendly. I'm not lonely at all; it's good here, much better than being in hospital. I was lonely there."

George laid a hand on Harry's shoulder.

"Well, son, I'm glad you like it here. I've been hearing from my boss, Kenny, what goes on at Sutton Court and the village at this time of year. I think we've all landed in a wonderful place. All we need now is for you to get your strength back."

Harry nodded.

"You certainly look at lot happier now, love," said Netta, looking at her son fondly. "I think being here will be good for you – good for all of us because we can come here whenever we like. Once the nursery closes tomorrow, your dad and I will be free for a couple of days because, unlike all the other businesses around, Kenny doesn't open Baxter's on Boxing Day. He says it's important for his workers to be able to enjoy a couple of days over Christmas with their families."

"Kenny is a very unusual boss, isn't he? Most business owners would be thinking of their profits, but not him," said Rowena, thoughtfully.

"The whole family are wonderful people," George agreed.

"Especially Lucy," put in Harry. Rowena looked at him and laughed.

"Oh my! I think Harry's got a thing for Lucy!"

"No I haven't!" he replied hotly. "It's just that she's helped us so much and it is because of her that I'm here now instead of in hospital."

"Don't tease your brother, Rowee," admonished their mother. "In fact, everyone has been so kind to us. Mrs Milton didn't have to bring Harry here. We should be thankful."

"Oh yes, Mum, we are thankful, aren't we Harry?"

"Yes. We've found a nice bunch of friends and a lovely place to be. I hope we can stay around here for always, even when I get better."

"We'll see," was Netta's non-committal reply but secretly she wanted to stay here just as much as her family did.

Chapter 13

The main living-room at Sutton Court was alive with happy anticipation. The residents had just had their Christmas dinner and were getting settled ready for the Carol singing. Lucy, Ken and other people from the village would be arriving at any moment to lead them in the singing. The beautiful baby grand piano had been especially tuned for this yearly event.

Harry and his family had also partaken of the Christmas dinner, invited by Cessy, as were other relatives of the residents. It had been a jolly occasion, with lovely food.

As they all gathered, some being pushed in special chairs, some walking slowly with zimmer frames, each person had a paper crown on their heads, many fallen askew, Harry grinned happily as his sister poked him, quietly giggling at some of the sights around them. One old chap was asleep already, mouth open, green crown over one eye.

Even though he wanted desperately to walk and be 'normal' again, Harry was glad he'd been given the opportunity to see for himself how these people were looked after at this rather special place for the elderly. He knew, from his conversations with various residents and workers, that Cessy and Neil often took in people like him, who were recuperating from operations or illnesses. He recalled one natter with a lady called Flo, who told him all about the man called Sam, whose bungalow his family were living in, and how DI Cooke had investigated when a body turned up in a field. The girl had been dead seventy-odd years but had been the sister of Joseph Baxter, Kenny's grandfather, and Sam had been in love with her.

Flo had also told him, delighted to be the source of so much information, about what happened when Lucy inherited River View farmhouse and all the mysterious things that had gone on.

Harry had learned a few people's secrets – which were really open secrets in the village. But, with a wisdom that most fifteen-year-old boys don't have, he refrained from repeating the stories to his family, especially about Sam. He didn't want his mother getting upset about the bungalow as he knew she loved it. In some ways, it made him sad to know that, once he recovered, they'd have to leave it because it just wasn't big enough for all four of them.

At the shouts of 'Hello!' from various parts of the room, Harry awoke from his deep train of thought and looked up to see people entering the room. He recognised Ken, who was carrying a small boy on his shoulders, and his mother Sheila, who had visited him in hospital. Following them came a middle-aged man with a much older man, walking carefully with a stick. His heart leaped when he saw Lucy and she smiled and waved. There followed quite a few other people he didn't know, but he felt it likely he soon would. A man who was obviously a clergyman was among them; although he wore a Christmas jumper with a reindeer with a big red nose, he still had his dog collar on, which looked a little strange. Harry noticed a very tall, thin man with a small, blonde woman. There were couples with children too.

A man sat down at the piano and the group of singers arranged themselves. The vicar was obviously not in charge of this event, for it was Sheila who spoke.

"Hello everyone, here we are again! We hope you've enjoyed your day so far. Was the dinner good?"

There were a few nods and a there were a few yesses in reply. Everyone was smiling (except for the chap who was asleep, whose hat had slid further down).

"That's good. Now, join in whenever you feel like it. All set, Dick?"

The pianist gave her the thumbs up and started to play. From the motley group before them, came enthusiastic singing in four parts, the joyful music of 'The First Noel.'

This roused the sleeping man, who came to with a jump and had a wrestle with the hat, which had slipped down further so it was over one eye, his nose and part of his mouth. Elderly voices and the younger voices of the carers and visitors soon joined in and the room was full of music. Harry and his family sang with gusto, helped by the carol sheets thrust into their hands.

There followed a great half an hour or so of singing. Harry's spirits lifted even more. He felt that this must surely be the best Christmas he'd had; his parents had never really done the religious side of it. Christmas Day had mostly been presents and telly. He liked this, he liked it a lot.

After it was over, the visitors talked with the residents, who obviously knew them well. Even the children joined in. Lucy came over to Harry, holding a small boy by the hand.

"Hello Harry, this is John. Say 'hello' to Harry, John."

"Lo, Hawee."

"Hello, John. I've wanted to meet you," said Harry, smiling at the little boy. John stuck his thumb in his mouth as he inspected the older lad.

"Why in push chair?"

"Harry has hurt his legs, John, so he can't walk just now." Lucy was patient with her little boy. She picked him up as the tall man and the short woman went out of the room.

"Oh! Stephanie and Alex are leaving. I wonder why? Must have something else going on."

She turned back to Harry.

"How are you getting on here, Harry? Do you like it?"

"I love it, Lucy. Everyone is so nice and I play games with some of the men and Flo has told me all sorts of things."

"Has she now? Bet she enjoyed that. She knows just about everything." Lucy laughed. Ken came over and took John to a table where there were some cakes and other things. "Oh, this is my dad, Tom," she said as a man walked towards them.

"Hello there, Harry, old chap, how are you getting on? Glad to meet you at last."

"I'm doing good, thanks, erm, Tom."

Lucy and Tom chatted with Harry and his family until it was time to go. Harry thought his dad was a bit quiet but thought it was probably because he was tired.

Chapter 14

It had been a lovely Christmas until now. Stephanie felt sick as she hurried down Sutton Court's drive, with Alex striding along, his arm around her.

"What's the matter, sweetheart?" Alex was concerned. He had noticed her suddenly sway while they were singing and that the colour had left her face.

"I – I don't know. I don't feel well; I just need to go home."

"There's a sickness bug going around, perhaps you have that?"

Stephanie was glad he thought she had a sickness bug. It meant she didn't have to try to explain anything.

"Good thing the restaurant is shut for a couple of days. You must stay upstairs until you're better, my love. I'm sure the others can manage. We can't have our customers going down with a bug from our kitchen."

"Thank you for your concern," she mumbled.

"Oh sweetheart, you know I'm concerned about you, of course I am. Oh goodness, I wish we'd brought the car."

"That would have been silly – it's such a short distance. Perhaps a bit of fresh air will help."

However, Stephanie knew that no amount of fresh air would help what assailed her. She just wanted to get home and lock the door and never set foot outside again. Of course, she knew that wouldn't be possible but at least today she could, and maybe tomorrow as well.

It didn't take long to arrive home and she climbed the stairs to their flat thankfully. She sank down onto the settee.

"Do you want to go to bed, darling?"

"No. I just want to sit here in front of the fire."

"Would you like a drink?"

"Perhaps a mint tea might help," she replied and he went off to put the kettle to boil.

Grateful for the few minutes alone, she curled her legs under her and let her head go back onto the rest behind her. She couldn't believe it! Of all the places in the world, he had to turn up here. This lovely place that she'd made her home had felt safe and never, in her wildest dreams, had she expected to see him here. The day when she had a cake with Lucy at the nursery and she'd him at a distance he'd seemed familiar but she hadn't given it any more thought because it was too ludicrous. A quirk of fate had brought him here, his son's accident. Now she knew for sure; it was him. She wondered if he'd recognised her; then she knew he had, for their eyes had connected, just for a moment and she'd seen it in his face.

As she sat there, she was flung back to a time, long before she'd met her beloved Alex. Life had been so different then...

"Here you are, darling." Alex appeared, carrying a mug of mint tea, which she sipped gratefully. Alex was always so good, making sure it wasn't too hot, so she didn't stop for one moment to ponder if it might be. It was beautiful and refreshing. She started to feel better, even though she was worried. But why was she worried? He wouldn't want his past revealed any more than she wanted hers. With that thought, she felt considerably brighter.

****

While the laughter and chat went on around him, George was also feeling shell-shocked. How could he have been living in this village for four months without being aware she was here? He knew she would be feeling worried, having realised his presence.

"Um, I was wondering who the couple was that left straight away?" he asked, carefully. "He was really tall and lanky and she was small and blonde."

"Oh," Lucy paused, "That was my friend Stephanie and her husband, Alex. They don't usually go early. I expect they have something else on."

"I thought she didn't look very well," piped up Rowena. "She was rather pale."

"Oh dear, I hope not," said Lucy, her face full of concern.

"Maybe she has a headache," suggested George. He thought it was highly likely, given that she'd just seen him. He wondered what he could do about it.

****

"Mum, Dad, I've got something I want to give you for Christmas. Will you all come upstairs with me please?"

Curiously, they went up in the lift with Harry. He was able to get himself around in his wheelchair, although the carpets in some areas made it more difficult. George lent a hand when the going was tricky.

Once in the room with the door shut, Harry asked his mum and sister to sit down and his dad to stand next to him.

"Is the brake on properly, Dad?" he asked and George checked.

"Yes."

Harry took a deep breath and, while George hovered with arms held out, he hoisted himself up so he was standing. Taking the crutches from the side where no one had noticed them, he proudly showed them how he could walk with them. His family congratulated him and clapped him on the back. George took him in his arms and they hugged.

"I really wanted to walk by Christmas as it is the only thing I could give us all. Sorry about letting you think I still needed the wheelchair."

"Oh, son, this is a wonderful present. I never thought we'd see you on your feet again." Netta had tears in her eyes as she hugged him. George ruffled the boy's hair and murmured, "I'm proud of you son."

Harry glowed and Rowena punched him lightly on the arm. "Get you! Well done, bro'."

"Linda says I still have to do lots of work to get strong. I'll still have to go to the hospital every day for a few months yet but at least I don't need to stay there any more."

When his family left, Harry sat by the window with a sigh. He couldn't see the river because of the dark. He was grateful to it though, for it had been instrumental in changing his family's life.

Chapter 15

Two days after New Year's Day, a letter arrived for Stephanie. It had been delivered by hand, much earlier than when the post normally arrived. Stephanie was always first down, although they never rose very early because of working late into the evening. Business was quiet this time of year and so she was up earlier than usual. She frowned as she looked at the envelope. It just said 'Stephanie' and in the top corner, it said *'personal and private.'*

She knew she'd have half an hour or so before Alex was down, so she went into her office and sat at her desk, reaching for a letter-opener. Inside was a single sheet and it read thus:

Stephanie,

It is important I speak with you. Can you meet me this evening in the lane to River View Farmhouse at 6.30? If you can come, please would you come into Baxter's as if you were going to meet Lucy at 10.30? I'll be working near the entrance. I won't be able to speak with you then but I'll know that you're willing to come this evening.

J.

The sound of Alex's footsteps on the stairs made Stephanie fold the letter away quickly. Not having time to put it back in the envelope, she stuffed them both under her bra strap so they were hidden by her blouse. She heard him go into the kitchen, quickly followed by the noise of the kettle being filled.

"Hello love," she called as she headed for the stairs. "I forgot something. Be right down."

Once upstairs, she stuffed the letter back in the envelope. Where to put it? She couldn't risk throwing it away, as it was Alex's job to empty the bins. Her eyes alighted on her jewellery box. It was an old box with a lock that she'd found in a junk shop. The wood was beautiful, and so she'd had it repaired and polished. It was one of her treasures. She put the letter inside and locked the box, returning the little key to her bedside table drawer. Alex never looked among her things. Satisfied that the letter was safe, she made her way back downstairs.

As she ate her breakfast, she argued in her thoughts about whether she would go to Baxter's. However, for all her misgivings, she knew she would. And she would meet Jimmy tomorrow evening; she had to hear what he had to say.

"I was thinking that I'd like to see if Lucy is free to have a cake with me at Baxter's this morning," she said to Alex.

"Oh, alright love. I have some work to do in the office. Why don't you call her now?"

"I've left my mobile upstairs. I'll use the house phone."

The house phone was the business phone and it was in the office so she went in there. Not long after, she came back into the kitchen.

"All arranged. I'm meeting her at ten thirty."

She felt a little guilty about the subterfuge but reasoned that, by actually meeting Lucy, at least she was telling Alex the truth about going out. Alex wouldn't think twice about it, he never minded her meeting her friends.

Just before ten thirty, Stephanie approached Baxter's. Her heart leaped when she spied a man working in a bed close to the entrance. She wasn't convinced he was actually doing anything but it didn't matter. Their eyes met briefly as she passed him and a moment of agreement sprang between them. She walked on into the shop and was immediately hailed by Lucy.

"Hi Steph! Come on into the café straight away. You look frozen! What a day to be out. I'm sure it's going to snow soon." Lucy hooked arms and the two women walked together towards the café. When Stephanie looked back towards the entrance, there was no sign of the man she knew as Jimmy.

****

Quarter past six that evening, Stephanie sighed, took her chef's hat off and turned to her kitchen staff.

"Sorry everyone, I have a headache. I'm going to step out for a short while, see if I can clear it. No need to tell Alex, I'll be back shortly. I just need some air – I'll take a walk round the block, or rather up the road and back again."

They nodded in reply. She knew they would be okay without her – they were all well-trained. They weren't to be busy that evening anyway so she could afford to take a few minutes. Donning her coat, scarf and gloves, she stepped out of the back door. Head down, she hurried through the passageway that led to the road from the back garden and hastened up the road, past the village shop, which was closed, and on to the lane. The village was dark and looked deserted and her flat shoes made no noise on the pavement.

A street lamp on the road illuminated the entrance to the lane but as she walked beyond the orange glow, the darkness felt more intense. She shivered, hoping she wouldn't have to go far up the lane. She jumped when a shadow detached itself from the black hedgerow.

"Sal! Shush, it's me!"

"Jimmy!"

Arms went around her, and for a moment she allowed him to snuggle her close, then pulled away from him.

"I couldn't believe it when I realised it was you," she whispered.

"Nor could I. I had to see you, have a chance to talk with you. So many years I wondered about you, if you were alright and happy."

"I am happy, very happy, Jimmy. More than I deserve. I have a good life here with Alex, he's a wonderful man."

He took hold of both her arms in his hands, looking down at her.

"You do deserve it, Sal. Never think you don't. The things that happened weren't your fault. I'm glad you've found happiness. I had to see you, to tell you that you must not worry. I'll never let anyone know – anything. I have as much to lose as you do."

"I know, Jimmy. You know I always trusted you."

"I know you do, Sal, and I trust you."

"But – George?"

"I am George James, Sal. Everyone called me Jimmy because my stepfather was George too, so I got called by my second name. I've just reverted back, that's all."

"Ah, I see." She nodded.

"I wanted rid of the association."

"I can understand that."

"Netta knows nothing about you so she won't recognise you at all. I'm the only one, so you're completely safe. We can live as neighbours and, as far as anyone knows, we are strangers."

"Thank you. It's hard to be strangers with you, Jimmy. I owe you so much. But I'm grateful, you know that?"

"I do. Now, we both need to get home before we're missed. You go first. I'll stay here a few minutes so we don't appear to be together."

Stephanie stood on tiptoe, put her arms around his neck and kissed his lips lightly.

"Thank you. I'll never forget what you did and now you're doing more for me. You're a wonderful man, Jimmy."

Then she turned and hurried away. When she arrived back in her kitchen, she felt as if a great burden had been lifted off her shoulders.

****

George watched Stephanie as she was briefly illuminated under the street lamp and then she turned the corner and was gone. He gave a deep sigh; she never did realise how much he loved her. Holding her in his arms so briefly and her soft kiss bruised his heart. Although it had been many years since he'd last seen her and she'd changed her appearance since then, she still had the power to melt him. He'd risked so much for her and he knew he'd risk as much again if it was needed.

He sighed again and headed for home, hoping that Netta wasn't wondering where he was.

****

Two people silently watched them, one behind them up the lane and another hidden in the shadows thrown by the hedging on the country road in the opposite direction to where the pair had gone. A car's engine started up and a dark saloon silently passed out of the village.

Chapter 16

A few minutes after the pair in the lane departed, Kenny came in through the kitchen door, shedding his thick coat and gloves and looking thoughtful.

Lucy immediately picked up his mood.

"What's the matter, my love?"

"I dunno. I just saw something but I'm not sure what."

"Would you care to run it by me?"

"I walked home as usual along the river path but as I was by the gate leading to it from the lane, I suddenly sensed someone there. I walked past the house and down the lane and I saw a shape . As I crept closer, the object split and I saw it was two people. They'd obviously been hugging or kissing. It was dark so I couldn't see clearly but, as I stood there, one of the figures walked away and under the lamplight I'm pretty sure it was Stephanie because the figure was not very tall and I was sure she had blond hair. I stayed where I was and the other one waited a few minutes and then walked away. I only saw him from the back but as you know, I know my men very well and I'm almost certain it was George."

Lucy was startled. "George? Harry's dad?"

"Yes. Thing is, I can't be sure what they were doing but they were very close."

"That's odd." Lucy sat down suddenly. Kenny pulled a chair from the table and sat too, pulling John, who was clamouring for his attention, onto his lap.

"Very. Surely they're not having an affair?" he said.

"I just can't imagine Steph having an affair. She loves Alex so much, you can see it in her eyes when she looks at him."

"Do you remember Christmas Day when we were at Sutton Court?" Lucy was thoughtful. "Steph went home early, looking very pale. Do you think it was because she'd just seen George? She may not have seen him before."

"Perhaps he's an old boyfriend? I remember him asking who they were."

"It's possible, I suppose. But why meet him in secret?"

"Well, George is in enough trouble with Netta already, after what happened to Harry. I can't imagine her being happy about discovering he has an ex-girlfriend living in the village!" Her husband laughed. "I wouldn't be happy if Jim came to live here!"

"Neither would I!" Lucy laughed too, rising to kiss him tenderly. "I'm hoping he's still safely locked away. In any case, I'm sure he wouldn't dare show his face here after what he did. I'll get your tea on the table."

As she set his meal before him, she said, "I would imagine that they met to assure each other that they wouldn't let anyone know about the past. I think George wanted to make sure she wouldn't say publicly that they'd known each other before. As you so rightly said, he's in the dog-house already. He wouldn't want any more trouble."

Later, when John was in bed and the pair relaxed together, Kenny's arm around her and her head on his shoulder, watching television, Lucy's mind wandered back to the earlier conversation. Try as she might, she couldn't imagine George and Stephanie being an item. Although she was sure they weren't having an affair, there was something about it that didn't feel right, although for the life of her she couldn't have said what it was.

****

George ate his dinner stoically. Netta never had been a great cook but he'd grown used to it over the years. She never said a word about him being late, although he hadn't been that late, only a few minutes and she didn't take much notice of his comings and goings anyway. She already had her coat on, car keys in her hand as he walked in, ready to visit Harry at Sutton Court

He was convinced he could have an affair and she wouldn't have any idea...

He grinned inside at the thought but he had no desire to do any such thing. In spite of everything, he loved her and he loved his son and daughter, even though Harry wasn't actually his son. The boy was two years old when he married Netta and Rowena had come along in the first year of their marriage. He thought Netta was wrong not to tell Harry that George wasn't his father; he felt the boy had a right to know. But he had to respect Netta's wishes. In any case, he was Harry's father in every way except conception. He loved Harry as if he was his own son and it would always grieve him what his recklessness had done to their boy.

Netta was visiting Harry alone that evening because George knew that sometimes she needed time with her son without anyone else. She was still working at the nursery shop because it was January sales time but she would finish in a couple of weeks and then she'd be able to visit Harry during the afternoons again. He was sorry really because she loved working for Baxter's, had made friends and enjoyed the work. She'd said it made her feel like a real person, someone of worth. He understood that because working at Baxter's had made him feel the same. He loved working with plants and learning more about them and how to grow things successfully. It wasn't just a job for him, it was a passion. He would be sorry when he had to leave, although when that would be he had no idea. Everything depended on Harry's progress.

Having finished his solitary meal, he put his plate in the sink and looked out of the window. Flakes of snow were drifting here and there and he hoped Netta would be sensible and not linger too long at Sutton Court. If snow was on its way, it might be difficult getting through the village. She wouldn't be happy if she couldn't visit Harry. He sighed, and wandered into the living room, where Rowena was engrossed in a television programme. She looked up as he came in.

"Hi Dad."

"Hello love."

That was the extent of the conversation as Rowena turned back to the television George rested his head against the chair back, closed his eyes and allowed himself to think of Sally, how she'd felt in his arms for a moment, the sweetness of her soft kiss. His mind then played out a dark scenario – what if she was discovered by – Him? He shuddered at the thought; it didn't do to dwell on the past. The past should never be allowed to invade the present and future. He resolved to watch over her, keep an eye out. Nothing should happen to her because of him, he'd do everything he could to protect her. He'd never forgive himself if anything bad happened to her. When he thought of what had gone on before, all those years ago...

He shook himself mentally, trying to dispel the dark fears that threatened to invade him and purposely trained his mind to concentrate on the programme Rowena was watching.

However, it suddenly occurred to him there was only one way of making sure Sally was safe, but he knew the family weren't going to like it.

Chapter 17

"Go back to Manchester?"

Three pairs of eyes turned towards George, showing shock. It was Rowena who had spoken.

"But Dad, we can't!" she wailed, "Our life is here now! I love being at Whitecross School."

"I want to continue working with Linda. I wouldn't feel right about someone new," Harry put in quietly but firmly.

"I can't believe you want to take us back there, George," said Netta. "The children are right, our lives are here now. You have a job. If we went back to Manchester, you'd be out of work again. Remember how depressed you got not having work?"

George saw the despair in her face. He thought about those times in Manchester and, as Netta prompted, about how down he had been having no job, being unable to maintain his family through his own efforts and how he'd started taking his bad moods out on them, especially Harry. With the benefit of hindsight, he could see what he'd been like and he didn't like himself for it. Normally, he was gentle and kind, and he was becoming the opposite – grumpy and ready to snap at any provocation. No, it had not been a good period in his life. He'd had worse ones but they had not reduced him to a bear-headed father and husband.

"Well," he began again, carefully. "Kenny only gave me that job temporarily until Harry came out of hospital. He's out now but not living with us! We can't expect Cessy to keep him at Sutton Court much longer so we have to do something. And we have a house in Manchester."

"But that house would be no good for Harry. He wouldn't be able to get up the stairs and there's no bathroom facility downstairs, not even a toilet."

George was stumped; that was certainly true. He nodded slowly.

"Well, we have to do something. We can't have Harry at the bungalow and we can't leave him here. Cessy will need the room for another resident."

"Perhaps we could rent a house in Hereford?" suggested Harry. We would still be in the area so Row can go to school and I can get to the hospital. If I had one of those scooter things, I could take myself instead of Mum having to take me every day, then perhaps she could find a job too."

"That's an idea," said Netta. "I'll be sorry to leave the bungalow but perhaps it would be better to live nearer town."

"We still have the problem of my work. We wouldn't be accepted for rental if we have no regular income."

Silence filled the room. George sat and watched the other three as they thought things through. He had been determined that the best way to protect Sal was to go back to Manchester. However, wouldn't it work to just be a few miles away? If he was found there, she would still be safe because 'he' wouldn't know she was in this village, would he? George nodded to himself. Yes, that would work if he could only find himself a permanent job. He would start searching when he got home and in the morning he would warn Kenny what they had decided to do.

"I'll look for houses for rent. I'll go into the city tomorrow and do a round of the estate agents," said Netta.

"You can do it online you know, Mum," said Rowena, rolling her eyes. Her mother laughed.

"Well, if you'd like to search for me, it will give me something to start on tomorrow."

"Looks like we have a plan," said George. He wasn't entirely happy, but could he really put Sally before his family? His Netta had never been as content before they came here and Rowena loved her school.

Because of Harry's accident, life had become good for them. If he'd only been able to tell Netta about the past, she would understand why they had to go. But he couldn't tell her now; she'd never understand why he hadn't told her years ago.

He didn't tell her because he wanted to protect her – and he wanted her to love him and he was afraid she wouldn't if she knew. He never dreamed that his past would come crashing into his present.

He thought about Sally, how lovely she'd been with her long, dark hair and remembered how his heart hammered whenever he was near her. But she wasn't his and her life was traumatic. She was so petite and delicate-looking; so often he'd longed to gather her up and protect her from the harm she was suffering. But he couldn't; he'd had to stand by and helplessly watch – literally watch sometimes. And his fists would curl in hate and longing to smash the face that mocked her, until at last he had been able to help her.

Now, she was happy, married to a man who loved and respected her. She looked different with her hair dyed blonde and her dark eyes blue because of the contact lenses she obviously wore. He felt a certain pride that he'd helped to bring that about for her.

Then, he looked at his wife and son and daughter who were his life. No, he really couldn't put Sally above them; he'd have to hope that things would be alright.

He stood up.

"Well, it's time we were away. We'll see you tomorrow, son."

He ruffled Harry's hair, Netta kissed her son and Rowena and Harry 'high fived', then left Sutton Court to go back to the bungalow which soon would no longer be their home.

****

Harry watched them go and sat on, deep in thought. He sensed there was something up with his dad, although he couldn't for the life of him work out what it could be. He finally concluded that his dad was worried about having to find other work.

He was well aware how much the job at Baxter's meant to George and he guessed that he didn't want to leave and was also worried that he wouldn't get work that he enjoyed half as much as working with the plants.

"Hello there, young man. All alone?" He looked up at the sound of Cessy's voice and smiled.

"Yes, everyone has just gone. They were talking about looking for a house to rent in Hereford so I can live with them again. Dad wanted us to go back to Manchester but we don't want to go."

"We lived there a long time, it's the only place I remember living. We still have our house there but it wouldn't be any good for me, the stairs are steep and narrow, I'd never manage them. Everyone loves living here, so they're going to look for a house in Hereford. Row doesn't want to leave Whitecross."

Cessy nodded.

"I can understand that. It wouldn't be a good time for her to move, in the middle of year nine, would it? She'll have to choose her options soon."

"Yes. Mind you, I've missed my last year."

"Perhaps you'll get the chance to do it."

"Maybe. I think Dad is worried because his job at Baxter's is only temporary."

"Oh? How's that?"

"Well, Kenny said until I came out of hospital and I'm out now."

"I see. So your dad has to look for another job?"

"Yes."

Cessy patted his knee.

"Don't worry, I'm sure things will work out. Don't be too long going up. You can watch television in your room of course."

"No, I won't be long. Thanks Cessy. I've no doubt you'll be glad when I've gone."

"Not at all. It's been like a breath of fresh air having you here. The residents love it. We're all going to miss you when you move out. But it will be good for you to be back with your family."

"Thank you. I can't tell you how grateful we all are to you for having me. We've had a lovely Christmas with you and everyone. Our other Christmases have been nothing like this year. In some ways, I'm glad my accident happened because it has brought us here. This village is special."

"I think so too and it's become even more so since Lucy came. Her Aunt Bea was a very special lady and Lucy takes after her in so many ways. It's lovely to see a family in River View again."

"I wish I could see River View. My family have seen it but I haven't."

"I'm sure you will. We'll keep in touch with you and your family once you've moved to your new home. You must come here often. We have a summer fair in one of Lucy's fields and it's great fun. And you will have heard about our Halloween party and our Bonfire Night display."

"Yes, Rowena loved the Halloween party and is looking forward to the next one. I'm hoping I'll be back to normal by then."

"I'm sure you will. In fact, I think another six months and you'll be running around as good as new."

"Linda says that too."

"Who's Linda?"

"Linda Cooke. She's my physio. Did you know her husband is a detective? She's brilliant. She's my second favourite person after..."

"After Lucy?" Cessy smiled gently.

"Well, yes – but you're my third favourite!" Harry's face coloured bright red.

Cessy patted his shoulder. "Don't worry, lad, I don't hold it against you! And you obviously have good taste in girls!

I think most of the males in this village are half in love with Lucy! But she is such a kind hearted, good friend, the rest of the females don't mind because we love her too. I think even DI Cooke is half in love with her along with everyone else, although I think perhaps he's in love with her cakes!" She giggled and Harry laughed too.

"Oh yes, Linda told me that! She says her cakes always sink in the middle."

"Oh dear! Well, we all have that problem sometimes, maybe even Lucy. Well now, it's time I went. Goodnight, Harry."

"G'night, Cessy."

He watched her leave the room and sat for a few minutes more. He did want to be at home with his family again and wondered how long it would take his mum to find somewhere suitable. He sighed and, grabbing his crutches, slowly rose from his chair, and made his way out of the room to the lift.

Chapter 18

The following day, as soon as he saw Kenny, George took the bull by the horns and asked if he could talk with him. Kenny readily agreed and they sat in the café area, which was quiet because as yet the café wasn't open.

"We have decided to look for a house to rent in Hereford because we need to get Harry out of Sutton Court. We love the bungalow but sadly, as you know, it isn't big enough for all of us. None of us wants to go back to Manchester. Rowena loves her school and Harry wants to continue working with the team at the hospital here. I've loved my job here but I knew this was only temporary until Harry was out of hospital. I'm so grateful to you and Lucy for the help you've given us but we can't rely on your charity any longer."

"It's a good idea for you to seek a house in Hereford. It will be more convenient for Harry and Rowena. But as for this job being temporary, I'd like you to stay, if you will. You're a good worker and I'm going to be losing one of my lads soon as his family are moving away. I'll be short without him. Would you consider staying with us? If you became permanent staff, I'll increase your wages too."

"Oh! I didn't expect that." Although excited at the thought of having a permanent job at Baxter's, he thought of Sally. Would she still be safe if he continued to work here? He didn't see why not, there was no reason why anyone would look for her just because he worked here. If he saw her, he wouldn't speak to her at all, just in case anyone was watching. He didn't usually see her as a rule anyway. He made up his mind suddenly.

"Thank you. I would be honoured to stay if you really do want me?"

"I'm not just saying it, believe me. I had been wondering what I would do once Ray left. He's worked with me a long time and I'll miss him sorely. But they have decided to emigrate, would you believe?

I really am going be a man down, so it'll be a relief to have you, George. I didn't offer before because I thought you'd go back to Manchester once Harry left hospital, but as you want to stay in the area I'm happy to offer you the job."

"Ah well then, that's great! Thank you very much indeed. I'm sure Netta will be pleased. I know the kids will be because they're determined to keep in touch with the village."

"That's settled then." Kenny rose to his feet and so did George. "I'll get the contract drawn up as soon as I can."

They shook hands and the two men parted. George went back to his job in the potting shed feeling optimistic about the future.

****

Netta was good with money, especially while George was unemployed. Living rent-free in the bungalow, she had saved and saved the past few months, knowing the time might well come when they would need to find another home. They'd only lived in Herefordshire about a month before she'd become determined that they wouldn't return to Manchester. She loved the countryside and the people around her and would be sorry to leave Having become friends with a few people and all the neighbours spoke to her when they saw her either in the garden or walking about. Although she could probably buy food cheaper in a supermarket than in the village shop, the food she bought from Madge was superior to anything she could get in a supermarket and so fresh, coming straight from the farms. Lucy's bread and cakes were sublime and she bought them regularly. Oh yes, she would really miss the community in Sutton-on-Wye. However, Netta was practical too and she knew they had to move so her family could be together. A house in Sutton-on-Wye but they didn't have the income for a mortgage. She could dream though…

There was no time to waste in her search for a new home. Rowena had shown her some houses and the names of the letting agents.

After she'd driven Rowena to school, she headed the car towards the city of Hereford and hoped she would be able to find somewhere to park. After driving around a little, she found a space in a car park and locked the car. Just as she did so, her phone rang.

"Hello? George? What's up?" She spoke sharply.

"I just called to tell you that Kenny has offered me a permanent job at the nurseries – and he's going to increase my wages too!"

"Oh George," Netta's voice softened. "That is good news! I'm in town now, about to go to the letting agents. I'll be able to tell them that we have a regular income. It'll make things so much easier."

"That's why I called you to let you know right away. I have to go now, love. Good luck in your search."

"Thanks. See you later."

Netta went over the details of each house, discarding them if they had steep steps up to the door or if it didn't have a downstairs toilet. Not familiar with the layout of the city, she needed to be shown by the letting agents where the houses were. In the end, she had selected three properties, one in Redhill, one in Hinton and a large flat in Bodenham Road. She really liked the house in Redhill but it was too far away from Rowena's school, being across the river. The house in Hinton's stairs were very steep and narrow, and she knew that Harry would never manage them. The downstairs toilet was pretty disgusting too. Wrinkling her nose, she hurried away. The agent looked discouraged as he followed her out.

The flat in Bodenham Road was surprisingly roomy and on the ground floor. It would be convenient for the hospital, the agent said, persuasively. She nodded, yes, it would be convenient for that but it was the other end of town for Rowena's school.

"I'll have to think about it. Can I bring my family to see it?"

"Of course. When?"

"This evening, if possible? My husband can try and leave work early. His boss knows we are house-hunting. Can I call you later?"

"Yes. Have a word with him if you can. Our office is open until five-thirty, although I could meet you later, it would be better if it's not too late."

Netta nodded. She watched him drive away and sat in her car, looking at the building they'd just come out of. It was large, built of sandy-coloured bricks with black ironwork around the edges of the roof. It was a well-presented building but inside she had noticed that the décor was looking rather sorry for itself and the bathroom suite was dated, although functional. There would be plenty of room for them but somehow it didn't 'call' her. It didn't seem right for a family like theirs to live in a flat. Although they were currently living in a bungalow, she thought it would feel odd living all on one floor, knowing there was a floor above. And what if their house mates were noisy and obtrusive? Also, George would get caught up in city traffic driving to work. She shook her head. No, she didn't need to bring the family, she already knew this place wasn't right.

Dispirited, she drove home. Well, she didn't really think she would find somewhere straight away, did she? Yes, she did! Under normal circumstances, she would probably have plumped for the house in Redhill because it was lovely, but George would have to cross the bridge to work every morning – and she rather thought that bridge could become a bottle-neck at busy traffic times. She recalled that the agent had said there weren't that many places for rent in January but they would start coming in over the next few weeks. She wouldn't give up, she would look on the internet every day to see if there were any new ones.

On reaching the village, she decided to pop into Madge's shop. Once she'd parked the car, she called the agent to say she'd changed her mind and wasn't going to bring her family to view the flat. It wasn't in the right place. Again, he promised to call if anything came onto their books that would fit her requirements.

"Hello there!" Madge's cheerful voice greeted her as she entered the shop. "How are you, Netta? My word, it's chilly! I shouldn't be surprised if we have snow soon. Got to expect it in January, I suppose. You're looking rosy – have you been out long?"

"Yes, I've been into Hereford looking at houses to rent. We need to move so that Harry can live back with us."

"Ah yes. Nothing suitable, I suppose?"

"No, not yet. I saw a lovely house in Redhill but it wasn't in the right place for Rowena's school. We need somewhere this side of the river."

Madge nodded understandingly. "Oh yes, you really should be in the school's catchment area, then the lass can get a bus to school. We're in the catchment area here but the bus doesn't come to the village. Hard for the villagers but I daresay they manage."

"Yes. The agent said more places should come up in the next few weeks go on. I guess we'll just have to be patient. But I do worry about keeping Harry at Sutton Court for too long because Cessy might well need the room."

"I understand that, dearie. Sutton Court is always so popular hereabouts. People know it's a good place, see? They look after their residents very well and make sure they have lots to do."

"I'm very impressed with it. Cessy does a wonderful job there."

"Try not to worry. Something will come up, it always does. Now, is there anything I can get you?"

Netta got her bits of shopping and made her way home. As she walked into the bungalow, it seemed to her like there was someone there, waiting to wrap their arms around her. She loved it and right now she was glad of the warmth as she went in. She had plenty to do because she'd gone out and left everything. But first, she would have a cup of tea and the cream bun, made by Lucy, that she had treated herself to from Madge's shop.

Chapter 19

News in a village like Sutton-on-Wye travels fast. Just how fast, George found out the day after Netta had had her disappointing house hunt.

"George."

He turned round and was surprised to see Ray standing there.

"Oh, hello Ray, I didn't see you there."

"I've only just come. I was looking for you."

"Oh?"

"I heard you're looking for a house to rent in Hereford."

"Well, I'm glad you've not found anywhere yet because I have a proposition to put to you."

"How's that?"

"Well, you've probably heard that I'm emigrating with my family to Australia."

George nodded, waiting for him to go on.

"Well, thing is, we decided not to sell out house in case we don't like it there and want to come back. How would you like to rent it? We'd be happy to know we have someone in our house we can trust not to trash the place. It would be very suitable for your lad, there's a loo downstairs and the stairs are wide and fairly shallow. It's four bedrooms but one is very small."

"It's good of you, Ray, but we decided we needed to be in Hereford rather than the village. To make it easier for Row to get to school, you know?"

"My house isn't in the village. I live in an area called Bobblestock; in fact, my house is very close to Whitecross School. It's easy to travel to work as you'd not have city traffic to drive through; in fact it only takes me ten minutes to get here of a morning."

"Oh! I didn't know that. Um, well, it sounds like a good solution."

"Tell you what, why don't the four of you come round to see the house this evening? Come about seven and we'll give you a tour."

"Brilliant. Thanks. I'll give Netta a call now."

****

They picked Harry up from Sutton Court at six-forty-five and set off for Ray's house. It was indeed only ten minutes later when they pulled up outside. Even in the dark they could see that it was pretty modern, surrounded by identical houses. There were two cars parked side by side on the drive.

The door opened at George's knock and Ray invited them in. As Ray shut the door behind them, a woman came into the hall with two children, a boy of about six and a girl about eight.

"This is my wife, Carol, and this is Megan and Andrew. We have another lad but he's doing homework at his friend's house. Carol, this is George, Netta, Rowena and Harry."

Carol smiled at them. "Hello there. Welcome. So this is the young man we've all been hearing about? I'm happy to see that you seem to be recovering well, Harry."

Harry gave her one of his grins.

"Right then, let's do the tour. Downstairs first," said Ray and led them into a door in front of them. "This is the main room, our lounge."

It was a lovely room of average size with laminate flooring but warm. It was 'L' shaped and round the corner on the short leg of the 'L' was a dining area. Through that there was a spacious galley kitchen. They then went upstairs, Harry very slowly, but managing, to the bedrooms. The master bedroom had an en-suite toilet and shower room but there was also a good-sized family bathroom with a shower cubicle as well as a bath. Harry nodded his head.

Two more bedrooms were single size but adequate. One of them had bunk beds but the other had a single bed. As Ray had said, the fourth so-called bedroom was barely big enough to be called a room. In here was a table with a computer and a shelf unit with various books, CDs, and other miscellaneous items.

"It's an everything and anything room," said Ray. "Let's go downstairs."

They went down, with Harry coming last, bumping down on his bottom. "Easier," he said with a laugh.

"Don't blame you, lad," said Ray. "I didn't show you the downstairs convenience. Here it is." He opened the door to show a toilet with a sink unit, a mirror above.

Ray led the way back into the lounge. "So, what do you think?"

"Let them sit down. I have drinks and biscuits for you," said Carol, and handed a tray around.

"What do you think, Harry?" George asked him. "Do you think you can manage those stairs?"

"So, what do you think, Netta? Would you be happy living here?"

She nodded slowly.

"Yes, I think so. Do you like it, Rowena?"

"Yes, Mum. As long as I don't have to sleep in a bunk bed!"

"A friend is going to have them," said Carol, "So don't worry about that. You probably noticed the house was looking a bit sparse in places. We've already sent a lot of our things, because it takes a long time. We will leave the larger pieces of furniture here because it's expensive to ship them, so the house will be pretty much as you've seen it, except for the bunk beds."

"Well, that'll be great. We have nothing because we left all our furniture in the house in Manchester. The bungalow we've been living in is fully furnished."

"So, when do you actually go?" asked George.

"In three weeks. We fly on the last day of January."

Carol grimaced. "It's scary stuff, but we're excited too, aren't we, kids?"

Megan and Andrew nodded, Andrew was pressed up against his mum, looking at them shyly. George couldn't help wondering how they would get on out there, especially the young one, he seemed so shy. Still, kids are very adaptable, he thought.

"Well, that's a load off our minds," remarked Ray. "It was getting so close to us going and we thought we'd have to leave it empty and use an agent. But we're glad we don't need to. We didn't want strangers in our house. Of course, we may well end up selling it if we become sure we're going to stay there but that won't be for a good while yet."

"It's a load off our minds too," said George. "Thank you for thinking of us. I've been astounded at how everyone here has done so much to help us. We're so grateful, aren't we, love?"

"Yes, very grateful. We'll leave you in peace now."

George heaved a sigh of relief; thank goodness that was another hurdle crossed! It got him out of the village but near enough for an easy drive to work. Someone must love him after all.

Chapter 20

Paul Engledow nervously ran his finger around the inside of his collar. He felt it was trying to strangle him as he watched the little ball dancing on the spinning roulette wheel. Where would it land? He'd already lost so much money, he was in debt up to his eyeballs. This was his one, last hope. If he didn't win this time, he knew he'd have to disappear, for it was only a matter of time before the heavies came down on him. He half-closed his eyes, scared to watch and yet afraid not to. He must win this time, he must!

"Number fourteen. Place your bets now, gentlemen."

Paul had nothing left. He was finished. The croupier looked at him and he shook his head and turned to walk away. He felt he might as well jump in the Thames, for he had no other means of escape, no money, nothing left to sell. He had enough money in his pocket for one more drink and then he would go and jump.

"Yes, Sir?"

"Isle of Islay, single malt, please."

"Right away, Sir."

Paul thought that this was the last time he would ever savour a posh whiskey, and he made the most of it, enjoying the taste and the burning as it slithered down his throat. He drained the last drop and turned to go. As he did so, a heavy hand landed on his shoulder. He looked up in surprise to see one of the club's heavies behind him. Beside him stood another, arms folded, standing akimbo, gazing intently at Paul. His heart dropped to his stomach. He shouldn't have stayed for that drink.

"The boss requests your presence, Mr Engledow," said the man with the heavy hand. Paul gave a deep sigh of regret; he had no choice. He straightened up and bowed his head slightly.

"Lead on, gentlemen."

His legs felt as if they were dissolving into jelly as he tried to look nonchalant, walking between the two burly men.

They left the gaming room and took him up an elegant flight of stairs, along a hallway and knocked on a door in front of them.

"Come."

When the door opened, Paul saw a sumptuously furnished room, manly but comfortable and elegant.

"Come in, Paul, take a seat."

The man who extended the greeting looked about in his late forties. Slim and neat with black hair and dark brown eyes, he was handsome in a smarmy sort of way. He was sitting in a black leather armchair and beside him was a small table.

When Paul hesitated, the man said. "Don't worry, I just want to have a little chat with you. Come, sit down. I understand you're partial to Isle of Islay, you have good taste. I always have some up here. Toby?"

A man Paul had not noticed, dressed in black, came forward with a tray, holding a crystal decanter and two whiskey glasses. He set it on the table beside his boss and poured it out, each with an ice cube and handed it one to the man in charge and then one to Paul, who took it gingerly as if it would bite him.

The man raised his glass to his companion and held it up in a 'cheers' motion towards Paul, who half-heartedly held his up too and gulped down a mouthful.

"You can go," said The Boss to the two heavies and Paul heard the door shut softly behind him. The other man, Toby, was nowhere to be seen.

"So, Paul. You've got yourself in a bit of a mess, haven't you, old fellow?"

Paul nodded miserably and looked down at his glass.

"You know what I should be doing, don't you?"

More sweat broke out on Paul's forehead as he looked into the expressionless eyes of the man before him. The Boss had a Reputation. He called all the shots and people had been known to disappear before turning up dead somewhere a long time later.

"Oh yes, I should be doing that, Paul. I've let you get away with things for far too long, because I'm kind, see?"

'Kind, my bottom' thought Paul.

"I am calling in my debt, Paul. I don't think you have anything left except your home, do you? I've always quite fancied that house, nice little pile it is, the ancestral home. Pity about the old woman though, she'd have to go."

Paul thought about his mother and feared what would happen to her. Would they kill her? Would they kill them both?

As much as he loved Isle of Islay, he couldn't seem to make his arm work to bring it to his mouth.

"What would you do with my mother? She's an old woman, she deserves to live in peace."

The Boss laughed, quite an unpleasant sound really.

"You should have thought about that before, shouldn't you, lad? Before you let your 'illness' get the better of you."

Paul nodded miserably.

"You can have everything I have left, only please don't hurt my mother."

"Well, I'm glad to hear that you care about something other than your habit. I'm not into hurting old ladies, even rich ones. But oh my, Paul, haven't you let her down? Does she know about your gambling and your –erm, energetic lifestyle?"

Paul shook his head. His other all-consuming vice was women. Lots of them, the more the merrier. He thought about how his mother kept asking him when he was going to settle down. But why should he, when he was having so much fun? Although that was all over now, wasn't it? If he had no money to flash around, the women wouldn't come either.

"Well, Paul, because I'm kind, I'm going to wipe out your debt."

Paul's head shot up – had he heard right? No, the whiskey must be going to his head. The Boss never wiped out debts, especially as big as his.

"Yes, you heard right. I will wipe out your debt. Not only that, I will give you five grand. But I want you to do a little job for me."

Fear trickled down Paul's neck. "A job? What sort of job?"

Although he was not above doing illegal stuff, he hated violence and hoped he wasn't being asked to hurt someone.

"I need someone with your particular – uh- talent, shall we say?"

"What talent is that? Not gambling"

He cringed when The Boss laughed heartily.

"No, lad. That's not your talent, that's your downfall. No, it's your talent with the ladies I'm talking about."

"I won't have to hurt a woman, will I? Or bait her so your heavies can get her? I can't do that."

"No, nothing like that. I want you to find a particular woman and give her a good night, you know what I mean?"

Paul brightened. Yes, he knew and it was definitely right up his street. The Boss was going to wipe out his debt and pay him for sleeping with a woman? Paul thought the gods must be smiling upon him; his ship had come in at last! Hang on, there had to be a catch, didn't there?

The man sitting before him was watching him intently, as if he could follow the thought processes running through his head.

"The only thing is, you'll have to disappear afterwards for quite a while."

Paul was confused and frowned into his glass. What could be so bad about the job? He raised a questioning look at the intimidating man in front of him.

"It's better you don't know. But I can assure you that no-one is going to get hurt. You have to go to Hereford but not in your own car. A vehicle will be provided. You will be booked into a hotel. When you arrive, you will be handed a package and you will then follow the instructions in that package. You must follow them exactly.

Do not allow yourself to be distracted by any other attractive women you may see. You only deal with the target woman, and then you disappear. Instructions for that will also be in the package. Make sure you take it with you when you leave and then destroy it at the first opportunity. Do I make myself clear?"

"Yes."

"Good. You will receive your travel instructions in the morning. Your mother will be looked after during your – erm – prolonged absence, so don't worry about her. You will leave tomorrow for Hereford. You will like it up there, it's very pretty. Pity you won't be able to stay long."

Paul shrugged. The Boss stood up and Paul took it as a sign he was being dismissed. The door opened and the heavy stood there, waiting to escort him away. As he turned towards the door, The Boss said,

"By the way, Paul, stay away from the tables until you've seen this job through, otherwise you may well end up in the Thames. Singleness of mind, one track vision, Paul, until you have done the job and left the country. Understand?"

Paul nodded. "I understand."

"Good." The man nodded to Paul's escort. Before Paul turned, he caught a look of amusement on The Boss's face and wondered why.

Chapter 21

Paul sat at a table in the bar of The Kerry Arms. It was busy, conversation hummed and music played. The door opened and in walked a woman on impossibly high heels. He noted her shapely legs, couldn't help noticing, because her leather skirt was tight and short. Her blonde hair curled down her back and she had a chest that would make a ship's figurehead feel insignificant. His eyes followed her, interested but not interested. He had a job to do and he was waiting for a woman called Ruby. How much longer she would be? It had been made clear that she would be here as she came to this pub every night without fail. He sipped his drink and watched the woman in a detached manner. One of the men at the bar hailed her.

"Hey Wiggy! Someone's been asking for you!"

"Oh yeah? Oo's that then?"

"Bloke over yonder." The man speaking indicated with his thumb behind him, in Paul's direction. Good looking chap – he might buy you a drink if you're lucky! The man roared with laughter and his mates did too, all three turning round to watch her walk towards him. Paul finally saw her face.

'Oh goodness, she's at least fifty!' he thought, taking in the blood-red lips on a heavily made-up face. Now he understood the reason behind The Boss's smile. He'd really been dropped in it.

"Yew bin askin' fer me?" she asked when she reached his table. "Oo are yer? I aint never seen yew afore."

"If you are Ruby Wiggington, yes, I've been asking for you. You don't know me but I've been told about you, from a good friend who passes this way sometimes. Travelling salesman." Mentally, he crossed his fingers. Had he hit on the right sort of story?

"Ooh, is it Arfur Smif? 'E' were one o' my reg'lers, like, but I hant seen 'im fer ages." She sat down on the bench next to Paul and he shimmied along to let her in.

She crossed her legs with difficulty, allowing her skirt to rise so it only just covered her modesty. She leaned towards him, and he couldn't help seeing down her deep cleavage. His head spun and he pretended to cough, turning away, hand to mouth. When he turned back to her, he made himself keep his eyes on her face.

"Yes. Arthur, that's right. I met him at a roadside café and when I told him where I was going, he winked at me and told me to look for you. He said that you were special and he always had the best times with you."

She preened a little at his story. "Did 'e really say that?"

"Oh yes indeed," said Paul, warming to his story. "And he said to tell you he's really sorry he hasn't seen you for so long but his firm has sent him to work in a different area. But he assured me that you would see me right. 'Treat her like a lady,' he said, 'And she will treat you like nothing you've had before. She knows a thing or two and you won't get anyone finer.'"

She brightened even more. "I knew that Arfur would be back fer me if 'e could. 'E's right, 'cos 'e always treated me like a lady, bought me drinks an' stuff."

Her face glowed so much at the thought of the unknown Arthur's fabricated praise, that Paul realised she was probably younger than he'd first thought and he was surprised to feel a pang of pity for her. She had probably been attractive in her younger days. He thought she would look much nicer if she didn't wear clothes more suited to a teenager but she probably saw her outfit as a tool for her trade.

He was acutely aware of the curious stares of the men at the bar, so he said suddenly,

"Look, shall we go?"

"Already? Yer aint even bought me a drink yet. Yer 'as ter git me at least one drink afore we goes inter the alley."

'Into the alley?' he thought, realisation coming to him. The thought made him feel nauseous. Paul had a voracious sexual appetite and he'd had many women, but the thought of what she was suggesting was sordid to him.

He told his stomach and throat to behave and made himself take her hand.

"You don't understand, Ruby. I don't do alleys. I do hotel rooms, champagne and luxury. You're worth more than a quick one in an alley. Will you come with me?"

Her eyes opened wider as she comprehended what he was saying. In spite of himself, he admitted she had beautiful eyes.

"Champagne? You want to give me champagne?"

"Yes, and any other drink you want."

"Lead on!" She got up and unsteadily tottered on her red high heels towards the bar.

"I've landed on me feet wi' this 'un. 'Ee's goin' ter give me champagne!"

"Way to go, Wiggy!"

Paul felt a slap on his back and, giving a sickly smile, he took her arm and the pair exited the pub to wolf whistles and jeers.

****

When they went into the hotel room, her eyes had widened with wonder at the sumptuousness. It was, after all, a high-class hotel. Give The Boss his due, he hadn't stinted on the expenses; he'd been booked into this hotel, The Grafton, which was gorgeous and he'd been given plenty of money to spend.

When Ruby saw the bathroom, her eyes widened. "Wow, just look at that bathroom! I'd give me eye-teeth to 'ave a bath in there."

"Why don't you then?" he'd said and her beautiful eyes opened wider.

"Are you serious?"

"Yes, go ahead, enjoy yourself while you can. Make the most of it."

He'd showered and changed upon arrival and already there were clean towels in place of the one he'd used.

While she was having her bath, he took a glass of champagne in to her and she smiled and held it up above the bubbles, which were doing a valiant job of hiding her voluptuous figure. The bath was very full!

"I en't never had champagne in a bubble-bath before – erm, what's yer name, by the way?"

"Peter. Peter Edwards," Paul made up the name hurriedly.

"Well, Petey-boy, you're makin' me feel really posh! This is wonderful."

"I'm glad you're happy, Ruby." He held up his own glass. "Cheers!"

She held up a soapy arm and mirrored his action and sipped at her glass daintily, trying to act like she thought a lady would. She wrinkled her nose when the bubbles went up it and laughed.

Paul couldn't help thinking that she reminded him of a child experiencing something she'd not been allowed before and smiled. In spite of his misgivings, he was quite enjoying it. *'You thought I was going to hate it but you're so wrong. Up yours,'* he mentally told The Boss.'

"What you smilin' at, Petey?"

"Oh nothing, just something someone said to me. Sometimes things come into your head that have nothing to do with what you're doing at the time, don't they?"

"Oh yeah."

"It was one of those times. Nothing to do with us. Have you finished your glass? Time to get out then, or you'll end up all wrinkly. There's more champagne in the bedroom. You can put this lovely robe on. It looks cosy. And it'll make things easier later." He winked.

"Oh yeah – yer wicked boy! 'And me that towel, would yer?"

He held out the towel and tried not to look as she stood up and wrapped it around herself.

"I'll go pour us out another glass. It'll be ready for when you come out." Making a quick exit, he couldn't make up his mind whether he was simply going to get her drunk and leave her to sleep it off, or to take advantage of her generous nature, it depended on how things went. Although fully aware of how potent champagne was, but he'd heard she was a hardened drinker of spirits and he might have to resort to them later. He poured her another glass, still having his because he'd only taken a small sip. He couldn't afford to drink because he would soon be driving.

When he had reached the hotel, there was a package for him. He'd taken it up to his room and found a wad of money and the instructions for finding Ruby. Once he'd found her, he had to keep her with him all night. That bit had been underlined and was the most important thing. 'It's up to you what you do,' the note had said, 'She is a pro, but as long as you keep her all night, you could just make her drunk, or do what you fancy.'

Another set of instructions told him to leave early in the morning and drive south towards a house in Monmouthshire, where he would be given tickets for travel and further instructions. It had all seemed simple enough.

When Ruby emerged from the bathroom, wrapped in the lovely, cosy gown, he handed her the full glass and, taking her hand, led her to the bed. They both sat on the bed, leaning against the pillows. He took off his jacket and tie and undid the buttons on his shirt. She drank her drink and he filled it again. She giggled.

"You're a naughty boy, spending all this on me! This is the first time someone has taken me to a place like this. I love it!" Her speech was beginning to slur. She was on her fourth glass of champagne. She sat up further and peered at him.

"You're an 'andsome man, Petey. You're very young too, aren't yer? How old are yer?"

"I'm twenty eight."

"Oh, yer older than yer look. Old enough to know what yer want, I daresay?" she giggled again and let the gown open more at the front. "Yes, you're very handsome. How old do yer fink I am?"

"Oh, about thirty…five?"

Again the giggle came. "You silly boy! I'm forty five! Do yer think I look forty-five, Petey?"

She leaned towards him and fluttered her eyelashes at him.

"Absolutely not, Ruby. As I said, you don't look a day over thirty five. If you wore more floaty dresses, you could look younger still."

"Don't yer like ma clothes then?" she pouted.

"They're fine, but they're not very lady-like, Ruby. I bet, if you wore something different, you'd look like a lady."

Her mood suddenly changed, and she laid back on her pillows again.

"I'll never be no lady. But I 'ope me dawta will."

"You have a daughter?"

"Yes, my Gloria. She is beautiful and clever, not like me, I ent clever."

"How old is Gloria?"

"Fourteen."

"Where is she now?"

"At 'ome. She's a good girl, she gets me breakfast when I come in of a mornin'."

"Who is her father? Are you married?"

"Noo," she giggled. "Although I was married once. 'E were a beast, used ter knock me about. 'Ee got banged up, fank God, fer armed robbery. I divorced 'im."

"He's not Gloria's father then?"

"Oh no, I don't know oo that is. Some bloke, one o' my clients. It were a shock, like, when I found out I was 'avin' a kid, like, but I 'ad her an' now I love 'er."

Paul held up the bottle of champagne. "Oh look, it's empty. Would you like something else?"

"Wouldn't mind."

"I'll see what's in the fridge. Paul hopped off the bed and a few moments later came back with a bottle of vodka and a bottle of lime cordial. "Vodka and lime?"

"Oo yeah, just the ticket."

He poured her a large glass, giving her a double measure of vodka. She took it eagerly and downed half of it right away.

"My word, tha's good." She was looking sleepy. He drank his own drink, which was only diluted lime cordial.

"Come 'ere," she said, and he came over with his drink. She put her hand to his chest and stroked him. "Mm, I love a hairy chest on a man, so much more manly than a smooth un."

He allowed her to stroke him, keeping himself in check, which was difficult because it was having an effect on him. He kept reminding himself of what she was and what she might give him if he allowed it to go too far.

"Drink up, love," he said and she drained her glass.

"Another one?" She nodded. He hopped off the bed and poured her another double which she downed quickly. He'd never known a woman to drink like she did.

"Come on, let's get you into the bed."

She giggled again as he undid the robe and slipped it from her and closing his eyes he lifted the duvet to let her slip under it. He went around the other side and shrugged off his shirt, shoes and trousers and climbed in beside her. She was already nearly asleep and she snuggled closer to him.

He put his arm around her. It took only a short time for her to fall into a deep sleep so he detached himself and got out of the bed, and, putting his clothes back on, made himself as comfortable as he could in the armchair and dozed off.

He awoke as the first weak sunlight of dawn crept into the room. He rubbed his neck, trying to relief the pain from his stiff neck from his head being at an awkward angle. He stretched and looked at the still sleeping Ruby. She didn't look drunk, just peacefully asleep and appeared much younger and vulnerable with her face in repose and half her makeup gone. His heart softened towards her. Yet again, he wondered why he'd had to keep her all night. From their conversation the previous night he understood that she was a broken woman. Abused by her husband and misused by men even before him she'd become an alcoholic. She hadn't actually said that, but only an alcoholic would prostitute herself for a few drinks night after night. He thought about the unknown daughter, Gloria, and wondered what sort of life the girl had with a mother like Ruby. He sincerely hoped she wouldn't follow in her mother's footsteps, for her mother was a deeply damaged individual.

Quietly, he tidied himself in the bathroom, cleaned his teeth and put his bag, which was packed and ready, by the door. Then he sat down at the small table and scribbled a note on the notepaper provided by the hotel, and left a handful of notes with it. He walked over to the woman, still deep in sleep. He gently stroked a few hairs that had fallen across her face away with his finger, noticing the grey roots for the first time in the dawn light, and kissed her cheek. She stirred, and he stood back, holding his breath, not moving until she settled down again. Heaving a quiet sigh of relief, he picked up his bag and crept out of the room, shutting the door softly behind him

.

****

An hour later, well on the way towards Monmouth, Paul listened to the news on the radio. They'd been talking about a kidnapped girl, Anita Brown, missing from Hereford. She was thirteen years old and had been walking her dog when she'd disappeared.

Paul had a light-bulb moment – could it be that The Boss was after young girls and had used him to secure one? He knew the man had been behind kidnappings before. This poor Anita had already been taken – had Gloria also been snatched while he'd been getting her mother drunk in a hotel room? Was The Boss stretching his fingers further afield from London?

"Gloria! Oh, my goodness, surely not? Oh, please, God, don't let Gloria be taken. It would kill poor Ruby!"

Paul was under no illusions about the man and knew that he did all kinds of unsavoury things, including selling children for prostitution. Paul had his faults, he was a womaniser and a compulsive gambler, but he wasn't cruel. It pulled at his heart to think he'd been used to get at another innocent kid. 'Oh God, I'm sorry." He hoped with all his heart that he was wrong, but deep down, he knew he wasn't. It posed a dilemma for him; should he go back to Hereford and tell the police? Maybe he could stop it happening. But no, it would have already happened, that's why he'd had to keep Ruby all night. It would take him an hour to get back there and another hour and the rest to get back to where he was supposed to meet his contact for the next set of instructions. In the end, his self-preservation won and he drove on, through Monmouth and found the minor road to Cwmcarvon. There, he came upon the deserted house that he'd been instructed to find. A man he didn't know waited in a car for him. He parked up the drive and got out. The man handed him an envelope.

"Your tickets and instructions. We'll swap cars, because yours was a hired car and I'm to take it back. You take the car I've come in. Wait until I've driven away and give me a few minutes, in case there's anyone around. You're to get a plane at Luton airport. Good luck."

"Thanks."

While he waited the few minutes the other guy had asked for, Paul opened the envelope. Inside was a plane ticket in the name of Jeremy Smith, destination, Rio. He smiled, returned the ticket to the envelope and put it on the passenger seat beside him. He turned the key to start the engine. Immediately, there was a big explosion and the car was enveloped in flames.

Chapter 22

"Have you heard the latest, Sir?" DS Grant greeted DI Dan Cooke as he entered the police station for work one late February morning.

"Give a man a chance to come in, why don't you?" Dan grumbled.

"Sorry. It's just that it's been a bit quiet for us lately so I've been gossiping."

"Oh yes? Who with?"

He pressed a button on his desk phone. "Get Johnson to bring me a coffee, will you please, Bert? Thanks."

"So, enlighten me."

"It seems we have a new crop of pushers on our streets. Dave Wilkins from Narcotics told me. Not local. They can't seem to pin them down. Slippery as eels, Dave says."

"Oh crap, that's all we need," groaned Dan. He looked up as the door opened and the young constable came in with a mug. "Ah, thanks very much. You know, often I think our beloved little Hereford is like a little London. We have everything here that they have, except for bombers. Thank goodness we've had none of them."

"Don't speak too soon, Gov," warned Grant.

"Oh, don't say that! Anyway, we can't do anything about it, it's not our province. Has there been any information on our missing girl?"

"No, Sir."

The phone rang Dan picked it up. "Cooke. Oh no! We'll be there right away. Give me the address."

He scribbled on a piece of paper, put the phone down.

"Another missing girl. We'll take my car."

Friar Street wasn't far. Dan groaned. "Oh no, I know who lives here."

The blue door was flaking and pealing; the window frames not much better. At their knock, the door was opened by a woman who, in spite of her high heeled shoes, tight skirt and red lipstick, looked as though she had definitely seen better days – a lot of days.

"Oh, it's you." She went back into the house, leaving the door open for them to follow her into a small room that held a brown settee and another chair, neither of which looked too clean. At the window hung a grubby net curtain that looked as though it should be consigned to a bin. The brown curtains hung on a rail that had come off the wall one end, so one curtain drooped lower than the other.

"Hello Wiggy, nice to see you."

"Well, I wish I wasn't seeing you. But I suppose I need you," she sighed, sinking into the lone armchair and lighting a cigarette with shaking hands. The two men sat gingerly on the edge of the settee and waited while she inhaled and blew out the smoke.

"So, Gloria has gone missing?"

"Yeah. I were out last night, on – erm, business and when I got 'ome, she'd gone. Trust 'er ter go missin', she always got my breakfast, see?"

Dan did see. While Hereford's most famous 'lady of the night,' Ruby Wigington, always known as Wiggy, was out working, her young daughter could be up to all sorts. However, Dan knew the girl, had watched her grow up and knew that actually, she was not a bad kid. Surprisingly, she was quite clever and doing well at school. She was bookish, not prone to being a good time girl and she did her best to look after her wayward mother, who was often not capable.

"Are you sure she's not with a friend?"

"Nah, she don't 'ave none really."

"Can I see her room?"

"Yeah." Wiggy led the way up stairs covered by a threadbare carpet of indeterminate colour a opened a door and stood back. Grant's eyes widened.

This room was a complete contrast to the one downstairs. It was painted white and had hand-drawn pictures of flowers on the walls. Piles of books sat neatly on a chest of drawers. The bed, however, was in disarray. Although the bedding was clean, the pillows had a dent where the girl had obviously been lying and the duvet in its pink cover was on the floor as if it had been dragged from the bed. A teddy bear and a toy rabbit were askew as if they had been knocked around. A book lay on the floor, open, some of its pages bent in contact with the floor.

"She done it 'erself," said Wiggy, proudly. "She bought a tin of paint wiv 'er pocket money and drew the flowers. Whoever her father was, 'e must 'ave bin arty, 'cos she don't get it from me. She gets 'er beauty from me."

Grant's eyebrows went up even further and Dan nudged him.

"Obviously, she was in or on the bed. Is anything missing? Clothes? Have you checked?"

"Of course I 'ave. It's all there, nuffing's gone. 'Ave a look."

Pulling on some latex gloves, Grant opened the small wardrobe which seemed to have no spaces. He opened the drawers, two of which were full of jumpers and underwear. The top one had a hairbrush and dryer on one side, on the other side was an artist's pad, pencils and water-colour pencils. He shut the last drawer.

"It certainly doesn't look like anything is missing, Gov."

Dan noticed a chair with a black pair of trousers, a white shirt and a navy school jumper

"Them's wot she was wearin' yesterday. Look!"

She pointed to a single pink slipper, which looked as though it had fallen off and landed on its side down beside the chest of drawers. Certainly, there had been violence in this room.

"What could she be wearing?" asked Dan.

"'Er's wearing 'er night fings, o'corse. Pyjamas aren't there, nor 'er dressing gown. She liked sitting up 'ere in 'er pjs and gown, it's pink and fluffy. I gave it 'er fer Christmas. She's bin taken, I tell yer."

"Let's go back down. Did you notice if your front or back door has been forced?"

"The b***** back door was wide open, letting all the cold in. B***** house is cold enuf, without leaving a b***** door open."

"Show us."

Dan expected the kitchen to be as filthy as the living room but surprisingly it was pretty clean and the only things in the sink were what Wiggy had probably used that morning. Obviously, Gloria made sure the kitchen was kept like her bedroom. Examining the door, Dan said to Grant, 'Get forensics over here, will you, Grant? Don't go outside until the team has done their stuff. And get a liason officer over here. Come on, Ruby, let's sit down."

He gently led her back to the scruffy living room and sat down again.

"Now, Ruby. Firstly, do you have a photo of Gloria that we can use?"

"Oh, yeah." She got up, went out and came back a few moments later with a framed photo which she handed to Dan.

"Thank you. When did you last see Gloria?"

"Last night, afore I went out, about eight."

"What was she doing?"

"Well, she 'ad already put 'er pjs and dressing gown on. She loved that dressing gown. I gave it to 'er fer Christmas, yer know?"

"Yes, you told me that already," Dan said, gently. "So, she was already in her night things. What do you think she'd have done after you went out?"

"Well, she'd watch a bit o' telly if there was something on she likes. Then she goes ter bed at about nine or ten an' reads for a bit. She loves readin', not like me. I don't read much. She were a good girl. I didn't mean to 'ave 'er, she was an accident, like, but I love 'er, she's all I've got. Please find 'er, Mr. Cooke."

She cried then. In all the years Dan had known Wiggy, he'd never seen her cry. He handed her his clean white handkerchief and she held it to her eyes. He held her hand and she gripped it. "I know I don't deserve 'er, Mr Cooke, but I love 'er. She's a good girl. Someone awful has taken 'er, I know it."

"I'll do my very best, Ruby. You know me well enough to know that."

"Oh, I do, Mr Cooke. I trust you! I know you can find 'er. I just 'ope they don' 'urt 'er."

'So do I,' thought Dan, grimly. "Someone will come and sit with you for a while, Ruby. I'm sorry I can't stay but you know I need to get onto this."

"Yeah. Yeah, I know that." She blew her nose and held the handkerchief out to him.

"You keep it," Dan said, hoping his inward shudder didn't show. The doorbell rang and he heard Grant opening the door.

"Ah, here's WPC Angela Griffin. She'll look after you now."

"The team is here too, Sir," said Grant.

"Good. Let's leave them to it. Can you take this photo and get some copies made. Find DC Coombs and PC Johnson and bring them back to help with a door to door. I'm going to stay here so I can look around the garden after the team have finished. Take my car."

"Righto."

Dan watched Grant drive off in his car and thought about Gloria. She was only fourteen, a very quiet and nice girl, in spite of her upbringing. Now, they had two missing girls of similar age.

He sighed heavily. He had a bad feeling about it, and felt this might just be the beginning.

Chapter 23

"Right. Anything from the house to house?"

The team were back in the incident room. Enlarged photographs of the two missing girls were on a board with their names, Anita Brown and Gloria Wiggington.

"Well Sir, the lady who lives next door, a Mrs White, said she heard some strange noises and a car at about two forty five last night. She looked out of her bedroom window but only saw its back lights disappearing." Detective Constable Collins said, reading from her notes.

"Not much there then, only helps to pin-point the time of the kidnap." DI Cooke frowned. "They must have been watching and knew Ruby's habits. The other girl, Anita, was snatched as she was walking her dog. She'd been seen at The Oval by a woman who knew her, a Mrs Hutchins, who spoke to her. After that, she disappeared off the face of the earth but the dog found its way home, trailing its lead. Mrs Hutchins seems to have been the last person to have seen her. As for Gloria, the back door was broken open – it wasn't in a very good state so it wouldn't have been hard and there were scuffed footprints leading to and from it in the garden. The girl was brought around the side of the house, probably carried and possibly drugged, into a waiting car. After that, there are apparently no witnesses, apart from the neighbour, Mrs White."

A knock on the door interrupted Dan's narration. "Yes?"

A WPC came in and handed Dan a piece of paper. "Sorry to interrupt, Sir, but Leominster police have just called in to say a young boy has gone missing this morning. They thought you'd want to know, Sir."

"Oh no! A boy, you say? How old and how did it happen?"

"They say he's a young-looking fourteen year old, name of Adam Monk. His mother says he left for school and didn't arrive."

"Boys truant."

"Not this one, sir. By all accounts, he's a good boy, studious, and has never missed school."

"We'll have to liaise with Leominster on this one. I'll inform the Chief then we'll go over, Grant, Coombs, be ready."

Detective Chief Inspector Richard Griffin groaned when he heard Dan's report.

"We have to get to the bottom of this, we can't have kids going missing wholesale. The press will have a field day."

"We're working on it, Sir, we have a few ideas. But now we need to get over to Leominster."

"Off you go then, let me know how you get on."

They went in Grant's car. Dan only vaguely noted the beauty of Dinmoor Hill and Queen's Wood as he sat, deep in thought, in the passenger seat. Fifteen minutes later they arrived at Leominster station. They were greeted by Inspector Ralf Turner, who ushered them into his office.

"They are combing Leominster right now. The boy in question left his house at the usual time, about quarter to eight. He attends the Westfields school and has quite a distance to walk, so he sets out early."

"On his own? Doesn't he have any friends to walk with?"

"Usually he does, but his friend, who lives in the same road, um…Steven Appleby, is off school with flu, has been off school for over a week."

"He had to walk all that way and no-one saw him? I find that hard to believe." Dan started pacing.

"As I said, a big hunt has started for him. All our officers are out, talking to people and many citizens have answered the call to form search parties. We're doing all we can."

Dan sighed. It was a repeat of when Anita went missing the previous week. The whole area was searched and they even dragged the river, although the current would have taken her downriver.

"Can we see the mother?"

"Yes. I'll give you the address."

"Come on then, Grant, let's go."

Adam's mother was naturally upset. Grant stayed in the car at Dan's request and Coombs went with her boss. Dan was gentle with Mrs Monk, who was a divorcee. She tearfully told him how Adam went off to school happily as he usually did.

"And he didn't show any signs of being distressed or anything? Anything you can remember, however insignificant, may well be helpful."

"We-ll, now I come to think of it, he did say one day that he thought someone was watching him."

"Really? When was that?"

"Um…two days ago, I think. Wednesday. Yes, that's right, it was Wednesday. I told him not to be so silly. I wish I'd taken more notice of him now, he wasn't a boy given to making up things. He's a good lad." She started to cry again and she groped for the box of tissues on a table near her. In her jeans and jumper, with her slight figure and dark, curly hair, she looked too young to be the mother of a fourteen-year-old.

"Well, I think that's all, Mrs Monk. We have a photo of your son. Please rest assured that we will do everything possible to find him."

She managed a tremulous slight smile and nodded. "Thank you."

****

Dan frowned at the three photos on the board, thoughtfully. He turned to his companions, DS Grant and DC Coombs, and PC Johnson, who was excited at being part of the investigation.

"Right. Let's brainstorm. What are your thoughts about these three young people and their disappearances?"

"Well, Sir…," began Coombs hesitantly.

"Yes?"

"I know it sounds silly, Sir, but they are all pretty. If you take the glasses off the boy, he's pretty."

Johnson gave a slight snigger and then reddened as Dan frowned at him.

"Good thought. I'm not sure if that would be a factor although it may be. Write it up there, Coombs."

"They are all children from one-parent families," said Grant. Dan nodded to Coombs, who wrote that too in her neat hand.

"Of similar age," said Johnson, wanting to redeem himself after his earlier gaffe.

"Yes, there are only months between them. Put it up, Julie."

There was silence as they all gazed at the board.

"Not much to go on really," commented Grant.

"Well," mused Julie Coombs, "Obviously, kidnap for ransom can't be the motive because none of these families are well off."

"Do you think these youngsters were picked at random because they happened to be in a place where they could be taken?"

Grant shook his head. "Not where the prostitute's daughter is concerned. That was a deliberate act, planned and carried out."

"Don't forget Adam's mum said he told her he thought someone was watching him," said Coombs.

Dan looked at her approvingly. She was learning to reason; that was good.

"So," he said. "we know Gloria was deliberately kidnapped, which means someone had been watching Ruby and her daughter and they knew Ruby is often out all night, giving them plenty of time to do their work. It also seems that someone was staking out Adam Monk from what he said. They must have known he was walking alone, although how I can't begin to guess, when his friend could have been with him at any time.
We have no way of knowing if they were also watching Anita but it's likely.

"She always walked her dog at the same time every day to help her mother who works full time. So, what can we conclude from that?"

"Given that the last two happened so close together, it's likely we're looking at a gang rather than one or two people," said Coombs, thoughtfully.

"Good, yes! Unfortunately, it does seem to be a gang, which makes it more difficult because they could strike anywhere at any time and at distance to each other. It makes it impossible to pre-empt their next move. There must be hundreds of one-parent families with a single child all over the county."

"Which bring us back to the 'why'," growled Grant. "And the 'where?' Where have they been taken?"

"Going back to how they look – and I hardly dare think about this – could they have been taken for – um, you know, young prostitutes?" Coombs cringed as if hardly daring to voice her thoughts.

The three men looked at her and her face turned red again. She hung her head. "Take no notice. Silly thought."

Dan frowned. "No, Julie, not a silly thought at all. In fact, it's something that's been running around in my mind since your earlier remark about how pretty they are, even Adam. I hate to say it, but we all know there's a certain type of person who would love to get their hands on a pretty young boy, especially an innocent one. Given that no bodies have turned up – and believe me, the tracker dogs would find them, that, to me, is the only possible solution. I know we've always had our share of doubtful nightlife but, to my knowledge there's never been anything like this here."

"Do you think it's anything to do with the new gang of pushers that seem to have arrived on our streets?" Grant said.

"It could well be. In fact, that might even be a kind of cover to lead up to this, their real motive."

"Horrible. Poor kids," shuddered Julie Coombs.

"Horrible indeed," remarked Dan. "I would imagine they are being held somewhere in the county, unless they have already been taken to London or somewhere else. For the time being, they should be okay but they'll be in for a shock when they find out why they've been taken. Right. Grant, I want you to take Johnson in plain clothes and get out into the streets of the city, see what you can find out. But, try not to give rise to suspicion and above all, don't do anything if you see something they don't want us to know about. Coombs, you come with me. We're going to see Anita's mother and then we'll call upon Ruby again. We have to find those kids before anything nasty happens to them."

****

Ruby was reticent at first to tell them where and who she'd been with that night. She was still smarting from the way she'd been treated by the staff of Grafton Bank when she'd walked out of the room and down to the foyer. The starchy, stuck-ups! Eventually, she told Dan about Peter Edwards and the wonderful night she'd had. She produced the note he'd left her.

'Dear Ruby, thank you for a wonderful night. Treat yourself to something nice. Peter'

"'E was gone when I woke up. 'E did say he'd got to get off early, like, and I did sort of oversleep. But I were sorry, 'cos 'e were that nice. I've never bin treated so good, 'e made me feel like a lady."

Dan refrained from comment on that. "May I keep this note? We may be able to find him through this."

"Yeah. Here, do ya think 'e did it a-purpose, like? To keep me outa the way so as they could take my girl?"

"I'm afraid it looks that way, Ruby," replied Dan gently.

She cried. "I'm so stupid. Gloria don' deserve to 'ave a mother like me."

Angela rose to comfort her charge while Dan and Julie let themselves out.

Chapter 24

George and the family soon settled down in the new house. Rowena loved that she could walk to school with her friends in a few minutes. Harry was able to catch a bus to the city from almost outside the house, so he took himself to the hospital every day. He was doing well. At first, the walk from the bus station to the hospital was a challenge, although it was only close behind the bus station. By mid-March, he was walking better, with only the aid of a couple of sticks rather than crutches. Netta had found herself a part-time job, working in the large supermarket a short distance away and George was happy working at the nursery. He was considering buying a moped or a motor-bike to go to work on. Things seemed to be looking up for the family.

Three more youngsters had disappeared, two girls and another boy. George looked at the news report about it on the television. Mary Brooke, aged fourteen, was taken from Ross-on-Wye, Sarah Randle, thirteen from Kington and Mark Hunt, who was only twelve, from Weobley. Their pictures were shown in a group of six on the screen.

"Terrible," remarked Netta. "Whatever is going on? They are so pretty, all of them, even the boys – and that Mark is only twelve too! Their parents must be going spare, poor things."

"Listen!"

'Detective Inspector Dan Cooke, of West Mercia Police, Hereford, has made an appeal.'

'These six young people have all gone missing within a period of two weeks. The police are doing all we can but we are appealing for witnesses to come forward. If you think back over those days and nights and can remember anything at all, however insignificant, please talk with us.

We are very concerned for the safety of these young people and we need you to help us. No bodies have been found, so we have reason to believe they are being held somewhere, either in the county of Hereford, or elsewhere.

If you have any suspicions, please talk with your local police. Although we don't want to panic you, we also appeal to parents of all young people of a similar age, especially if you are a one-parent family, to please be especially vigilant at this worrying time. Thank you.'

"That's Linda's husband," said Harry. "I know she's been worried about him because he's working practically round the clock, although she wouldn't tell me what it was. It must be bad indeed if he's put out a warning."

"Oh, we must keep an eye on Rowena!" said Netta, her eyes darting to where their daughter was sitting sideways in a chair, her legs over the arm, eyes closed, listening to music through her earphones.

"I don't think we need to worry. She walks to school with a crowd of friends, otherwise she's either here or with friends at their home. In any case, all those children are from one-parent families."

"No, they're not! That last girl, Sarah something, has two parents and a younger sibling."

"But the father is away somewhere with the SAS."

"Ah! But anyway, it's awful."

"I agree," said George, quietly. As the music for the end of the news came on and Netta rose to make hot chocolate, he thought how these terrible kidnappings reminded him of another time and another place...

****

Gloria put her arm around the sobbing little boy. Mark had joined the group two days ago. He was younger than the rest of them and obviously was not dealing with his situation very well. Adam was the eldest of the group but he spent his days sitting in a corner, silent and morose.

"Why are we here? What are they going to do with us?" Mark sobbed, taking in great gulps of air as he fought to control his emotions.

"I don't know. I don't know where we are and I don't know why they've taken us, I wish I did know."

Actually, Gloria had an idea why, but she wasn't about to tell the others. She was a sensible and resourceful girl; she'd had to be with a mother like Ruby. Although she didn't know what she could do to help them out of their situation. They were in a large room, what she imagined a dormitory in a boarding school to be like, with four beds along one wall with a bedside cabinet in between each one and the same on the opposite side. The windows were boarded up, except for at the very top of each one to let in light. She knew it was an upstairs room because she could hear movement below them.

When she had first arrived, she'd found Anita already here, alone and frightened. She couldn't believe there were now six of them. She had more or less become the leader, the comforter, the one that tried to keep up their spirits. She had to admit, they were well looked after, provided with clean clothes and the food was good too. A shelf at the far end of the room had books and games, and there were a couple of tables and eight chairs where they could play or eat. The only difficult bit was the bathroom facilities as there was only one with sinks and four toilet cubicles. So the boys and girls took turns. Towels and night clothes and everything had been provided for them to live in relative comfort. They all thought it was strange but there was nothing they could do about it. Gloria wondered about the other two beds – did that mean there were going to be two more coming?

Two women brought their meals. They wore identical masks that looked like women's faces so they couldn't tell what they actually looked like. They were always accompanied by two burly men wearing balaclavas and carrying guns to make sure the youngsters didn't try anything. The women didn't speak, they just brought the food and left, one of the men locking the door behind them.

"Why don't they speak to us?" Mary paced around the room. "We're just left here, day after day and they're not telling us anything."

"I guess they don't want us to hear their voices, afraid we might be able to identify them somehow."

"You – you don't think it's anyone we know?" Mary was wide-eyed at the thought.

"Don't be silly!" Adam spoke from his corner, making them turn to look at him. "How could they be people we know? We all come from different places, we attend different schools and we don't know each other. We don't even have friends who know each other. We were just easy to take, that's all." He raised his book in front of his face, effectively shutting them out.

"Anyone fancy a game of Cluedo?" Gloria held up the box.

"Might as well, I suppose. Better than doing nothing," agreed Anita. Gloria set the box on a table and the five of them gathered their chairs around and set out the game.

"Want to play, Adam?"

Adam looked up from his book. "Only if I can be Colonel Mustard."

"Okay. Come on then."

They brought another chair in for Adam and the six of them were soon involved in trying to find out who committed murder with what weapon in which room.

****

George wasn't the only one to have his thoughts cast back to the past by the news item. Stephanie felt her blood run cold as she listened to DI Cooke's appeal while she was getting ready to go down to the restaurant kitchen. It seemed that this year her past was fast catching up with her and she didn't know what to do about it.

Chapter 25

The Tuesday after the police appeal had been made, George was working in the potting shed. He'd only been at work for a couple of hours when Sheila came to the shed.

"Oh George! I'm glad I've found you! You need to go home right away. Apparently Netta's not well or had an accident or something. A neighbour of yours called, he didn't give his name and didn't seem sure about what's actually happened. He said his wife gave him our number and told him to leave a message for you to come home."

What could have happened?

As George dithered about what to do, Sheila said, "Go on, lad! Your wife needs you. I'll square it with Kenny, he'll be fine. Get gone, now."

George left, feeling in his pocket for his car keys as he went. He had his fleecy jacket on because it wasn't terribly warm in the potting sheds. As he drove, he searched his mind for what could have happened to Netta. He finally concluded she must have had a fall, for she had seemed well that morning. An illness doesn't come on that quickly – unless it was a heart attack or stroke. That thought alarmed him even more and he put his foot down further on the accelerator.

The ten minutes that it took to get home seemed more like an hour to George. Surely another member of his family hasn't had an accident, not after what had happened to Harry?

He pulled into the drive, and, slamming the car door, ran into the house, calling "Netta! Netta, where are you?"

He went into the kitchen first and looked out to the back garden. There was no sign of her and no answer. He flew up the stairs and went from room to room calling her. Perhaps she'd been taken to the hospital already? He went down and into the sitting-room and stopped short.

"Luke! What are you doing here? Where's Netta? I had a message that she needed me to come home."

"Just a little ploy to get you here, Jimmy. Don't worry, Netta's at work. It's Tuesday, lad. She always works on Tuesdays."

George felt a moment of relief – Netta was okay. But what did his step-brother want? George had gone to great lengths to get away from his him and had not seen him for – well- since *that* time.

"So, what do you want, Luke? I should be at work."

"Isn't it enough that I wanted to see my little brother?" The calm voice answered. "Why don't you sit down, take the weight off?"

George sat, glad of it, for his legs were turning a bit wobbly. He had a bad feeling about this.

"You haven't bothered with me for years, Luke. What do you want?" George asked for the third time.

"Well, I haven't needed to, have I? I thought you may as well be left in peace. Weren't doing too well, though, were you?"

George felt a little shiver run up his spine.

"You know what I've been doing, where we've been living?"

"Oh yes, Jimmy. I've known for a good while. No one disappears from Lucian Avery, unless I order the disappearance." The darkly handsome face gave George a sardonic smile. George's shivers ran up his spine again. He was only too well aware of how people disappeared from Lucian's sight. Their bodies were sometimes never found. He was suddenly very grateful for the fourteen years he'd been allowed to live his life free of this man.

"Of course, you weren't very clever really, going back to your proper first name and taking your mother's maiden name. No, not clever at all. I found you easily. And of course, you were brought to my mind again when your lad had his accident."

George regretted all over again the part he'd played in Harry's canoeing disaster, if it had brought his abominable step-brother's attentions upon them.

Why couldn't he just go back to his plush London casino and leave them alone? He wished his mother had never married this terrible man's father. He never had been able to see the attraction. He wished his own dad hadn't died. He only had vague memories of him and sometimes he wasn't sure whether he was remembering right or if it was wishful thinking. He did have a faded photograph of him and was almost the image of him. He thought he remembered playing with him and riding on his shoulders.

When George's mum, Elsie, had married George Avery, little George had only been five. Lucian Avery was seventeen, already self-assured, already a bully, but a bully who got others to do his dirty work. George Avery already had his 'empire', the casino and all sorts of other things that he had his fingers in, many of them illegal. Lucian had simply stepped into his father's shoes when George senior had an aneurism and died. George's mother had slipped into dementia and had died six years after her husband. George missed his gentle mother more than he would ever admit to anyone, least of all Lucian, who looked down on any weakness of character, as he would see it. Young George had his mother's gentle nature.

George had not liked George Avery and was happy to be called Jimmy instead of having the same name as his hated stepfather. Lucian was exactly like his father. There was a sister too, called Hannah, who had married a rich American and gone to live in California.

Jimmy had fallen into working for Lucian but had eventually broken away because he was sickened at the way Lucian dealt with people who crossed him. He decided he would rather be poor but free from being one of The Boss's gang of heavies. He hadn't done badly either, until he'd been made redundant. Frankly, he was surprised that Lucian had let him go – and unharmed at that, which was something he never did.

George was broken out of his reverie by his brother getting up and walking leisurely round the room, stopping to look at an ornament here, a picture there. George's scalp prickled; he expected something to happen, although he had no idea what. Eventually, Lucian picked up a framed photograph off a shelf. He examined it closely as his younger brother looked on nervously, aware of exactly which picture it was. It had been taken by Cessy and it was of himself, Netta, Rowena and Harry smiling happily beside one of the Christmas trees at Sutton Court. It depicted one of the happiest times in the family's life. George couldn't help wondering if the happiness was coming to an end…

"Nice picture, Jimmy. Is that your lad who had the accident? Nice looking boy. Not yours though, is he?"

George shook his head.

"Looks a lot like his mum, doesn't he? What's he really like?"

"He's a nice lad. Clever, also like his mum."

"Uh-ha. He's what – sixteen?"

"Almost, yes."

"And this is Netta. Nice piece. You did well there, lad."

"I did."

"This your daughter? What's her name?"

"Rowena."

"Pretty name. Pretty girl. Love her blonde curls. Can't think how you managed to sire such a pretty one." Again, the sardonic laugh. George only allowed his lips to twitch slightly in a nervous half-smile.

Lucian sat down again, still holding the photograph. He drew a clean, white handkerchief from his pocket and, slowly and deliberately, wiped the frame all over, very thoroughly. The effect his movements had on George were indescribable. The room, suddenly felt hot.

"So, what are you doing here?"

"Tell me about your work, Jimmy-boy. You like working for the country bumpkin?"

"He's not a country bumpkin at all! He's very knowledgeable and a great boss. He and his wife have been very kind to us."

"Ah, yes. The lovely Lucy! I've been watching her. Let you live in a place she owns, didn't she?"

George's heart gave a leap – surely he couldn't be after Lucy, could he? What could he possibly want with her?

"Relax, lad! I'm not after your precious Lucy. But I am interested in one of her friends."

George stood up abruptly and turned his back on Lucian as if he was going to the kitchen. He didn't want his brother to see the distress on his face – Sally!

"One of Lucy's friends? How's that then? Why would you be interested in one of her friends?" he said, as he walked towards the kitchen. Getting a cup out of the cupboard, he poured cold water into it.

"I think you know, Jimmy. In fact, I know that you know. You've been holding out on me, haven't you, little brother? You should know that's a dangerous thing to do, a very dangerous thing."

George knocked back the water, appreciating the coldness slipping down his throat. He wiped his wet forehead on the kitchen towel, before going back towards the living room, where Lucian was still calmly sitting.

"I don't know what you mean. I was offered the job at the nurseries to help us through a problem while Harry was in hospital. I don't know any of Lucy's friends."

"*Au contraire*, Jimmy-boy. I think you know one friend very well. A friend of hers who used to belong to me, Jimmy. One that made a terrible mistake. I don't know how she did it but you have led me into finding her."

"How's that then? We came upon the village by accident – literally. So how could I have led you to someone, whoever it is?"

At that remark, Lucian's previously calm face turned dark. "Don't pretend with me! We've been watching you ever since you went to live in the village and we know Sally is there. We know you've had contact with her and met her one night. You should have notified me, Jimmy! Why didn't you?"

George shrugged. "She's changed her life. She's happily married and is a businesswoman. Why would I want to spoil that for her?"

"Hmm. Well, you're going to spoil it. I want to talk with her. I want her back, Jimmy. She was the best thing I ever had and I will have her back. What's more, you're going to get her for me."

"No!"

"Oh yes."

"I won't do it. You can't make me do it."

"Oh, can't I?" The voice was icy calm now and the man in black picked up the picture again, with the handkerchief.

"Lovely wife you have. Bet she doesn't know about your past, does she?"

"And Harry. It would be such a pity if he were to meet with another accident, wouldn't it? Hmm? He might not survive another one, do you think?"

"No!" George was on his feet now, his fists clenched.

"Good to see you're attached to the lad, George. My father wasn't very attached to you, was he? Don't worry, nothing is going to happen to Harry."

George relaxed a little, then tensed again as he watched Lucian look at the photo again and stroke the image of Rowena.

"Beautiful girl. Lovely blonde hair, gorgeous big blue eyes, little breasts budding. A real rose, just ripe for the picking. I'd like to add her to my bower; I've quite a collection of pretty little Herefordians now."

George gasped. "That's you?"

Lucian smiled enigmatically.

"How could you do that in this day and age?"

"Don't forget, this is a business I've been in for a long time. I know exactly what to do with those youngsters. Especially now I've completed the set. I have seven, just the right number."

"Seven?"

Lucian stroked the photograph again. "Mmm, yes. I have the prize now, the one I've been waiting for."

George's veins turned to ice. "Rowena? You have my Rowena? I don't believe you, she's at school."

"Is she? Are you sure?"

George tapped the buttons on his phone with shaking hands. He had the school's phone number already in it.

"Hello. This is Mr Thompson. My daughter, Rowena Thompson is in 8b. Can you send someone to bring her to the phone, please? It's very urgent."

There was a momentary silence.

"Mr. Thompson, I received a phone-call from yourself saying that Rowena was sick. Don't you remember?"

"Oh! Yes of course. I clean forgot. I called this morning, yes, yes."

"Are you alright, sir?"

"Yes, yes I'm fine. Thank you." He rang off and looked wild-eyed at his brother, who smiled back at him calmly. George, who was a very peaceable person, longed to smash his fist into that face. For a split second, he imagined those perfect teeth knocked out and that face bloody and bruised.

"Don't worry. No harm will come to her – if you do what I say. In fact, I give you the chance to set them all free, all seven of them. All you have to do is give me Sally."

George put his face in his hands. How could he betray Sally? And yet, there were those children, imprisoned somewhere – and now they had his daughter. How distressed would Netta be when she found out their girl had been snatched and how terrified his little girl would be right now.

He could hardly bear the thought of his beautiful Sally once more in the hands of this monster, his own step-brother.

He saw what had been done to her before at Lucian's cruel hands; he'd not borne to see her pain and humiliation. Did Lucian know he'd helped her escape? Was that why he'd always kept an eye on George?

His question was answered a moment later. That calm voice came again.

"You should know that no-one is allowed to cross me, Jimmy, you made a bad mistake fifteen years ago, along with Sally. I suspected you helped her, that's why I've always kept track of you. I've been very patient. You two almost got away with it, you know. I thought she was dead for a long time – until this last year, in fact. That's when I realised, put two and two together and actually made four. When I really thought about it, I knew it could only have been you, Jimmy that helped her. No one else would have dared. But you had the hots for her, didn't you?"

George looked up then, startled. Lucian laughed that small, self-satisfied chuckle.

"Oh yes. You thought I didn't know, didn't you? But it was plastered all over your face, every time you were in the same room. I couldn't fail to notice, you never were an actor. But you're going to do some acting for me shortly. Oh yes, you are. If you don't, your lovely little girl will be taken in Sally's place and the others will go with her. I know several rich men who will pay real good money for them. Think about that, Jimmy. Think of Rowena taking over Sally's role and there will be no-one around like you to save her as you saved Sally."

The quiet laugh that rankled George so much came again.

"How fortuitous that you should end up, literally by accident, in the very place where Sally now lives! What's the odds on that happening, I wonder? Lady Luck certainly smiled upon me, didn't she? And I've had such fun setting the scene!"

Knowing he was entirely defeated, George bowed his head.

"What do you want me to do?"

"That's more like it, Jimmy-boy! The first thing you have to do is introduce me to your lovely wife when she gets home."

Chapter 26

Rowena was frightened. When she woke up from her drugged sleep, she was lying on a bed that she knew wasn't her own. Her head felt heavy, as did her limbs. Opening one eye, she squinted to see a wooden chair and a small table. A small shelf above the table held some books. She opened the other eye and looked around the room. It wasn't very big, about the size of her bedroom at the bungalow but where that had been cosy and homely, this wasn't. The walls were bricks that had been painted over in a dirty white. The single small window was high up and bare, the bed was old-fashioned, rather like a hospital bed without any moving parts and the mattress was fairly unforgiving. However, someone had made an effort and the two pillows were soft and comfortable and the white sheets and green blankets were clean. She stretched tentatively and sat up. Resting her head against the tubular steel bed head, she tried to recall what had happened.

Rowena always left the house at the same time every school morning. Her parents had both already gone to work. It being Tuesday, her mum started work at the supermarket at eight. Harry was in his room, waiting to get up after everyone had left because he still took him a while to do things. He would have his breakfast and then catch the bus to the hospital. She always left via the back door, for the garden led to a shortcut between the houses and came out opposite the school.

Shouting cheerio to Harry, who always shouted back, Rowena had slammed the back door and run down the garden path, slinging her bag onto her back as she went. No sooner had she passed through the gate when someone had wrapped their hand around her mouth. She'd struggled for a few moments, kicking out, and remembered no more until she'd come to in this room.

As she sat there, her mind running around, trying to figure out what had happened, the door opened and a woman came in with a tray. Her heart missed a beat. Why was the woman wearing a mask with a woman's face?

"Who are you? Where am I?" Rowena's voice came out as a croak, her throat felt stiff and dry.

The woman shook her head and proceeded to put a jug of water and a plastic cup on the table and a plate of something with cling-film over it. She indicated with her hand that Rowena could come over to the table and eat. Then she backed away towards the door.

"No, no, please don't go!" pleaded Rowena, to no avail because the woman disappeared through the door and a moment later, she heard the sound of a key being turned in the lock.

She sighed and carefully swung her legs over the side of the bed and gingerly stood up. She felt wobbly but the need for a drink spurred her on to move the couple of steps to the chair. The water was cool and welcome; it slid down her parched throat, healing the rawness.

She looked at the plate of food. It was sandwiches and a cake. She realised she was hungry and so immediately started to eat. The bread was fresh and lovely, the ham inside tasty and the cake was homemade.

Feeling better after the food, she stood on tiptoe at the window but it was too high and all she could see was sky and part of a branch of a tree.

She wondered if her bag was here somewhere. She looked under the bed and there it was. Excitedly, she pulled it out and hunted through her things. After searching thoroughly, she sat back disappointed. All her school things were there but not her phone. Darn it! That was one good idea gone. Oh well, she wasn't surprised. She checked out the books on the shelf and found one she might like. However, instead of reading, she sat and thought.

Recalling the news, she wondered if she was the latest victim of the kidnap gang. She was of similar age to those others and she wondered where they were. Was she in the same place or had they been taken somewhere else? If they were in the same house, where were they? Were they all in little cells alone like her? How they were coping? She was scared enough and some of them had been taken two or three weeks ago.

What was going to happen to her? The room was furnished and she was warm in bed with books to read. The food was good. Did that mean there were people there all the time, making meals and looking after them all? Or was it just her? They didn't seem to want to harm her and that was a slight relief but she did worry about where she might end up and what they might ultimately do with her. Would she ever see her mum, dad and Harry again?

****

That day was one of the slowest and most difficult of George's life. Harry returned home from the hospital a couple of hours later and was surprised to see his dad at home with a stranger.

"I've been given a day off because of this surprise visit, Harry. This is your Uncle Luke." Lucian had told George exactly what to say. "He's been living abroad and we haven't seen each other in, oh, years, long before I met your mother."

"Hello there, Harry," said Lucian, shaking hands with the lad. "It's good to meet you. I've been hearing all about you. How are you getting on after your accident?"

"As you can see, I'm doing good. I only need one stick now and can pretty much manage to do everything. Still can't run though." He pulled a face. "I didn't know I had an uncle. You never talk about him, Dad."

"No, well, we lost touch, you see? I just never thought, I suppose."

"And I was too busy living a great life and never thought to get in touch, to my shame. I've been looking at that photograph of you all and you look great. I can't wait to meet your mum and sister too."

"Well, Rowena gets home around four and Mum just after five. I'm starving! Have you eaten, Dad, Uncle Luke?"

"No, not yet. We were waiting for you. You know I'm not very domesticated, Harry, can you see if you can find anything?"

"Erm, of course. Won't be long." His walk was slow and deliberate as he went towards the kitchen.

"He's a good boy," remarked George.

"Do you like pizza?" shouted Harry from the kitchen.

"Love it," called Lucian back, smiling at George, who didn't smile back.

"Loosen up," said Lucian quietly, "Or he'll suspect something."

Soon, the smell of cooked pizza reached them.

"Dad, can you help me please? I can't carry all this stuff and my stick."

Both men jumped up and put the food and plates on the table and sat down to eat. George could hardly swallow his slice of pizza but he valiantly chewed on. He must not appear to be nervous in front of Lucian. He'd already given Harry a subtle hint that all was not well by saying he wasn't domesticated and Harry had got the message by the puzzled frown on his face.

Things were easier with Harry there as the lad asked his uncle questions about his travels, which Lucian answered easily. George suspected there weren't many places Lucian hadn't been, after all, he had the money to go anywhere he wanted. It made it easy to give the impression he'd lived abroad. And Harry was a great listener, asking questions and paying eager attention to the answers.

"You and Dad are not very alike, seeing as you're brothers," Harry suddenly remarked.

"We're step-brothers," Lucian replied, cool as ever. "My father married your dad's mother when your dad was little. I had almost left home then as I'm a lot older than your father. We were never that close really, because of the big age gap. I guess that's the reason why we let our contact slip."

Harry nodded understandingly. "So, are you staying here for a while?"

"No, just passing through, lad. I'm up this way on business and thought I'd look you all up. I wouldn't have known where you were, except I'd read about your accident and recognised your father's picture in the paper and knew you were in this area."

'*Cool answer*,' thought George. Doesn't anything faze the man?

"Do you fancy a game of chess?"

"Love to."

"It's up in my room, would you like to come up?"

"Why don't you bring it down here, then we can continue our chat with your dad too?"

"Uh…"

"I'll get it. In fact, I don't need to, there's another set in the sideboard. I think it's all there." George got up quickly and went over to the sideboard. He found the game and brought it out. Harry set it up on the table.

"Black or white?" Harry asked.

"Black, I think."

'*Appropriate*,' thought George and settled down for another nerve-wracking hour, although it was interesting watching them play, for Harry was every bit as good, if not better, than Lucian.

"You're very good," Lucian said, admiringly. "I really thought I had you there but you managed to outwit me, lad. Can we have a cuppa tea? I'm parched."

"I'll do it," said George, getting up.

"No, let Harry do it. You don't mind, do you, Harry? Let your old man and uncle have the chance to catch up some more. I won't be around much longer. I'll just wait to say hello to your mum when she comes and then I'll be off. I have to be in Leeds tonight because I've a big business meeting in the morning."

"Of course I don't mind, although you'll have to help me carry it through. Do you like a cup and saucer, or will a mug be okay?"

"Mug's fine. Black with one sugar, please."

"Okay." Harry walked carefully towards the kitchen and George heard the click of the kettle. It seemed an age until he came back, carefully carrying a mug which he handed to Lucian.

"I'll fetch yours, Dad."

"Just pop it on the table there, thanks. I'll get it when I want it. You have yours.

And so the afternoon ticked slowly by. Normally, Harry would have gone up to his bedroom by now to work on the computer but he seemed to know that George wanted him to stay. George was thankful that he had such a sensitive son and the remembrance of forcing him to go canoeing turned a knife in his heart again. How could he have done that? He'd turned into such a bad-tempered person, so unlike his usual self and all because he'd been out of work for so long. They were really paying the price for it now, and Sally too.

It was with relief when George heard the back door open and in breezed his wife. She came straight through to the living room, where she stopped dead.

"Oh! George, what are you doing home from work? And who is this?"

"This is my step-brother, Luke, Netta. He's been paying me a visit but he'll be going soon."

Lucian stood and took her hand and kissed it in an old-fashioned gesture. "I'm pleased to meet you, Annette. You are even more beautiful than in your picture. I can see I've missed out these past fifteen years or so. I've enjoyed meeting Harry, we've had a game of chess and he beat me!"

"Oh," Netta was flustered at such flattering words. "Harry's good at chess."

"So, when will I meet your lovely daughter? I can't go until I've met her too."

"Isn't she here yet?" Netta turned to George. "She usually comes straight from school. She should have been home an hour ago."

"Well, she's not home, my love. Could she be at a friend's house?"

"Try not to worry, Annette. Kids go off to their friends' houses without a thought about their mothers worrying about them. Perhaps she had a project she needed to do with someone."

"I'll call her."

Netta tapped her phone and held it to her ear. "It's gone to answer phone. She must have it switched off. I know her friends' numbers. I have them written down somewhere."

She went out of the room and came back ten minutes later with a worried look on her face.

"I called Fiona, her best friend. She said Rowena wasn't at school today. Oh, my goodness! Where can she be? She's been missing all day!"

"Well, she definitely set off this morning because she called cheerio to me as she usually does," said Harry. "Do you think she decided to go into town instead?"

"Why would she? She went there on Saturday with her friends."

"Maybe she has a boyfriend?" suggested Lucian.

"I believe there is a boy she likes but I have no idea who it is."

"There you are then! She's gone off somewhere with him. She'll be back soon, I'm sure. Why not give her until six, then, if she's not back, George and I will go out and look for her. How about that?"

Netta nodded. "If that is what she's done, I'll give her what-for when she gets home. I'll get tea ready. Will you have some with us, Luke?"

"I'd be honoured, thank you. Can I give you a hand?"

"Oh no, I'll manage. The kitchen isn't really big enough for two people to work. Harry can give me a hand if I need it. I made a cottage pie yesterday so I only need to heat it up. Won't be long."

Fifteen minutes later, a cottage pie with carrots, peas, corn and gravy was presented. Only Lucian ate heartily, complimenting Netta on her wonderful cooking. She nodded absent-mindedly, obviously her thoughts were elsewhere.

Just before six, Lucian said. "Why not try her phone again? She might have switched it on by now."

Still sitting at the table, Netta touched her phone and held it to her ear. She put it down. "Nothing."

"It may have run out of charge, of course." Lucian pushed his chair back. "I think we should go look for her. We'll take my car. We'll call you if we find her. Come on, George, let's go."

George fetched his coat and kissed Netta. "I'll call you. Stay here in case she comes home. If she does, send me a message."

Netta nodded dumbly and grabbed his hand. He turned to look at her and she opened her mouth to speak, then, glancing behind him, she shook her head slightly and he knew Lucian was watching. He kissed her again. "I love you", he whispered, and was gone

.

****

Netta watched the door close and flung her arms around Harry, who was standing behind her.

"Oh Harry! I have such a bad feeling about this! Do you think Row has been taken, like those other poor kids?"

"I don't know, Mum, but I do know something funny is going on. I don't like that guy who says he's Dad's brother and Dad was definitely acting strange around him."

"I know what you mean. He acted charmingly but when I looked in his eyes, he gave me the creeps. Do you think he's really Dad's brother?"

"If he isn't, he knows a lot about him as a little boy and Dad's mother."

"I suppose he must be then. I wonder why we didn't know about him?"

"Well, he and Dad gave the reason as him being so much older that they weren't really like brothers and so never kept in touch. But, thinking about the way Dad has acted all afternoon, I'd say the real reason Dad's never kept in touch with Luke is because he's afraid of him."

Netta nodded slowly, remembering the 'hunted' look in George's eyes as he'd bade her goodbye. When he'd told her he loved her, it was as if he thought he wasn't going to see her again. Netta's heart jumped in fear. She'd been horrible to him over Harry's accident but she loved him. He'd been a good husband to her and a good step-father to her little lad and to their daughter. It was unbearable to think she'd never see him again.

She let Harry lead her back into the living room, where she sank down on the sofa. Harry put his arms around her and she sobbed. Was this the end of her family?

Chapter 26

"Now, Jimmy. The first thing you're going to do is write a note to Sally. I'll tell you what to write."

They were in the back of a car with blackened windows, in a country lane. George hadn't clue where.

Lucian pulled a shelf out from the door and gave him a pen and paper.

George wrote what Lucian dictated, then the man took it, read it, and put it in an envelope.

"Good. Jake will see to that." He knocked on the window and the car started up again. They came to a deserted house with a small Fiesta parked outside. A man got out of their car and went to the Fiesta and drove it away. They stayed where they were. About fifteen minutes later, Lucian's phone rang. 'yes?' He listened and smiled. 'Good'. He snapped the phone shut and looked at his watch.

"Right. The plan is set. We'll wait for Jake to come back."

Another fifteen minutes later, the Fiesta reappeared and the man called Jake got out and came over to the car they were in. He got in the front seat, and Lucian picked up the car's intercom.

"Any trouble?"

"No, Boss. That village is so quiet, there wasn't a soul around. I posted the note and drove away without anyone seeing."

A few moments later, George's phone rang. He took it out of his pocket. It was a number he didn't know. Receiving a nod from Lucian, he answered it.

"Hello? Yes."

At the sound of Sally's voice on the other end, his heart beat faster. He didn't want to do this, he really didn't. For a moment, he didn't speak but Lucian held up the photo from the sideboard and scratched one of his large rings across Rowena's smiling face, cutting the glass. George swallowed hard, getting the message loud and clear.

"Sal, I have to speak with you, it's very urgent. No, I can't tell you over the phone, it's too dangerous. When can you meet me? Yes. Yes, that would be okay. I'm not sure what I'll tell Netta for being out so late but I'll manage somehow. No need to worry, but please do come. Don't tell anyone, not even Alex. This is dangerous but I'll risk it for you, Sally. Same place as last time? Yes, I'll be there. See you later."

He closed the phone, feeling sick. He shut his eyes as Lucian patted him on the shoulder. "Well done. What time?"

"She said around half eleven. They'll be closing then and she can make the excuse of needing some air as she often walks outside at that time."

"Perfect. Now, ring Netta and tell her to call the police."

"What?"

"Call your wife and tell her to report Rowena's disappearance to the police. Tell her that you are going to continue searching and will call her again later. Tell her that I'm still with you but I will have to go soon to Leeds."

George did as Lucian said.

Lucian held out his hand. "Give me your phone."

He handed it over reluctantly. Lucian opened the window and threw the phone out. It landed amid the undergrowth at the side of the road. George opened his mouth to protest, then thought better of it.

"Drive." Lucian ordered and the car pulled out of the gateway. As they did so, the Fiesta that Jake had used, burst into flames. It looked like there would be no one to see it being scorched to death. George had a moment of sympathy for whoever had lost their car, for he had no doubt it had been stolen.

****

Dan received the message just after eight o'clock that evening.

"Oh no! Not another kid gone missing," he groaned. "Come on, Grant, Coombs, let's go. At least we don't have to go far, only up to Bobblestock."

When the Thompsons' door opened, Dan nearly fell over in surprise.

"Lucy! What are you doing here?"

"Oh, Inspector Cooke, I'm glad to see you! I came to be with Netta and Harry."

"Harry?" Dan frowned. "Not Harry from hospital?"

"Yes. It's his sister, Rowena, that's gone missing. Come on in."

Grant and Collins followed their boss into the living room, where they found Kenny, Harry and Netta. Harry had his arm around his mother, who sat, tears running down her cheeks.

"Mrs Thompson," said Dan gently. "I'm so sorry about your daughter. This is Detective Sergeant Grant and Detective Constable Coombs. Are you up to answering some questions?"

She nodded, sniffing back another sob.

"I'm sure I can probably tell you more than Mum," said Harry.

Dan nodded. "Okay, then, Harry. You answer my questions, then if your mum wants to add anything, she can. Is that okay with you, Mrs Thompson?"

She nodded again. Grant and Coombs both took out notebooks, discreetly sitting on chairs at the back of the room. Dan sat on an armchair, the very one that Lucian had sat on earlier.

"Now, did Rowena go off to school as usual?"

"Yes," said Harry. "Mum goes to work for eight o'clock on Tuesdays, so she was already out. Row always hollars 'cheerio' to me as she leaves because I'm usually still upstairs when she goes out."

"What time does she leave?"

"About eight-fifteen. She has to be there at eight-thirty but it only takes five minutes to get there."

"Does she go to Whitecross School?"

"Yes."

Dan nodded. "So, was she as usual this morning? She's not had any upsets with anyone, no rows at school?"

"No. She's always cheerful and loves school. There hasn't been any trouble as far as we're concerned. She was as she always is."

"Right. So, when did you become aware that she was missing?"

"Not until this afternoon when Mum got home from work and Rowena wasn't at home."

"Does she always come home, or does she sometimes go to a friend's house after school?"

"She sometimes goes to a friend's house but if she does, she usually texts Mum, or me if Mum is at work."

"And you didn't get a text?"

"No. Mum tried to call her but it went straight to answer phone."

"What did you do then?"

"Mum has the number of Row's friends. Row's best friend Fiona told Mum that she hadn't been at school all day."

"The school didn't call you, Mrs Thompson, to ask where she was?"

Netta looked up for a moment and shook her head.

"We'll talk to the school in the morning." Dan looked towards Grant, who nodded slightly.

"So, once you knew she hadn't been to school, what did you do?"

"We had tea."

Dan looked up in surprise. They knew their daughter was missing and they had tea?

"I know what you're thinking, Sir, and you're right really. It was Uncle Luke's fault…"

"Uncle Luke?"

"Yes. When I got back from the hospital, Dad was here with a man, who he said was Luke, his step-brother. He hadn't seen him for years because Luke has been abroad but he was going to Leeds on business and thought he'd look Dad up on his way there."

"And where is your dad? And this Luke?"

"They went out to look for Rowena. Luke told Mum that teenagers are often inconsiderate and play truant or go off somewhere, not giving a thought to their mothers worrying about where they are. He suggested that we give it until six o'clock, then if she wasn't home by then, he and Dad would go out and look for her.

"So, we ate, and then she tried calling Rowena again and got no answer, so Dad and Uncle Luke went out to look for her. Then, about quarter to eight, Dad called and said to ring the police but he was going to keep looking. That's when we called the police, and I called Lucy because I thought having Lucy here would help Mum."

"I see. So, where is Uncle Luke now?"

"He had to leave Dad to get to Leeds. That's why he called us, I guess."

"Your dad went off in Luke's car?"

Harry frowned. "He must have done, because Dad's car is still here."

"So, if this man had to go on to Leeds, your dad must be on foot."

"I suppose he is. But the bus service is good, so I suppose he'll catch one to come home."

"Why don't you call him and tell him to come home? Your mother needs him."

Harry pulled out his phone and tapped around on it. He listened for a while, then said,

"His phone's ringing but he's not picking up."

At that, Netta started crying again. "It's that man! He's done something to George! I know it, he was awful, he made my flesh creep."

Dan looked at her and then at Harry, a questioning look on his face. Harry nodded empathically.

"Yes. Mum is right. There was something very wrong about that man – my so-called 'uncle'. I spent all afternoon with him and Dad, and I got a strong impression that Dad was afraid of him. It was also strange that, at lunch-time, Dad asked me to get the food. He said to me 'you know I'm not very domesticated' and looked at me intensely for a minute. It puzzled me because Dad is very domesticated, he can cook a meal and do all sorts in the house. It was as if he was trying to tell me something."

"Trying to tell you that something wasn't right?"

"Yes! Yes, that's it! Although Luke was friendly and played a game of chess with me, I definitely got the feeling that he was something other than what he was trying to show me. I suppose I watch too many films, but he kindof made me think of a mafia boss, or something. Like he was used to people obeying him. Certainly Dad was complying with everything he said and did."

"A mafia boss eh?" Dan stroked his chin thoughtfully.

Kenny suddenly said, "I've just remembered. My mother told me that someone called with a message for George. He said Netta needed him at home because she'd either been taken ill or had an accident. Apparently, the caller wasn't sure what had happened. He said his wife gave him the number of the nursery and told him to call for George. Mum took the message to George and he left work straight away."

Netta looked up, shocked. "But I was fine! I was at work."

"Yes," said Dan, grimly. "It was a ploy to get George to come home."

"Oh, Mr Cooke, do you think my George is in danger?"

"I don't know, Mrs Thompson."

"Oh, please find him! He's a kind and gentle man, wouldn't hurt a fly. I was so horrible to him when Harry had his accident but I love him. Please, please, find him."

"We'll do our best. I'll have uniform search the streets of Hereford for him. We'll find him, don't worry."

He nodded to Grant, who slipped into the kitchen to make the phone call.

Harry got up. "I have something, Sir. It might be useful." He made his way out of the room. Lucy took his place beside Netta, who gripped her hand. "Oh Lucy, I've lost Rowena and George in one day! What will I do?"

"I'm sure Mr Cooke and his team will do everything they can, Netta."

"Do you have a picture of your husband and daughter, Mrs Thompson?"

Netta looked around the room. "Oh! I had a photograph of us all on the sideboard and it's gone! Why has it gone?"

Harry came slowly back into the room. "What's up, Mum?"

"The picture that was on the sideboard, Harry. It's gone."

Harry frowned. "It was on that little table beside you, Inspector Cooke. That man was looking at it. He must have taken it. Don't worry about that, Mum. I'm sure Cessy will give us another one."

"What did you have for me, Harry?"

"This." Harry held up an A-4 sheet of paper.

Dan took it and whistled. "My word! Did you do this, Harry? You have quite a talent. Is this 'Uncle Luke?'"

"Yes. I have a very good memory for faces. I would have tried to take a photo of him with my phone but somehow I knew he'd not allow it.

"As soon as he and Dad left, I went up and did this drawing while the details were fresh in my mind. I had an idea it might be needed."

"Clever lad! Look at this, Grant and Coombs, Lucy and Ken, isn't it amazing?"

"I see what Harry means," said Lucy. "He does remind me of a mafia boss."

"He does indeed. Did he have any kind of accent?"

"Not markedly so but I was certain I recognised a slight London twang. The occasional word, you know?"

Dan did know. "Can we keep this?"

"Of course. That's what I did it for."

"I don't suppose...?"

Harry handed him two more papers. One was a drawing of Rowena, the other, his dad. Dan nodded in satisfaction. "Brilliant. These will help our officers. Now, can you think of anything else that might help us?"

Netta spoke then. "Not really, Mr Cooke. But I do know that George was not at all happy when he went out. He kissed me and told me he loved me. He hardly ever tells me that. Oh, I know he loves me and he cuddles me and so on but doesn't often tell me. He had a look on his face that made me think he didn't expect to see me again." She started to cry again, and Lucy put her arms around her.

"Did you call the doctor, Julie?"

"Yes sir. He'll be here shortly."

"Good. Mrs Thompson, we'll get the doctor to give you a mild sedative to help you to sleep. It'll head off the worry for a while. I have a feeling that we'll have news for you in the morning."

As he spoke, the doorbell rang and Julie Coombs went to answer it. She came back, followed by a man in a coat and hat, carrying a bag.

"Ah, Doctor, thank you for coming out. This lady has had a shock. Her daughter and husband have gone missing. Can you give her something to help her sleep, please?"

"Yes indeed. Hello, Mrs Thompson. I'm Doctor Gillard, a police doctor. Would you like something to help you sleep?"

Netta nodded. Overwhelmed, she just wanted to stop thinking. "Yes please."

He gave her two tablets and she took them with water that Kenny brought from the kitchen.

"Will you help her to bed?" the doctor asked Lucy and she nodded "Of course."

He gave her the eye. "Don't you overdo it, young lady. I see you are near your time and you're looking tired. Get this lady to bed and then you should go home to yours. I'll see myself out. Goodnight, everyone."

****

Kenny helped Netta up the stairs and Lucy helped her to undress and into bed. After she was covered up, Lucy smoothed Netta's hair from her forehead. "Try not to worry. I'm sure there will be news in the morning."

Netta nodded sleepily. She was practically asleep and Lucy crept out, quietly shutting the door behind her.

Dan and his team had gone. Harry sat with Kenny, talking softly. Lucy's heart went out to the lad. He'd already been through so much and now this, two terrible things happening at once.

"Shall we stay with Harry, Ken? I don't like to leave you, my lad."

"The doctor is right, Lucy, you should go to bed," said Harry. "I'll be fine. I'm here if Mum wants anything, or, or if we get a call."

"Well, if you need us again, just ring. Let us know if you get any news."

"I will. Don't worry about me. I'm very grateful to you for being here with us and for looking after Mum."

"Lock the door after us," said Kenny as he picked up his coat. He and Lucy made their way to the front door, with Harry just behind.

Lucy enveloped him in a big hug. "We're here for you, Harry. Just call us."

Kenny helped Lucy into the car. Harry briefly waved and shut the door.

"Poor kid. First his accident, now this."

"I know. It's strange how everything seems to happen to some people, isn't it? I do hope his sister will be found, and George."

"It's odd, isn't it? I mean, if the sister has been taken by the kidnapping gang, why has George gone missing too?"

"No good asking me, my love. I'm not the detective. Poor Mr Cooke was looking tired, don't you think?"

"Not surprising, with all those youngsters missing. I bet he can hardly bear to go home to sleep."

Chapter 28

On the way out of the Thompson house, Dan ordered his team home to bed.

"We can't do anything else right now. I don't think there'll be any point in getting search parties out again. They never turned up anything with the last six and I don't think they'll have any luck with this one. In the morning, Grant and Coombs, I want you to team up with Johnson and another constable, maybe Tanner, and do some house to house round the area at the back of the Thompson house. I'm going to send this drawing to Thames Valley Police and the Met to see if this man is known to them. I'll ask uniform to continue searching Hereford for George Thompson. Now, go home. We need to be fresh for the morning."

****

George had no idea where they were going but it seemed they drove a long time. The black outlines of hills and trees meant they must be near the border of Wales, or even over the border. At last they pulled into a dark driveway of a large building that looked deserted. Some of the windows had been broken and others were boarded up. It had a desolate air, made worse by the deep shadows cast by tall trees all around. George shivered; there was something about the place that spooked him.

"Cold, Jimmy?" Lucian was amused.

"No, not really. It's this place, gives me the creeps. What is it?"

"That's for us to know and for you to wonder. Get out."

Startled, George got out of the car. Could he make a run for it? But when he felt the poke in his back from Jake behind him, he thought better of it.

"Walk."

George didn't have to walk far. In front of the house stood another dark coloured saloon, the number plate obscured by what he assumed was mud.

"In."

He bent his head and got into the back seat of the car. It didn't have the luxury of the first car, but then he realised a vehicle like the first one would attract a lot of attention if anyone spotted it in the village. Lucian got in beside him.

"Now. You're going with Jake and Butcher to Sutton-on-Wye and you'll meet with Sally in the lane. You will arrive before her so she doesn't see a car and you'll embrace her. No funny stuff mind, or you will be punished – and you will never see your girl again, understand?"

George nodded miserably.

"Don't worry about the kids, they're okay. I don't deal in that kind of business now, although that kid called Gloria is Something; I could do a deal with her. Her old woman is a pro and I'd like to bet Gloria would be a good one too, given the chance. She could make me a few quid. Your girl is great too. If you do anything stupid, I'll keep her. She'll be a good replacement for Sally."

George leaped on him then, and his fist smashed into that smug face. Strong hands pulled him off and he was held in a vice-like grip. Lucian put his hand to his mouth and felt the blood.

"You'll pay for that, Jimmy-boy. I didn't think you were stupid, but I can see you are. Butcher here is dying to get his hands on you, aren't you, Butch?"

George heard the cracking of knuckles and blanched. He braced himself for what was coming. But all that happened was Lucian got out of the car and Jake got in beside him. Butcher climbed into the driving seat and they pulled away, leaving Lucian standing on the cracked tarmac.

George was uncomfortably aware of his silent companions, but smiled to himself, glad he'd punched his step-brother's smarmy face, he'd wanted to do it years ago. It was about eleven twenty when Butcher drove into the village of Sutton-on-Wye and pulled his car around the corner from River View Lane, out of sight. Pushing the revolver into George's back, Jake ordered him out of the car. Keeping in the shadows, they went into the lane.

"Right. Stay here, and don't try anything, otherwise you will get a bullet. The woman won't see us in the shadows."

It seemed an age to George as he shuffled from foot to foot just inside the lane, out of range of the lamplight. He wished and prayed she wouldn't come. But come she did. He heard the sound of light footsteps and saw her in the light of the street lamp. Taking his courage in both hands, he ran towards her.

"Run, Sally, run!"

He just had time to see her turn and run and a shot rang out. George felt an explosion of pain and he hit the ground.

****

The phone was ringing. Kenny opened one eye and peered at the clock. It was just after twelve. Who could it be? Perhaps it was Harry, having heard something. He picked up the phone.

"Hello? Alex? Calm down, man! Stephanie's disappeared? How? When? Oh, my goodness! Have you called the police? Well, call them! I'll come right away, don't panic! I'll be there in a few minutes."

"Wha's going on?" said a sleepy voice beside him.

"It's Alex. He says Stephanie's disappeared!"

"Are you serious?" Lucy was wide awake and sitting up.

She watched Kenny get out of bed and started to follow him.

"No, Lucy, you stay, you need your rest."

"I'm coming! Stephanie is my friend!"

As they pulled on the clothes they had not long taken off, Lucy put her hand to her mouth and gasped.

"What is it?"

"You – you don't think Stephanie and George have run away together? You did say you saw them that time!"

Kenny paused for a moment, then, "No, I don't. In any case, Alex needs us. Are you ready?"

They hastened downstairs. "We'll take the car as it's so dark."

"I'm so relieved your mum took John home with her." Said Lucy as Kenny drove, grim-faced, out of the drive.

"What's that?" Kenny said, as the headlights picked out a dark shape in the middle of the lane. He stopped the car and ran to the still form. He bent down to look closer. Lucy had climbed out, holding a torch. She shone it on the figure.

"It's George! He's badly hurt – don't move him! Call an ambulance."

With shaking hands, Lucy dialled 999 and swiftly gave directions then asked for the police.

"Leave me here with him! You go to Alex."

"No! I don't want to leave you here in the dark on your own. What if whoever did this to him is still around?"

"They won't be! They'll be long gone. They probably think he's dead – he almost is. I'll be alright. Alex needs you and someone must be here to signal the ambulance or they'll run him over! I've got my phone, I'll keep in touch! We can't get the car around him so you'll have to go to Alex's on foot. Don't worry, darling. Go on – go!"

Kenny kissed her. "Don't be a hero, don't do anything stupid."

"I won't! I'll sit in the car until I think they might be near. There are a couple of blankets in there. I'll cover him up."

Kenny hugged her again and left her. Lucy watched him jogging under the lamplight. She went to the car and pulled out a couple of blankets she always kept there in case John was cold and carried them back to tuck around George, careful not to move him. A dark pool of blood had seeped into the rough tarmac under his lower body. She went back to sit in the car, shivering a little, but whether from cold or nervousness, she didn't know. It seemed a long time until the ambulance came, although it was only about twenty minutes.

The police arrived before the ambulance, along with the paramedics. While they saw to the injured man, Lucy told the police what she knew. They called in for DI Cooke, who arrived in remarkably quick time, looking dishevelled and driven by his wife, Linda.

"I sent my team home," he explained, "and I'm not fit to drive. So my darling wife here brought me. So, we've found George then? What's the verdict, gentlemen?"

"He's been shot," said a paramedic. "He's bleeding badly and he looks like he has a head wound too, likely caused when he fell. We've no way of knowing how long he's been here, but he needs to get to hospital right away, he's in a bad state."

"Right. Constable, would you go with him, please?" The man climbed into the ambulance and it drove away, blue light flashing silently.

"Dare I ask what you are doing here in the middle of the night?" said Dan to Lucy.

"Well, I was in bed, we both were. We had a phone call from Alex, who runs the restaurant here. His wife, my friend Stephanie, has disappeared."

"What? Another disappearance? This is getting beyond a joke!" Dan growled. "Where is this restaurant? Oh, don't bother, I know! Linda, will you go to Lucy's place with her and wait until I come back for you?"

"Oh, but I was going to join Kenny at Alex's," protested Lucy.

"You are not! You are going home and Linda is going with you. I'm going there now. Get off back up the lane, do as you're told, girl!"

He stomped off, giving her no chance to object. Linda took her arm. "Come on, better do as the boss says."

Lucy had to drive down the lane and turn round in the road, grimacing as she had to drive over George's blood, which was a dark puddle creeping across the lane. Moments later, they were back in the farmhouse.

"Wow! This is a lovely place," said Linda, looking around.

"It is. I'm very lucky my Aunt Bea left it to me. Even luckier that I found Kenny."

"Well, I've always wanted to come out here to visit you, but I never thought it would be in the middle of the night!" laughed Linda. "Harry told me so much about you and so has Dan. He's very fond of you, you know."

"Who is?" Lucy was startled. "Harry?"

"Well, yes, certainly Harry has a crush on you, but I think Dan is fond of you too."

"Oh, he just likes my cakes!" Lucy flapped her hand at Linda, embarrassed.

"That could be it!" Linda laughed again.

"Do you fancy a hot chocolate or a Horlicks or something?"

"That would be lovely. But you should sit down and rest. I'm sure I can find my way around your kitchen."

"No, I'll do it. I have a lot of cupboards and things and I know where everything is."

Linda sat at the table while Lucy busied herself.

"Don't you have a little boy?"

"Yes. Fortunately, his grandma, Kenny's mum, took him to sleep at her house because Harry called us go there. At least I don't have to worry he'll wake up. I wonder how DI Cooke, Kenny and Alex are getting along. Poor DI Cooke, he looks so tired."

"Oh, do call him Dan to me! Yes, he is tired, he's been working practically non-stop since those youngsters started disappearing. He's so frustrated, there seems to be so few leads."

"And now Harry's sister's disappeared and George has been shot and Stephanie has disappeared too. It's all very strange, don't you think?"

"Yes, I have to admit, I can't make head nor tail of it, can you?"

Chapter 29

Dan was thinking something very similar, When he reached the Wyeview Restaurant, the place was ablaze with light. Kenny was there with a man that rather resembled a human spider, so tall and lanky was he. The spider was pacing about restlessly.

"Please, Sir, come and sit down," Dan said in a commanding voice. He felt sorry for the man but he needed to get to the bottom of things.

They all sat down. The other officer who had attended the scene of George's shooting was also there, notebook at the ready.

"Now, as calmly as you can, tell me the events of this evening. When did you know your wife was missing?"

"She was here until the restaurant closed at eleven thirty, I think. Although the kitchen staff told me she left them to finish clearing up and said she needed a few minutes' air. They didn't think anything of it because she does that sometimes. They finished cleaning the kitchen and left. They probably thought she would come back in and go straight up – we live in a flat above here. But she hasn't come back. Oh goodness, what shall I do? Where can she be?"

"Is it possible she could have left home of her own accord?"

"Why would she? She loves this restaurant, it was her dream, and she loves me. We're very happy together. At least, I thought we were."

He sank his head into his hands.

"Um, I don't know if this is any help, but back in January, I saw Stephanie and George in our lane, about where we found George," said Kenny.

Alex's head shot up. "George? Who's George? And why would Steph be meeting him?"

"You know George, Alex. He works for me. It was his lad who had the canoeing accident last year."

"Oh yes, of course. But why would he and Stephanie be meeting? He was a stranger here."

"He was indeed a stranger here," murmured Kenny. "But they didn't look like they were strangers."

"What do you mean?"

"Well, at one point, they embraced. However, it didn't look like a lovers' embrace, they didn't kiss or anything. It looked, well, it looked like a 'I haven't seen you for a long time' sort of embrace. I've thought about it a lot since then. I've never heard of them associating again since. George always leaves and goes home straight after work. He's a straight up sort of guy, a family man. Not the sort to play around with other women."

"What's this about finding him in the lane?"

"Lucy and I found George lying in our lane when we were on our way to you just now," explained Kenny. "He'd been shot and was in a bad way."

"Maybe George was shot trying to help Stephanie..." said Dan, slowly.

"That makes sense, to some degree. Someone took Stephanie and George tried to stop them and was shot. It doesn't explain why he was there."

"Maybe he was the bait."

"Do you think all this has something to do with the man who was at his house today, the one Harry called Luke?"

"Shouldn't be surprised. It would explain quite a few things. Harry didn't like him, nor did Netta. And Netta said George behaved as if he thought he wouldn't see her again when he left. Yes," Dan nodded, "That would explain a lot. Still more to explain. I'm sorry, MrTownsend, we need to search among Stephanie's things. We might find a clue or two. But that can wait until tomorrow, I think. It's very late now. Try not to worry, although I know you will. I am hopeful we will find your wife, we have some clues to go on. Right now, I need to get my wife home. Ken, are you coming back now?"

"I will stay with Alex, he should have someone with him. Would you let Lucy know, please?"

"Of course. Goodnight for now."

Back at the farmhouse, Dan was welcomed by Linda and Lucy.

"Come, Linda, my love. Lucy, Ken is staying with Alex for the night. We have some clues and ideas to go on but I need to go home so I can get started on them early tomorrow."

"Goodnight, Lucy. Thank you for letting me come here while I waited for Dan." She hugged Lucy.

"You must come back when all this is over – during the day! We have each other's phone numbers now. I'll send you an invite. It's been lovely to meet you, if under such horrible circumstances. How is Alex, Dan?"

"Not good, as you may imagine. But I have every confidence in Kenny. Come along, woman, I'm practically asleep on my feet."

Dan got into the passenger seat, thankful to let Linda drive. He closed his eyes and started to think around the case. He also prayed that, wherever Stephanie was, that she was safe and wouldn't be harmed. Dan couldn't help wondering why, if this Luke person was the one behind it all, did he let George's family see him? After all, they hadn't known him before. Did he think it wouldn't matter? He suddenly opened his eyes and sat up. "Where are we?"

"Just about to reach the Whitecross Roundabout. Why?"

"Go up the Three Elms Road! We have to get Harry and Netta out of that house!"

Chapter 30

Harry was startled when his phone rang. He'd just dozed off, after lying awake for a while, worrying about his sister and father. Groping blindly for it, he picked it up as it rang off in the annoying way that mobile phones have. As he squinted to see who it was, it started up again.

"Hello?"

"Harry, this is Dan Cooke. Get your mother up. You both have to leave your house. We will be there for you in less than five minutes."

Thoroughly awake now, Harry reached for his stick and hobbled as quickly as he could to his mother's room.

"Mum! Mum, wake up" He shook her hard. "Mum, you have to wake up!"

She stirred but then settled down again. Harry finished dressing and threw some clean clothes into a bag. His phone rang again.

"Harry! We are outside the door, we don't want to make any noise. Come down and unlock it."

Harry went down the stairs on his bottom, knowing there was no time to waste. He opened the door to admit Dan and Linda.

"Linda! What are you doing here?"

"Not time to explain now. Where's your mum?"

"She wouldn't wake up. You know she had those tablets."

"Oh bother, yes!"

Dan took to the stairs, swiftly followed by Linda. Harry followed as fast as he could, cursing silently. Dan and Linda were trying to waken his mum. He went in to help them.

"Mum, get up!" He shouted. "The Inspector says we have to leave."

That seemed to do the trick, for she opened her eyes. "Wha'?"

"Come on, Netta," said Linda. "Let me help you get dressed, we have to go, quickly."

The two men left the room.

"Who are you?" Netta slurred, peering at Linda with half-closed eyes. "I don't know you."

"Yes, you do. I'm Harry's therapist. We've met, remember? Now come on, get these trousers on. That's good. Now, drink this water, it will help you wake up."

"Take her, Dan. I'm going to grab some clothes for her."

Dan took Netta and helped her down the stairs and a short time later, Linda came out with a pile of clothes.

"Do you have a bag for these, Harry?"

"Yes, downstairs."

Harry found a shopping bag the clothes.

"Lock the door, Harry," said Dan and the lad obeyed and climbed into the car in the front because Linda was in the back supporting Netta, who was already dozing off again. Now fully awake, Dan drove off quickly towards the quiet city and their home.

"I'm glad the spare bed is made up," remarked Linda as she helped Netta out of the car. They managed somehow to get Netta up the stairs and into the bed, Linda just slipping off her shoes, before the woman was once again sound asleep.

'She won't know where she is when she in the morning', thought Harry.

"Sorry, Harry, but we only have the one spare bed but the sofa is quite comfortable."

"Doesn't matter, Sir, there's not much of the night left now anyway." Harry grinned. "I'll be fine, don't worry."

"We'll have to take you and your mum to a safe house until all this is over. No explanations now, Linda will fill you in tomorrow. Now, we must all get some sleep; I have a busy day ahead of me."

Certain he and his mum were safe, in spite of being concerned about the other half of his family, Harry drew on that talent teenagers have and fell asleep almost as soon as the light went out.

****

Stephanie was very frightened. When she heard George's voice shouting to her to run, she turned immediately and ran.

However, when the shot rang out, she hesitated and that was her undoing. Two men overpowered her. One of them knocked her senseless and when she came to, she was in a car, bound and gagged. Her face hurt and she had no idea how long she had been out but it was still dark.

As the car slowed. she tried to lift her head to try to see where they were but she saw nothing, only dark trees.

The car stopped. The door opened and she was hauled out by a man wearing a black balaclava.

"Walk."

Pushed from behind, she stumbled.

"Careful," growled another voice. "She has to be unharmed."

"Not much chance of that after that punch you gave her."

"Quiet! Let's get her in. I need some shut-eye."

She was dragged by the two men towards what looked like a deserted mansion. Even in the dark she could see that windows were boarded and others were broken. They went in through a side door, which led into a plain hallway and shoved her into a room. They picked her up and laid her on a hospital-type bed against the wall. She started to scream and kick them. Someone else came in, a woman, who a mask on like a woman's face. She stopped, surprised. The men held her down and the woman put something over her mouth and nose. Eyes wide, she tried to struggle but a moment later, she heard a door slam and closed them to the blackness.

****

Rowena awoke with a jump. Was that a car and voices! Was she being rescued? Straining her ears, ready to scream and shout if necessary, she ran to the door and listened. Then she heard a scream and her heart sank. Surely they hadn't taken another victim? The door that slammed was not far away, in fact, she could have sworn it was next to hers. Apart from the woman who came with her meals and the masked heavies standing on guard at the door, she never heard or saw anything. This was new. If it her meals were made in this building, it was quite a way from where she was because she never heard anything of life at all.

Convinced that they had another prisoner and she was not being rescued, with her hopes dashed, she crept back to her bed and pulled the covers up to her chin. Tears of despondency trickled down, landing on her pillow. She brushed them away angrily and lay there, determined to find a way to escape.

Chapter 30

In spite of his late night, Dan was at his desk early, having grabbed a cup of coffee on his way in.

A young constable came into the room. "Message for you, Sir."

"Oh, thank you, erm, Constable Brown isn't it?"

"Yes, Sir. The fire chief wants a word, Sir."

"Is he here?"

"Yes, sir."

"Ask him to come in, please."

Dan stood up to wring the hand of the burly fireman who came in.

"Trevor! Good to see you, mate. Take a seat."

"My department attended two fires last night. One was a burning car, or rather, it was pretty much burnt out when we got there and more importantly, a house in Bobblestock, where I believe a family called Thompson live?"

"Oh my! We got them out in time! Thank the Lord!"

"I understand you are investigating an incident involving the family?"

Dan gave the chief a quick run-down of the events of the previous night and he whistled.

"My word, Dan, you've got a job on!"

Dan nodded, grimly.

"I'm glad the boy and his mother are safe. And the father is in hospital, is he?"

"Yes. We're worried about the girl but we have a lead now, thanks to Harry."

"What if...?"

"What if what?"

"I was just thinking. If we put out a news bulletin about the fire and the shooting and give the impression that the three are dead, would that help to relieve the pressure on protecting them? If the perpetrators of these crimes think they've succeeded in their purpose to wipe out the family, they might well let down their guard.

"Good thinking! We'll do that. I'll have a word with Superintendent Keating, get his approval, then we'll get onto the local television right away."

"I'll be happy to add weight, let them interview me at the scene, so to speak."

"Great! We'll take the family to a safe place as soon as we're able but if the gang, or whoever they are, are no longer watching for them, it will make moving them easier."

"Do you know where you will send them?"

"I have an idea but I'll have to arrange it."

"Great. That's a plan then."

"Let me know what your investigators find at the fire."

"That's another thing. I don't know if the house fire and car fire are connected but we are pretty certain, although we'll have to investigate further, that both fires were set the same way, with a detonator of some sort. We'll know more before long."

"Keep me posted. I'll get men out to the burnt-out car too, to have a look around."

The others arrived as the Chief was leaving.

"Incident room, now," he barked. "And I want Johnson and Tanner too – and WPC Griffin."

Once in the Incident room and everyone assembled, Dan gave his team the low-down on the happenings of the night before. The board not only had the pictures of the six previously missing youngsters, it also held Harry's drawings of Rowena and George.

"Right. This is what today is going to look like. Griffin, who is your partner?

"Symonds, Sir."

"Right. I have permission from your CO to use uniformed officers. I want you and your partner to go to my house and escort Mrs Thompson to the hospital to see her husband. Not yet, though, not until I've heard from my wife. She has the unenviable task of telling young Harry and his mother what's happened to George. I want a twenty-four-hour guard on George and I want to know the moment he comes to."

"The picture of 'Uncle Luke' has already been sent to Thames Valley and Scotland Yard to see if they know him. It's imperative that all this is kept under wraps; we don't want any leaking to the press. The perpetrators of this set of crimes must not know we are onto them, nor that George and his family are alive. They think they're dead so let them think that. In view of that, I want you and your partner to collect Mrs Thompson out of uniform. Does one of you have a car here?"

"Yes, Sir, we both have."

"Use the one most inconspicuous."

"Yes, Sir."

"We have to find a safe house for Harry and his mother, and maybe George too, if he needs to leave hospital before this is done. In fact, the sooner we can get him out of the hospital, the better."

"Do you think all these kidnappings are connected?" asked Tanner.

"I'm certain of it. I'm not sure why, it's just a gut feeling. Johnson, I want you and Tanner to do a house to house around the Thompson house before eight. In fact, go now, so you can catch anyone going out around eight. Take a look at that alley-way that's by their garden gate, it's likely that's where she was snatched. Also, talk to the person who called the fire brigade, um, a Mrs Broadgate, number 96, next door to the Thompson."

"Sir." Johnson and Tanner left the room swiftly.

"Grant, you're with me, we're going out to see Mr Townsend and do a search. Coombs, you come too."

"Sir."

Dan pressed a button on his desk. The voice of his civilian secretary came through. "Yes?"

"Babs, I am going out to Sutton-on-Wye. I need to know the minute we receive any information on that picture you sent over to London."

"Right you are."

"And, I need you to send a statement to the local television, stating it's believed that two people died in a fire last night, just hours after the husband was found shot dead in a country lane. You know the sort of thing, you're good at it. Let me know if they want to speak to me."

"Yes Sir."

"Let's go! We'll take your car, Grant. I'm still spaced out from last night."

****

Linda did not look forward to telling Netta and Harry about George. Normally, something like that would be done by a police officer or by a detective like Dan. For the first time, she had an idea how he and other officers might feel about such a task. At least she hadn't to tell them he was dead, although apparently he had been pretty close to it last night.

Dan had hugged her and kissed her before he left, which was pretty unusual. He usually kissed her but it was often a quick peck. She realised he was feeling the pressure. It had been bad enough before with those missing youngsters but this was worse. It involved a family they knew and a close friend of Lucy's.

Linda smiled for a moment at the thought of Lucy and their midnight visit. She and her husband Ken were obviously remarkable people who were friends indeed when others needed them. She hadn't met Ken but she hoped she would before long.

Remembering her twinge of jealousy when she and Dan had been talking about Lucy that evening and she smiled again. She knew she had nothing to fear there and in fact, after all this was over, Linda could see her and Dan becoming good friends with Lucy and Kenny.

As she sat in the kitchen, hugging her morning mug of tea, trying to be quiet so as not to waken Harry who was still sleeping on the couch in the living room, she wondered where they would be sent for safety. She also prayed that George would recover. Making a sudden decision, she walked quietly out into the back garden and down to the end, where she could be sure her voice wouldn't be heard, and called the hospital. She was well-known there and had no difficulty in obtaining the information she wanted. George was in Intensive Care and was very poorly but was still alive. Thank goodness! The last thing she wanted to do was send Netta off to discover her husband had died. She sent a text to Dan: *'Called hosp. G in ICU, poorly but alive.'*

She went back into the house and, checking the clock, filled the kettle and switched it on. As she did so, Harry appeared in the doorway, looking dishevelled and hardly awake.

"Good morning."

"Yeah. Maybe." He ran his fingers through his hair in a distracted manner. Linda's heart went out to him. *'Not for the first time,'* she thought, ruefully. This boy had always pulled at her heart strings but when he was in hospital, she never dreamed they would be involved in something like this.

"I'm just making some fresh tea, or would you like coffee?"

"Actually, I'd love some orange juice, do you have any?"

"I do indeed." She opened the fridge and, taking out a carton, poured some in a glass for him.

"Thanks." He downed half of it straight away, then grinned at her. "That's better, just what I needed."

"Happy to help." She smiled back at him and he stepped closer and wrapped his arms around her and hugged her. "Thank you, Linda, for everything. I have so much to be grateful to you for and you just keep on adding things!"

She hugged him, holding him tightly for a few moments, then drew back.

"Go on with you! I was doing my job and doing my duty as a detective's wife! Now, do you think your mum is awake yet? Would you like to see while I make her a drink? What does she like?"

"Coffee. I'll go and see. I need to use the bathroom anyway."

Twenty minutes later Harry reappeared with his mother. Linda looked up and smiled.

"Hello, Mrs Thompson, or may I call you Netta? We have met before, I'm Harry's physiotherapist but my husband is DI Cooke."

"Oh, yes. I was confused when I woke up but Harry's explained what happened. Thank you for having us, Mrs Cooke."

"Linda, please. I've made coffee, would you like a cup?"

"Yes, please."

"We'll have breakfast and then we must talk."

After breakfast, during which time they made small talk, Linda said, "Now that you've eaten, I have something to tell you. I wanted to make sure you'd eaten, because you are going to be taken to the hospital. Last night, George was found. However, I'm afraid he's very ill. He's been shot."

"Shot?" Netta's face blanched. "How? Where?"

Linda related to them the happenings of the previous night. Netta stood up.

"I must go to him."

Linda put her hand on Netta's shoulder. "You are going to be escorted there, I cannot let you go on your own, my husband would kill me! I have to let them know you're ready."

Half an hour later, Linda saw them off in a car with PC Symonds and WPC Griffin.

She switched on the television, needing to have a short time of relaxation to unwind before she tackled the rest of her day. A picture of a burnt-out house and a fireman talking to the reporter burst onto the screen.

"We have found evidence that this fire was set deliberately. The two occupants wouldn't have stood a chance against such a furious blaze, even if they survived the smoke inhalation. My investigators will be examining the building thoroughly."

"Thank you, Fire Chief Evans. The police have sent a statement to us: 'This fire is the latest in a series of worrying events following the disappearance of the family's young daughter, Rowena Thompson yesterday morning. Late last night, Mr Thompson was found shot in a country lane and another woman, unrelated to the family, has also gone missing. It is not known if the assassination of this family and the woman's disappearance are connected. The police are doing everything possible to get to the bottom of this worrying series of events. This is Ben Warren for West Mercia News."

Yet again, Linda's heart went out to Harry and his parents. As if dealing with a kidnapped daughter and a seriously ill husband wasn't enough, they had now lost everything. Thank the Lord that she and Dan had got them out in time.

****

In a seemingly deserted building about an hour or so away from Hereford, someone else watched the news with satisfaction. Everything had gone beautifully, his men had done well. Now, it was time for the next step in his plans.

Chapter 32

"So, Mr Townsend, tell me about your wife. Everything you know about her. How long have you known her?"

"We met at Catering College in Hereford, oh, eleven years ago. We have been married ten years."

"That's quite a long time. So, you married soon after you met?"

"Well, about a year, after we'd finished the course – we were in the same year. We found jobs in different establishments in Hereford. As soon as I met her I knew I wanted to marry her. She wasn't quite so sure, because of the age gap, she's quite a bit older than me, you know. But I persuaded her."

"What do you know of her life before then?"

"Well, she told me she had no relatives as far as she knew. She said she had lived in London and her mother died so she couldn't afford to stay, so she moved away. She worked as a waitress to earn money so she could finally go to catering college."

"She didn't tell you where in London she lived? Or what her mother's name was?"

"She once told me her mother's name was Jane. She has a picture of her somewhere."

"Father?"

"Apparently he hopped it when he found out Jane was pregnant. Her mother brought her up alone."

"Hmm. Now, do you mind if we search amongst her things? It might give us some clues."

Alex waved his hand. "Yes. Do whatever it takes. I have a really bad feeling about this. There has to be something in Steph's life that she hasn't told me. Why didn't she? Surely she could trust me?"

"I have no answer for that, Mr Townsend, I'm afraid. Maybe she had something happen in her life that has made it difficult for her to trust. Has she been acting normally lately? Anything you noticed?"

"Well, there was that incident on Christmas day, although she said she was ill."

"What happened?"

"We went to Sutton Court to sing Christmas Carols like we do every year. Suddenly, she turned white and said she needed to go home. Not like her, she's almost rudely healthy."

"And was she ill?"

"No, I don't think so. But she wasn't *right*. I can't quite explain what I mean but I noticed she definitely wasn't herself and she didn't want to go out. She would curl herself up on the sofa and just – lie there. I've never known her do that. She often sat next to me and we'd cuddle, but she took to curling herself up in the foetal position and stay like that for ages."

"Was she still doing that until last night?"

"No, it stopped a few nights later. She became herself again. I thought it was a bit odd but I was so glad to see her back to normal I didn't comment. I just thought that perhaps she had been feeling a bit unwell then felt okay again."

"I think that's all for now. May we have a look around?"

"Yes of course, I'll show you where to go."

The three detectives worked swiftly and thoroughly but neatly. Julie Coombs was looking through a set of drawers in the bedroom. She'd found a wooden jewellery box, which she'd opened.

"Look at this, sir."

She help up a piece of paper, the note George had sent to Stephanie in January. "Hmm, it says here that if she was willing to meet him in the evening, to go to the nursery in the morning and have a meet-up with Lucy."

"Yes, I remember that. She suddenly said she was going to call Lucy and see if she could have a coffee with her and later she went and met Lucy. The next day, she was herself again."

"That must have been when Kenny Baxter saw them in his lane. Obviously, he must have told her something that set her mind at rest and so she stopped worrying."

"But why is the note signed 'J'?" Alex asked.

"Maybe Stephanie knew George by another name," said Dan, frowning. This case was getting more puzzling by the minute!

Alex clicked his fingers. "Yes! When we went to Sutton Court on Christmas Day, that must have been when she first saw him. It was shock she had – she was shocked to see him!"

"Then they met to talk a few nights later and she was happy again. Yes, that makes a lot of sense."

"I think she got another note last night! She saw me coming and shoved something in her pocket. I also saw her make a phone call, although she didn't notice me looking."

"Hmm. I'm getting the idea that George was used as bait. This Luke fellow, whoever he is, is behind this, I'm sure. He must have some hold over George, perhaps the daughter. It's obvious Stephanie trusted George, that's why she was happy again after she met him. Whatever secret they share, they must have agreed to keep quiet so she knew she was okay. Because she trusted George, she would have agreed to slip out to meet him if she thought he had something important to tell her. Then, they shot George and snatched her."

Alex paced the room. "But why? What has she kept secret from me? And why come after her now, after all these years?"

"I'm afraid we don't have the answers to those questions as yet, Mr Townsend, but rest assured I will do everything in my power to find out."

****

"Sir, we've had a reply from Scotland Yard."

Jennings was waiting for Dan as he and the others arrived at the police headquarters. He handed a handful of papers to Dan.

"The man is Lucian Avery. He is well-known to the police in London sir. He owns a private casino and is suspected to have fingers in all sorts, from protection to prostitution and drugs. But as yet they have not found any proof to put him away."

"Hmm, so Harry's observation was pretty accurate when he said the man reminded him of a mafia boss. Interesting. Julie, will you find us some food please, while I read these papers? Grant, contact Johnson and Tanner and see if they have anything. Get an investigation team out to that car fire, out on the Canon Pyon Road. And Jennings, see what you can find out about George Thompson and Stephanie Townsend.

"Right away, Sir."

It took Dan a good half an hour to read all the information sent to him from London. DC Coombs came back with sandwiches and sausage rolls and Grant brought more coffee for them.

"This makes very interesting reading," said Dan. "Lucian Avery inherited the casino from his father, who died suddenly of an aneurism. There is a sister living in America who never comes here. The father, George Avery, married a woman called Christine Malloy, nee Thompson, a widow, who had a three year old son, George James. Avery senior adopted the boy and everyone called him Jimmy so as not to confuse him with his step-father. Lucian Avery was seventeen when his father married Mrs Malloy."

"Jimmy?" said JulieCoombs. "Could that be the 'J' on the note? Apologies for interrupting, Sir."

"That's okay. Yes, it looks like George Thompson is George James Malloy/Avery. He and Lucian are indeed step-brothers."

"It says Avery had a mistress who had a daughter called Sarah. The mistress died in suspicious circumstances and Avery married the girl, who was only just sixteen."

"Rather indecent," remarked Grant. "Why on earth would she do that?"

"Well, from the sort of character he is, she may not have had a choice."

Julie Collins shivered. "Horrible."

"Yes. It also says that Sarah Avery committed suicide by driving her car, a gift from her husband, over the edge of a cliff."

"Oh goodness, poor woman. She must have had a terrible life to do that."

"Yes, but it also says her body was never found. The car was discovered smashed on rocks in the sea below the cliff but it was assumed her body had been thrown clear and washed away by the tide."

"Jimmy Avery used to work for his brother. He wasn't thought to be involved with any of the illegal stuff but worked in the casino and kept the books. He left his brother's employ not long after the wife's suicide and seemed to disappear too."

"Until he turns up here after his son's accident." commented Grant. Dan nodded.

At that moment, Jennings came back. "I've looked into those two people you gave me and George Thompson is indeed Jimmy Avery. He changed his name to his mother's maiden name and moved around the country. He met and married Annette Smith, who had a small son called Harry and eventually settled in Manchester. They have a thirteen year old daughter, Rowena. I think you know most of that anyway, Sir."

"I did, thank you, at least, we guessed most of it, having read about Lucian Avery. I didn't know Harry isn't George's natural son though. You can't tell, you can see he loves the lad."

"Yes, Sir. About Stephanie Townsend, maiden name Miller. I couldn't find much about her. She seemed to just turn up fourteen years ago. I couldn't find anyone of that name that would fit her and I couldn't find any relatives. She lived for a short time in Bristol and then came to Hereford to the Catering College. She married Alexander Townsend ten years ago in Hereford registry office."

"Hmm. Are you thinking what I'm thinking, Grant, Coombs?"

"Yes," answered Grant. "Stephanie Townsend is Sarah Avery."

Chapter 33

When Stephanie awoke from her drug-induced sleep, she opened her eyes and knew immediately that she'd been dropped into hell. In her sightline was an immaculate set of black clothes sitting on a chair close by. Her eyes travelled up to the face and felt another tremor of fear as she looked at the features she had not seen for fifteen years. Strangely, he didn't look much different although obviously slightly older.

"Ah, my dear, you are awake. So nice of you to drop in to see me," the smooth voice she had come to hate and hoped never to hear again, dripped into her brain like ice-cold needles. She said not a word; her throat had closed up, rendering her speechless.

"I hope you like your accommodation." His hand waved towards her bed and around the room. "It was the best I could do at such short notice. He leaned towards her and her eyes opened wider in fear, her heart thumping painfully in her chest. His hand stroked her hair. She lay still, resisting the temptation to pull away.

"Your beautiful black tresses, I missed them so, they were wonderful to run my fingers through, like caressing silken threads." His fingers fastened around her hair, holding her in a vice-like grip. Unable to stop it, she gasped as he twisted her head so she had to look straight into his eyes and his face came close to hers.

"Sally has been a naughty girl, hasn't she, *Stephanie?*" He spat her new name. His grip forced her head to and fro. "*Hasn't she?*" He moved her head around and around. "*Hasn't* she? *Speak* to me! Say, 'Yes Lucian'!"

In pain, she couldn't help the tears. She managed "Y-yes, Lu-cian."

He flung her down, letting go of her hair. She lay still, tears still trickling down her face onto the pillow. But she couldn't close her eyes, dare not close her eyes, aware how helpless she was, still tied up. He got up and paced the room.

"I thought you were dead, Sal! All these years, I thought you were dead. I grieved for you."

When he reached her bed again, he stopped to peer at her.

"Do you believe I grieved for you, do you?"

She made a movement that could have been a nod.

"I loved you, Sally."

He resumed his walking. "Yes, I loved you, Sally. But you deceived me and you know what happens to people who deceive me, don't you, Sally?

Her heart, that had started to calm down, started up harder. She did indeed know what happened to people who crossed Lucian.

"Hm, yes. You and Jimmy deceived me. He helped you, didn't he?".

He was beside her again. His hand shot out, the slap on her face ringing loud in the room. She gave an involuntary scream and couldn't even hold her hand to her cheek because her hands were bound. She didn't want to get Jimmy into trouble, so she did nothing, said nothing.

"No matter. He's been dealt with. Quick and clean, he got off lightly. His family too, at least his wife and son."

"No!" She gasped.

"Ah, she speaks at last! I thought that might do the trick! I met them, you know. Very nice wife and the son, Harry was it? Great boy. Shame really, especially as he's done so much hard work to get over that accident of his. I wonder if he knows yet that his dad is dead? Oh silly me! Of course he will know, they are all together in heaven. Dear, dear, such a shame the house caught fire."

"Fire? You killed that poor boy and his mother in a fire? How could you do that to innocent people? They had nothing to do with what Jimmy and I did!"

"They didn't, did they? But my lad, he does so like fires! And why should I stop him having a bit of fun? But at least they are together again, if not here on earth. I'm quite kind really, when you think of it.

""Hum, that'll be the day. Kind is not a word anyone associates with you, Lucian."

Lucian laughed delightedly.

"I see my Sally is coming back! That's more like you, girl! I can see I'm going to have more fun with you. I always did enjoy our little spats."

"Gentlemen, I'd like you to meet my wife, Sarah. Lovely, isn't she?"

"Looks a bit of a mess really, Luke," said one of them. Lucian laughed again.

"Yes Jake, you're right. We haven't been treating her right, have we? Let's see what we can do about that. Go on then."

Stephanie prayed that she would die quickly. However, all that happened was, the heavies cut her loose and helped her to sit up. A woman came in and set food on the table.

Lucian waved his hand at the food. "You need refreshment, my dear. Help yourself. There is a bathroom through there. The boys will escort you. You'll find everything you need, then come back and eat. I'll visit you again later and we'll have a proper talk."

Stephanie held back the sigh of relief at the sight of his back, then she felt a finger in her back, propelling her towards the door. She went willingly, knowing she needed the facilities of the bathroom.

After tidying herself up, she returned to her cell, watched over by Jake and his friend. Once inside, the door was shut and locked behind her.

She decided she may as well eat, since there wasn't much else she could do and who knew what she might have to face; she would need all the strength she could muster and it wouldn't help if she was faint for lack of food.

Stephanie was indeed becoming Sally again; she was under no illusions – she knew she would probably soon be fighting for her life.

****

When Netta and Harry arrived and gowned up, they found George looking dreadful with all sorts of lines around him, monitoring everything and dripping blood into him. Netta's hands rose to her mouth, Harry put his arm around her and she turned and rested her head on his forehead.

A few minutes later, a doctor came in. "Mrs Thompson?"

"Yes."

"Could I have a word, please?"

They went into the corridor, and the doctor explained that George had lost a lot of blood but it was the head injury they were really concerned about.

"He's already had surgery to remove the bullet. He was fortunate that it just missed his left kidney. He will recover from that, he's a lucky man really. When his head hit the ground, with no control, it took a lot of impact. It could have killed him outright. We won't know how much damage there is until he wakes up."

"How long will that take?"

"We don't know. It's a matter of waiting. It could take days. We can't say. The best thing is for you to talk to him, both you and your son."

"What about?"

"Anything that comes into your mind, it doesn't matter what."

Netta thought back to when they'd done the same thing with Harry, and nodded. "Yes, I'll do that. Thank you, Doctor."

DI Cooke and his ever-faithful sergeant came up the corridor. He and the doctor nodded to each other and Dan came up to Netta.

"Mrs Thompson, Harry. How is George?"

"Well, the doctor just told us that the bullet wound is going to be okay. They are worried about his head injury and say it's a matter of waiting."

Dan nodded. "Let's hope he will be okay. I'm afraid I have some further bad news for you. I had to come and tell you myself."

"What else could there be?" Her hands flew towards him. "Oh no, not about Rowena, is it? Is she hurt? Is she dead? Where is she?"

He put his hand out and gripped hers. "No, it's not about Rowena. I'm sorry to say we don't as yet know where she is. It's about your home. I'm afraid it was set on fire last night an hour or so after you left."

Netta thought she would fall over. "Someone set our house on fire? We could have died." She reached for Harry's hand.

"That was the intention, I believe."

"Oh, Mr Cooke! You saved our lives! I can't thank you enough! Oh Harry, how lucky we are! All these terrible things happening to our family! We've lost everything now but we're still alive and hopefully your dad will recover and, God willing, we'll get our Rowena back."

"I certainly hope you will. We have leads now, thanks to you and Harry here. Now, I must tell you that we've put out a news bulletin, giving the impression that the three of you have died. We want the criminals to believe that, so we have arranged for you to go to a safe place until this is over."

"Oh, but I can't leave George!"

"Not right away, we'll give you time to spend with him. As soon as the doctors say it's safe to move him, he will go too, either to another hospital or, if he can cope, to the safe house with you.

"You need to understand we are dealing with a very dangerous man, who seems to have eyes and ears everywhere.

The sooner we can get you three out of harm's way, the freer we will be to carry on our investigations without having to worry about your safety."

Netta could see the sense of what the detective-inspector was telling her. She had no idea what had happened to Rowena but she had to do whatever it took to keep the rest of her family safe.

"Yes. Yes, I see. We will do whatever you say. Can we go in to my husband now?"

"Of course. He will be guarded all the time while he is here and my officers have been instructed to inform me as soon as George comes round and is able to speak."

Netta took his hand again. "Thank you. Thank you for everything you are doing for us. I hope you catch that wicked man who is causing so much trouble."

"We'll get him, Mrs Thompson. He has got away with numerous crimes over many years. He won't get away with this one."

Chapter 34

Rowena heard the shout and the scream from next door and sat up straight. What could be happening? Was someone being hurt? Would she be next? Then she heard footsteps. Were they coming towards her? She held her breath and listened but her door didn't open. Someone walked past, she knew, but they didn't stop at her door. She didn't know whether to be glad or sorry. She was terribly bored and wished something would happen.

Okay, so the food was nice and they hadn't hurt her at all. Everything she needed to be reasonably comfortable, even puzzle books containing word searches and crosswords was provided although she couldn't concentrate on reading and there was a limit to how many word searches one could tolerate. She missed her phone with the music she'd always listened to and had even scratched 'Row T' on the wall with her knife before they took away her dinner things.

She'd tried talking to the woman again but all she got was a shake of the head. For the life of her, Rowena couldn't think what was going on. They couldn't be holding her for ransom because Dad and Mum never had any money. And what about the other kids that had been taken before her? Where were they? Why wasn't she with them? Was it only yesterday morning she'd been taken? Time was going so slowly, she'd swear her watch was going backwards.

Rowena nearly drove herself mad, trying to think of a solution, a way to get help. But every time she drew a blank. Why didn't they rescue her? She flung herself down on the bed in disgust.

****

In the room next to Rowena, Stephanie sat on the single chair with nothing to do. There were no books and the bed was hard and uninviting. She knew this was an interval and soon she'd have to face Lucian again. She got up and paced the room. What could she do?

"Oh Alex," she whispered, "I'm so sorry. I hope you know how much I love you and will always love you. I'm going to die. I know he won't let me live. I'm not worried about dying, it will be better than to be at his mercy for the rest of my life. But I'm afraid of what he'll do to me though before he kills me, how much pain he'll give me and even how he will do it. Because I'm sure it won't be quick. He'll have to have his pound of flesh, his revenge. and his money's worth out of me, fifteen years' worth. But it'll be worth it because I've had a wonderful ten years with you, my darling. You showed me what true love really is and I'm grateful. I love you, Alex, I love you."

She sat down again and rocked, whispering 'I love you Alex, I love you Alex,' over and over until she was almost in a trance.

So much so, that she didn't hear the door open, didn't know anyone was there, until she once again felt his hands in her hair, tugging her head upright. She looked at him, wild-eyed and stopped rocking. She flung out her arms, making him let her hair go.

He laughed. "That's my girl."

"I'm not your girl!" she spat. "I'm done with being your girl – I'd rather die!"

"Oh, that can be arranged! But I'd like to give you a chance first. Get up!"

She stood and braced herself, ready for his fist. But it never came. Instead, she was shown the open door. The man she knew as Jake came in. Lucian said, "Follow me, and don't try any funny stuff, or I'll let Jake enjoy himself."

He went out and she followed with Jake behind her. They carried on beyond the bathroom. She marvelled at how long the corridor was, or was it a hallway? She couldn't guess.

But eventually, they came to another door and Lucian opened it and they went in. Stephanie looked around in amazement at the large room, comfortably furnished, with a bright fire burning in the grate. It was lit by a chandelier that looked old and not particularly attractive. A modern standard lamp stood in a corner.

The big picture windows looked out onto large, rather overgrown garden which was more like a field than a garden. Although the chairs looked comfortable, they didn't match and she noticed that the walls had no adornments, except for one picture that looked like a group of school boys, posing for the camera.

Lucian saw her looking at the picture. "Ah yes. It seemed a shame to take it down, it's been here so long, part of the place, you might say." He indicated the room in a large arm sweep. "Welcome to our temporary home. We didn't have much time, so we put in what we could. I'm sure the charity shops were grateful for the custom, especially as they didn't have to deliver. Do you like the garden? This was a school once, out there is the school field. I hope you don't get hay-fever, although it's too early in the year for that, so no need to worry."

If she only had hay-fever to worry about in the future, that would be wonderful. She wasn't at all sure she'd still be alive in hay-fever season.

"Do sit down, my dear. I have another guest I want you to meet. Would you care for a drink while we wait? No?"

He clicked his fingers and a woman appeared. "My usual, please, Flora." She went out and came back a few minutes later with a glass of whiskey.

Stephanie thought that this was the woman who brought her food. She looked around twenty five, attractive in a quiet sort of way and looked familiar but Stephanie couldn't place her. The woman didn't look at her. Stephanie thought that it was likely she was being allowed to see their faces because she was going to die anyway and wouldn't be able to identify them. She sat in a dark purple armchair, her hands in her lap, waiting to see what was going to happen next.

****

Rowena woke with a jump when someone shook her.

"Get up! You're wanted." She opened her eyes, her heart beating rapidly from the shock of being woken and looked into the eyes of a man. He had a bulbous nose and a scar running down his right cheek, from his eyebrow to his chin. He was not an attractive fellow.

She got up hurriedly in case he laid his hands on her again and went towards the door. He put his finger in her back and propelled her along the long corridor. While she walked, her mind puzzled about why she was now being confronted by a man who no longer wore a balaclava but found she had absolutely no idea. She was pushed into a big room and the door shut behind her. She stood by it, wondering what this was about.

"Ah, here she is! Come on in, my dear. Come and join us."

Rowena moved forward, eyeing the man who had spoken. Dressed all in black, with black hair and dark eyes, he reminded her of the devil. She'd never believed in the tales and pictures of the devil, or Satan, all red with horns and a tail, but had always thought of him like this, all in black, suave and sophisticated.

When he smiled, he was even more so. Even though he had perfect white teeth, reminding her of a picture she'd seen of Donny Osmond, he was the epitome of the devil. That smile worried her; it was like a snake ready to pounce but wanting to lull his potential victim into a false sense of security before making his strike. If anything, she was even more afraid of this man that she was of Scarface, although the burly man was obviously a vicious bully. No one needed to tell her that she was face to face with the man behind everything and Scarface was just one of his minions.

"Rowena, we haven't met. But I'm your Uncle Luke."

Rowena gasped, "My uncle? How can you be?"

"Oh, I am indeed. I'm your father's brother."

"I didn't know he had a brother. You're lying."

The Devil man laughed. "Oh, I like this girl! She's much braver than her father. Must get it from her mother."

"He's your step-uncle," said Stephanie, quietly.

"Yes, that's right. Your father and I are step-brothers. This is your step-aunt, Sarah, although you might know her as Stephanie of Wye View Restaurant."

For the first time, Rowena looked at Stephanie. The woman kept looking down at her lap so Rowena couldn't see her face properly.

"You're Lucy's friend?"

"Yes."

"I've heard her talk about you. But, how can you be his – wife?"

"Long story," said Lucian, getting up and walking over to Stephanie and putting his arm across her shoulders. Rowena saw the woman stiffen, then she noticed the bruised face. Her eyes narrowed. Was it this woman she'd heard scream? Rowena realised that Stephanie was a prisoner, like she was. What was this all about?

"I went to see your dad yesterday, Rowena. I met your mother and brother. A good looking woman and a fine lad."

Rowena didn't answer. He sat on the settee beside her and she flinched and tried to edge away. He ran his fingers through her hair, or tried to but it was knotty. He tutted and clicked his fingers. The door opened silently and a woman came in. Rowena wondered how on earth she would have known he wanted her. Did she stand on the other side of the door with her ear glued to it so she wouldn't miss the summons?

"I need a hairbrush, Flora."

While the minutes ticked by in silence as the three waited for her to return. Rowena looked at the top of Stephanie's bowed head and realised that darker roots were showing in the woman's blonde hair. The woman called Flora came back and handed a hairbrush to her boss, then hurried out.

Rowena stiffened again when Lucian started to brush her hair. Obviously, it was something he'd done often, for he brushed expertly and gently. Rowena had to admit that she rather liked it and it relaxed her. Eventually, he put the brush down and ran his fingers through her long tresses.

"Ah, that's much better. Like silk, I knew it would be. Did you like that, Rowena?"

Nodding her head, because she felt it was expected, she was relieved when he got up and crossed the room to sit on the arm of Stephanie's chair.

"Sally used to have long hair like yours, didn't you, Sally, my dear? Long, beautiful and dark as night. She's not a natural blonde, like you, Rowena. I like blondes, but have always adored girls with black hair. 'Gentlemen prefer blondes', they say!" He laughed. "But of course, I'm not a gentleman, am I, Sally?"

He put his finger under Stephanie's chin when he spoke and tipped her head up so she had to look at him. Rowena suddenly felt she'd been brought in to witness something horrible. She wished she were back in her cell.

"I see your dark is showing through your disguise. I will have my mysterious brunette wife back." Again, the clicked fingers and this time, two men appeared and another woman followed, not Flora. The two men, one of which was Scarface, picked Stephanie up and placed her on a kitchen-type chair and put a strap around her body so she couldn't move. Rowena's heart was in her mouth. What were they going to do? She didn't want to watch.

The woman and one of the men had scissors and, in spite of Stephanie trying to move away, they chopped at her hair, while Rowena cried "No, don't, don't do that!"

She tried to run over to her, but Scarface held her back and she was forced to watch while they hacked Stephanie's hair until all the blonde had gone and more. She was bald in places and what was left of her hair stuck up in black tufts. When they were done, the woman and one of the men left and Scarface untied Stephanie and man-handled her back to the chair she'd been in before, where she sat, defiant, although tears ran down her cheeks.

Rowena got up and put her arms around Stephanie, actually surprised that The Devil let her. She felt like a bird under her arm and the girl wondered how she didn't break under the rough treatment she'd obviously had.

Without thinking, she glared at Lucian. "You, you devil! What did you do that for? You're nothing but a bully! You're nothing like my dad – he's kind and gentle."

Lucian laughed heartily. "That's my girl! You've got spunk! I've never heard anyone talk to me like that before. I rather like it."

"I'm not your girl!"

"Oh, but that's where you're wrong, my dear Rowena. You are mine, because I'm now all the family you have left."

Chapter 35

"Wha – what do you mean?" stammered Rowena, wide-eyed.

"I mean, my dear niece, that your father, mother and brother are all dead."

"Dead?" Rowena's voice rose to a high note. "How can they be dead? What have you done, you wicked man?"

"I've done nothing. Your father got himself shot somehow and your house burst into flames in the middle of the night. Must have been an electrical fault or something."

"What? Our house was safe, the electricity and everything was checked before we moved in. It was you, wasn't it – or your ruffians, who did it. How could you?"

Heedless of danger, Rowena ran across the room and beat her fists against his chest. He caught them and held them fast so she couldn't move and had to look at him. All the fight went out of her and she slumped. He let go of her one wrist and twisted the other so she was forced to sit down. There she sat and cried and it was Stephanie who got up and comforted her this time.

Lucian looked at them in disgust but left them and went to sit the other side of the room. He clicked his fingers and the woman called Flora came in with another drink for him. Rowena briefly wondered how she knew he wanted a drink but was too busy trying to deal with the knowledge that her family was all gone, and dealing with the pain in her heart.

****

"Sir, the team who went out to the car fire did a thorough search of the area. They found this."

Grant held out a plastic bag which held a mobile phone.

"When they found it, it still had charge, so it hadn't been there all that long."

"Send it down to Technology and get them to do their stuff. I want to know what's on it."

Grant went off with the phone.

"Can you find me a coffee, please, Julie? I need some caffeine to help me think."

"Sir."

Before Julie left, the phone rang.

"Cooke." Dan listened for a moment "Thanks, we'll be there right away."

"Forget the coffee, Julie. We need to get to the hospital, George has woken up. Get Grant and meet me there, I'm going right now."

It only took a few minutes to get from the police station to the hospital, with Dan tapping his fingers impatiently on the steering wheel waiting for the traffic lights. He ran along the corridors to ICU until he came to the door where two policemen were sitting outside. They stood up as he reached them and one opened the door for him. He thanked them quickly as he passed through and donned a white gown before going through the second door into George's room. Netta and Harry sat together, side by side, next to the bed. Dan went round the other side. George was indeed awake. He wasn't exactly lively and raring to go but he did have his eyes open.

"Mr Thompson, I'm Detective Inspector Cooke. I'm glad to see you awake."

"I'm glad to be awake, Mr Cooke. When I felt the shot, I thought my time was up." The voice was weak but he seemed to be lucid.

"Are you up to answering some questions, sir? Let me do the talking and you tell me if I'm right, okay?"

"Yeah."

"Right. We believe you are George James Avery, known as Jimmy, adopted by Lucian Avery's father, George, when he married your mother. You left his employ and took the name of George Thompson, your mother's maiden name.

We also believe Stephanie Townsend to be Sarah Avery, known as Sally. Is that correct?"

"Yes."

"Sally faked her own death but somehow Lucian Avery discovered that she was alive and living in Sutton-on-Wye."

"Yes. Through me, it's my fault. And now he has her. He forced me to lure her and I tried to warn her but they shot me." Tears flowed from the man's eyes and Netta rose to dab his face with a tissue

"Okay, don't get upset. We need you to help us. Do you have any idea where they might have taken her?"

"No. But you have to find her, Mr Cooke. Lucian will kill her, or worse. He has Rowena and the other kids too. He told me he'd let them go if I helped him. I had to choose between my own daughter and Sally."

Dan put his hand on the man's shoulder. "An impossible choice, George."

"I had to choose our Rowena, didn't I?"

"Of course you did."

"But it meant I had to betray Sally."

"Try not to worry, George. You made the same decision any father would."

The doctor came in.

"Mr Thompson really needs to rest, Mr Cooke. He's still very weak and we also need to do a brain scan to check there's no brain damage."

"I'm okay, doctor, really." The voice from the bed was weak.

"I'll be the judge of that. I'm going to arrange the scan now. I'll see you later."

Dan went out with the doctor. "When can we move him to a safe house?"

"If the scan shows there's no brain damage, he can be moved but he must have proper medical care wherever you move him to."

"It will be arranged. Can you contact me when you consider him able to move, please? Or tell one of our officers so he can call me."

"Will do. Must get on now."

Dan poked his head round the door and signalled to Netta and told her what he and the doctor had discussed.

"You and Harry should have a break. My officers will keep an eye on him while you're gone. If the doctor gives the clearance, we will move you all tonight. The sooner we can get you away from here, the better. I'm going back to the station now, but I'll be in touch."

Grant and Collins joined him in the car park.

"Interesting news, Sir. That phone is George Thompson's. The contacts are all George's family and his work. The last two calls he made, were to his wife. Of the last three incoming calls, one was from an unknown number, which might be Stephanie Townsend's and the other two were from his wife but weren't answered."

"So, he was out on the Canon Pyon Road. I wonder where they went from there. Grant, I want you to go into the hospital and ask George if he knows where they went after his phone was thrown away."

Dan returned to police headquarters with Julie Coombs.

"Julie, I want you to go home and get some rest. Tomorrow is going to be a hard day. Time is of the essence. The longer Mrs Townsend is in the hands of that evil man, the less our chances of rescuing her alive. There's also all those kids. We have to find them, Julie, and we have to find them fast."

Chapter 35

The respite Lucian gave Rowena and Stephanie was only temporary. Once Rowena's tears had slowed down, he strode over to them.

"Right. You are under my care now that all your family are no more. No, don't start crying again, I can't be doing with emotional females. We have to make plans. I'm going to give you a choice. I'll give you a chance to save Sally here. I will let her go if you will agree to take her place as my, erm, my right-hand woman. What do you say? I could use a bright girl like you."

"No! Don't do it, Rowena. You don't know what he's like – don't," Stephanie screamed then because Lucian had grabbed her arm and twisted it behind her back. It didn't stop her though. "He's wicked, he'll use you like he used me – and he'll do unspeakable things to you, he likes young girls. Ahh!"

She was silenced by him twisting her arm further. Rowena heard a crack and Stephanie screamed again.

"Don't hurt her again! I'll do anything you want! Just don't hurt her anymore." Rowena cried.

"No! Don't say that, Rowena! Don't worry about me. He's going to kill me anyway! Don't believe that he'll let me go, he won't! He's a monster! Oh!" This time Lucian hit her across the face. Rowena screamed and rushed at Lucian, kicking and hitting him.

The door opened and the two burly men came in and grabbed Rowena, holding her fast. Lucian caught hold of her round her jaw and held her so she was eye to eye with him. His eyes were ice cold.

"I like a girl with spirit, but you go too far. I will *not* tolerate such behaviour, understand? Don't think I won't punish you, because I will. Never underestimate me, Rowena. Get that?"

She blinked, the only thing she could do. He let her face go and she spat at him.

"Oh! We have a little wildcat, do we? Well, I'll enjoy taming you, my girl!" He swiped her a vicious back-hander and she gasped. The sting made her eyes water and she looked down, sniffing, trying to hold back the tears. She cast a glance at Stephanie under her eyelashes. The woman was sitting on a chair, nursing her arm and looking very pale under the purple of the bruises on her face. Rowena was desperate to help her but she was helpless. What could she do? Rowena realised that Stephanie was right. It didn't matter what she agreed to, that monster was going to kill Steph. He'd already broken her arm, what else would he do to her before he killed her? Rowena didn't dare to think. All she could do was pray that this nightmare would end and that somehow, someone would find them.

****

"Sir, I've spoken to George. After they left the deserted cottage where the car was burnt, they travelled for around an hour, where, he didn't know, because it was dark but they went to a large, derelict building with a wide drive and an impressive front door. He saw some broken windows and others boarded up. He was made to get out of the car and into another one. He also mentioned two names, Jake and Butcher. Oh, and the doc says there's no brain damage and we can move him to the safe house, provided he has proper nursing."

"Great. I'll arrange that. As for the derelict building, I don't see how they could keep anyone there for a couple of weeks as there wouldn't be any facilities. But we will look for possibilities. If they were using it as a meeting place, we might gain some forensic evidence from it that might give us leads. Let's look at the map."

They looked at a detailed map of Herefordshire on the wall.

"George mentioned seeing hills," said Grant.

"Well, that could have been the Malverns but it's more likely, as they were on the Canon Pyon Road and Sutton-on-Wye is also over that side of the county, they probably went in the direction of Wales. We need to contact the Dwfed and Powys force and ask for their help. They may know of the kind of building we're looking for. Can you get in touch with them, Grant and I'll make the arrangements for the Thompsons to be taken to their safe house."

****

It was only an hour later that Netta and Harry were on their way to the safe house. Netta hadn't wanted to leave George but had been assured that he would be joining them very shortly, travelling separately, for safety's sake.

They were driven in an ordinary Ford Mondeo, which had darkened rear windows. After a drive of around an hour, they arrived at some big gates. The driver spoke into an intercom and the gate swung open to reveal a large house up a long drive.

A man and woman welcomed them. The man held out his hand to Netta.

"Hello, Mrs Thompson, I'm Dave Blackwood and this is my wife, Margaret. And you must be Harry? Welcome to Castle Farm. Come on in."

Feeling rather shy and out of her depth, Netta followed the couple into their house. It was a lovely, welcoming house, reminding her of River View Farmhouse, although this was vastly different, having large, square rooms with high ceilings and luxurious without being too opulent. Margaret Blackwood, a pleasant woman, made her feel welcome very quickly.

"I'm sorry to put upon you like this," she began, but Margaret waved her apologies away.

"Don't you worry, my dear," she said, in her soft Shropshire accent. "We're happy to have you both and your husband when he gets here. I have a close friend who will nurse him. She's single so she can stay for as long as he needs her. We love having visitors, don't we, dear?"

"We do indeed, my dear. Is this all the luggage you have?"

"Yes, I'm afraid we lost everything in the house fire," replied Netta. Margaret gasped.

"Your house caught fire?"

"Yes, it was set on fire. Fortunately, we'd already left but I think they meant us to die."

"Oh, you poor things! You have been through a dreadful time. Well, you can relax here, you'll be quite safe. This place is like Fort Knox."

Netta felt her tensions easing away. She really liked this woman.

"Now, my dearies, would you care for some food? It's about four o'clock and I have sandwiches and things prepared."

Netta and Harry agreed they would indeed because they hadn't eaten for ages. Soon, they were enjoying their afternoon tea with Margaret. Dave had gone back to his work on the farm. Although they appreciated the food and the company, Netta wouldn't feel happy until George was at the farm with them.

Chapter 36

Lucian pulled Rowena up roughly as the two heavies came into the room.

"Take her to the others. There's a change of plan; we're not going to let them go, they're coming with us. We'll leave after dark. Make the arrangements."

"Yes, Boss," the one called Jake said and nodded to Butcher, who grabbed Rowena's arm.

"When you've seen to her, you can come back and escort my lovely wife to her room."

Butcher smiled, revealing a set of yellowed teeth with one of the front ones missing. It was not a pleasant sight. He pulled her arm and took her out of the room and up some stairs. In spite of the uncomfortable position she had to walk in, Rowena noticed that the staircase had an elegant sweep in the wide hallway and the banisters had once been attractive and ornate, although now they were scratched and in a bad way. Upstairs, the upper hallway was long, with several doors along the stretch. They stopped at last and Butcher unlocked and opened a door, pushing her in so that she fell. She heard the door slam shut behind her.

Footsteps ran to her and arms helped her to stand up. "Are you alright? Oh!" The girl who was speaking had obviously seen the reddening of her face where she'd been slapped. Her hand went to her face, then to her knees. "Oh, my knees! He's such a brute!"

"Mark, bring a chair please!"

A boy brought a chair over and Rowena sat thankfully, still shaking.

"Here, have some water. It's all we have to give you, I'm afraid."

"Thank you." Rowena took the cup and took a sip or two. Feeling better, she looked around at the group of young people.

"Hello. Are you the kids who've been kidnapped?"

"Yeah. I'm Gloria, and this is Mark, who brought the chair. This is Sarah, Mary and Alison and that's Adam over there. Who are you?"

"I'm Rowena. Have you all been here together all the time?"

"Yes," replied Gloria, who seemed to be the self-appointed leader and speaker. "Alison was taken first, then me, then Adam, Mary, Mark and Sarah last. Did they just take you?"

"No, I was taken yesterday morning, at least, I think it was only yesterday. I was in a room on my own downstairs."

"I wonder why?"

"Well, apparently, the dreadful man who's in charge is my dad's step-brother. He specially wanted me, but I put up a fight. He's also got a lady who was his wife. She ran away from him years ago and he's just found her. I think that was my dad's fault somehow. She lived in the village where we lived after my brother had his accident in the river last year."

"Was it your brother that had the canoeing accident?" The boy called Adam came towards them. "I remember hearing about that. He was rescued in Sutton-on-Wye, wasn't he?"

"Yes, that's right. I wish it had never happened, that's what's caused this, I think. And I have something awful to tell you."

"What?"

"Well, from something *he* said before I was brought up here, I think they were going to let you all go but now I don't think they are."

"What are they going to do with us then?"

"They're going to take us somewhere but I don't know why."

"Hm. Not hard to guess," muttered Gloria. Rowena gave her a sharp look. She was obviously intelligent. The other girl met her eyes and a message passed between them: 'Don't tell them.'

'Yes,' thought Rowena, '*she knows as well as I do. I wish to goodness I could work out how to get us out of here.*'

****

Flora stood silently in the corridor not far from Stephanie's room. Butch had taken the woman back to her cell and locked the door half an hour previously. Lucian had gone in a few moments ago. Flora pressed her ear up against the door after it had locked behind him. She heard him say,

"Now. You're my wife and I'm going to remind you of that fact."

Flora pulled her head away from the door and closed her eyes. She knew only too well what that man could do. He was evil. He got others to do his dirty work when it involved men but he loved to do unspeakable things to women. When the screams started, she put her hands to her ears and ran. She thought of those kids upstairs and her own life. Afraid as she was of the Boss, Flora decided she would do something. If he killed her, at least that would be a way out. But he didn't kill. He abused and maimed but didn't kill. No, he liked his victims to suffer as much as possible, just as that poor woman was suffering now. She already had a broken arm and Flora knew the wretched creature would suffer a lot more than that before he finished.

Butcher and Jake were in the kitchen, laughing and joking. Karen looked up and the two women's eyes met. Karen gave an imperceptible nod.

"Hey, you two! It's getting dusk, don't you have things to do?" Karen spoke, sharply.

"Oh yeah, 'spose. C'mon, Butch, let's get on."

They stood up.

"Don't forget we have to feed the kids before we go," said Karen.

"Oh yeah. Get it ready and we'll be back. They'll just have to hurry up and eat, won't they?"

When the men had gone, Flora ran to a cupboard, grabbed something and handed it to Karen, who put it in a plastic bag. They had made sandwiches a short time ago and they laid trays, ready to take them up. Flora prepared another tray with mugs of tea, which one of the men would carry. Karen knocked on the window, and Jake came in.

"Ready, are yer?" he said.

"Yes, let's get this up to them and then we've gotta get ready ter leave," replied Flora.

Karen led the way, with Flora and Jake following. He had to put his tray down to unlock the door and they went in, setting the trays down on the tables. Jake immediately returned to the door, but Karen said,

"Make sure you eat all your food because we're moving out tonight."

"Yes. You need to make sure you do the job quickly," added Flora, looking meaningfully at Gloria but avoiding Rowena's eye.

The two women hastened out and the door was locked behind them. Karen and Flora crossed their fingers behind Jake's back and linked their little fingers for a moment, then followed him down the stairs.

Chapter 38

The youngsters waited until the door was locked and the footsteps died away. They looked at each other, curiously.

"What do you make of that?" asked Mary. "They've never let us see their faces before."

"It means it doesn't matter anymore," came a voice from the back of the room. They turned to look at Adam. He shrugged. "I think they were going to let us go, that's why they didn't want us to see their faces. Something's gone wrong and now the plans have changed. So it doesn't matter if we see them."

After making that statement, Adam put his nose back into his book.

"Well, there's no point in worrying about it now. We'd better eat. There won't be a cooked meal for us tonight, obviously."

Adam sat with them as they gathered around the tables to eat. There was a large pile of sandwiches and another plate with a sausage roll each. There were cakes and a packet of biscuits.

"We should eat the sandwiches but we could take the biscuits with us," said Gloria. They tucked into the mountain of sandwiches and silence reined for a while. Before very long, there were only a few left on the plate.

"What's that?" said Mark suddenly. He leaned forward and took something from underneath the bread. He held it up.

"It's a mobile phone! Does it belong to one of us? Whose is it?"

"It's mine!" said Rowena. She took it and slid it out of the bag. A slip of paper came with it and Adam picked it up.

"What does it say?" asked Mark.

"It says, 'Old boarding school, near Kinnerton. Destroy this note.'"

Rowena looked at him and then at Gloria. She switched on the phone and scrolled down her contacts.

"It's not safe to make a call. You'll have to send a text and hope someone sees it."

Who should she send a text to? Not her mum, dad or Harry, because they weren't there anymore. Fighting back the tears, she scrolled past her friends; they were no good. Lucy! She'd message Lucy, she would do something.

Her fingers flew over the letters. The signal wasn't very strong but she prayed that it would reach Lucy. In fact, Rowena had never prayed so hard in her life.

****

"Sir, you have a visitor. It's one of the kid's dads, you know, the one in the SAS?"

"Bring him in, Julie, thank you."

A man strode in. He was of average height but powerfully built. His hair was cut short and he wore combats.

"Mr Randle?" Dan rose to shake hands.

"I've just returned from our last assignment and found my daughter's gone missing. My wife couldn't contact me because she's not allowed to know my whereabouts. I'm here to find out what you're doing about it."

"I'm glad to be able to tell you that at long last we have a positive clue as to where the youngsters might be. We have to find the place and then hopefully we'll be able to gather more clues as to where they've been taken."

His phone rang. "Excuse me," he said as he picked it up. "Cooke!" he barked. Then his face softened, "Lucy? Really? Tell me!" He scribbled on a pad in front of him as he listened. "Good girl! Thank you." He put the phone down. "Grant, Collins! We have a real lead! Apparently, Rowena Thompson has sent a text to Lucy – Mrs Baxter! It said: 'Prisoners. Old Boarding School, near Kinnerton. Moving out tonight, please hurry.'"

"Kinnerton?" Grant frowned.

"Near New Radnor," said Mr Randle

"Get onto the Welsh police, it's in their territory. We need an armed squad. Get onto it, Grant!"

Grant picked up his phone and gave rapid instructions.

"I can help! My squad, or some of them can help!" Mr Randle was on his feet. "We are trained marksmen and we have experience of this kind of thing."

Dan only took a moment to consider. Then he shook his head. "Sorry, I can't allow it, Mr Randle. If anyone gets shot, one of your friends could be accused of manslaughter or murder. We have to let the firearms officers handle it."

Dan's phone rang. He listened, then,

"They know the place! It was once a boarding school for boys just outside Kinnerton. It's been empty for a while. Apparently, a local farmer has seen activity there, vehicles coming and going, and thought the place had been sold." He relayed the message to his team then spoke into the phone, "We need somewhere to assemble our men." He listened again and nodded. "Yes, where that farmer lives, ask him if we can use his place."

Via a conference phone-call with the Radnor police, they informed Dan the farmer had agreed to let them use his property. He had a field where the helicopter bringing the armed squad could land, well out of sight of the old school. Dan instructed them to move out immediately, for it would take them an hour to get there.

"As swift as we can, but no sirens or flashing lights," he warned, "Nothing to give them any indication that we are on to them."

"We'll send scouts in to check it out," replied the Welsh voice on the other end. "See you as soon as possible. Over and out."

"Grant, Julie, you're with me. We'll take your car, Grant as it's the fastest. Tanner, Johnson, and all you others, in your own cars. We'll relay the postcode to all cars en route."

"Can I go with you? I want to rescue my girl."

"Yes, but you must stay away from operations, or my head will be on the block."

****

The police headquarters emptied rapidly as cars sped out of the car park. Bert the desk sergeant sighed heavily as he watched them go and hoped fervently that no major crimes would be reported in between then and the evening shift coming on at seven or there would be no one to attend.

Chapter 39

When they pulled into the large farmyard it was dark but the farmhouse was ablaze with light and loud, thumping music could be heard. A man came to them and introduced himself as Inspector Williams.

"What the heck is going on?" Dan waved his hand at the illuminated house.

"Oh, the farmer's wife, Mrs Llewellyn, had the bright idea of pretending to have a party, in case anyone from the old school noticed lots of cars arriving here."

Dan nodded approvingly. "Clever woman! Now, who have we got?"

"I have ten men. They are over there, assembled in that barn. Two are scouting the old school; they should be reporting back soon. The armed unit is here too."

"Great. Let's join them."

Once in the barn, Dan looked at the assembled company. They all wore dark clothes rather than uniforms. The armed squad were with their commander, who came and shook hands with Dan, introducing himself as Morgan Lloyd.

The two scouts came in.

"The building does look derelict on the front side. However, round the back, it's a different story, there's a large area, once the playground, I imagine, and it's full of cars," said one, in his Welsh lilt.

"I went around the other side, Sir, and, as Evans said, it looks very much lived in. It's a huge building, forming an L-shape. On the L, there are rooms, obviously a kitchen and other living quarters. One big room is furnished. I could see in the windows easily at the end of the L, which had French windows looking out across the field. I could see at least twenty men, sir."

"No young people?"

"No, Sir, not that I could make out. There were a couple of women. It looked like they were having a meeting as one man stood out from them and seemed to be talking to them. Then they went out, leaving him behind with two others."

"Right. That sounds like what we're doing now — receiving instructions. We need a softly, softly approach, no blaring loudspeakers and threats, we don't know what they're up to in there, nor do we know where the kids are. Morgan, do you have any suggestions?"

"Yes. We'll have two of my men watching that room, six surrounding the car park and three in the front. We all have night goggles."

" How many cars do we have? I need a driver with each car. So, how many men do we have left? Ten? How many of you have bullet-proof vests on?" Okay. That's everyone except myself, Grant, Collins and Inspector Williams. I think the best way we can do this – there were no large vehicles?" Dan said, looking at the scouts.

"No Sir, they were all cars."

"Good. Pair up and silently get in between the cars and capture the drivers quietly. You have truncheons? They're probably going to take the kids in different cars, possibly with a driver and another man to guard them. Morgan's men will make sure none of them get away. We don't know if Mrs Townsend is in there. so we also need to look out for her. Keep an ear to your radios and obey all instructions. Above all, keep your heads down. We hope not to use any bullets but it may come to that. Right, we will let Sergeant Lloyd's men get into place first then make our way to the building. Morgan, if your men see any cars leaving before we get there, feel free to shoot at the tyres, but don't take any risks of injuring one of our youngsters. Okay?"

He turned, then added, "Oh, and a couple of police vans will be here shortly. They'll be parked in the lane on the farm side so the thugs don't see them."

"Okay. Come on men."

The group of skilled armed men went first, out of the barn and onto the lane, moving silently and keeping in the shadows.

Ten minutes later, Morgan's voice came over Dan's radio. "All in place. No movement from the house as yet. Bring your men in, we have all areas covered."

The policemen moved as quietly as the others, creeping through the gateway one by one. Silent dark figures could barely be seen as they crept around, keeping under the shadows of the hedgerows alongside the house and disappearing behind the building.

Then, the first of the vans arrived and Dan went to instruct the drivers quietly. When he came back, he said,

"Julie, I want you to stay out of the way, I don't want you getting hurt. I'll need your help with the kids."

"Sir." She answered, and took a step back.

"Grant, I want you to go round the right side. I don't want anyone escaping out of that room at the end of the side wing. Look for any outside doors and make sure there are no escape routes we don't know about."

He nodded and silently made his way through the shadows.

"Keep an eye on the front door please, Inspector Williams? I don't think anyone has used that door in many a year but someone might try to use it to give us the slip."

"Absolutely." The Welshman crept silently along the inside of the front hedge. Dan then took himself along the left side towards the car park area. Julie crept just inside the gates and stood in the shadows there.

Everything was in place and the men were poised and ready. Dan looked at his illuminated watch. Eight forty nine. How long would they have to wait?

Chapter 39

The door to the dormitory opened and the two heavies, Jake and Butcher came in.

"We're moving out. Get in line and follow Butcher down the stairs. No funny stuff, we both have guns and we love to use them. You first, Goldie." Jake waved at Gloria, who grabbed her dressing gown 'I aint leavin' that behind, me mum give it me.'

Having been kidnapped in her night clothes, she had been provided with jeans and a jumper.

When Rowena tried to take her place in the line, she was stopped. "Not you, Blondie. You gotta wait, special arrangements for you." He winked and laughed. Standing back, she silently watched the others leaving the room and the door was shut and locked again. She sat down on the nearest bed, wishing she was going with the others and wondering what the 'special arrangements' were, hoping she wasn't going with *him*. A shudder ran through her and she hoped against hope they would yet be rescued.

****

Half an hour passed and Dan felt as if his legs had seized up. He shuffled about, trying to relieve the pins and needles, just as light flooded out through a doorway that had just opened. He stiffened.

"Here we go, lads," he whispered into his radio.

He watched as some figures appeared, a girl, with a man behind her, followed by another girl and man. As they came closer, he realised the girls had their hands tied behind their backs and were being pushed along by the men. As they went towards a car nearest the exit to the car park, he realised the men had guns.

"Get out of there, quickly! They have guns! Don't let them see you," he instructed his men. He radioed Morgan. "We need you, these guys have guns. Let the car come to the front of the house and catch them before they get out the gate. Julie! Can you shut the gates?"

"Already did it, Gov," came the reply.

"Good," he breathed. "Get out of sight and keep down."

Although the two guys and girls got into the car, there was no more movement in the open doorway.

As the car took off, throwing up dust and turning slowly to go alongside the house towards the drive, Dan moved to follow the car, keeping at a safe distance. He heard a low pop, pop, and it stopped. The driver's side door opened and the man got out. 'Dammit! Punctures! How did that happen? Get the girls out, we'll have to take another car."

The passenger door opened and the other man got out to open the back doors. Before they knew what had happened, both men had two officers onto them, holding them fast. They were searched and disarmed, then frog-marched away. Julie opened the back door.

"Okay, girls, I'm a police officer. You're safe now. Come with me."

The two youngsters got out and Julie took them both to one side, well away from the men. Dan nodded in approval and he saw Julie put a finger to her lips to indicate they should be quiet. They nodded. He radioed for car one. The men at the front would keep the prisoners safe until the car came. Inspector Williams drove the disabled car expertly over to the far side of the house and left it close to the dark, derelict part of the building.

"Gov, the next ones are coming out. It's four guys, don't think it's any of the kids," came a voice through his radio. Dan made his way back to see.

"You're right. It's just four yobbos. We'll nab them round the corner. I need three officers to help take care of the prisoners. The vans are in the lane for them. Morgan, I think we might need more marksmen around the front."

"Wilco."

Dark shapes moved and Dan retrained his sight on the door.

"It looks like they very helpfully are leaving at intervals. That will make our job much easier. No need for storming. We'll just pop them off as they go through."

The system worked like a dream. One by one, the cars were disabled by discreet popping of tyres and prisoners were taken quietly with no fuss. Guns were collected and each man was handcuffed to an officer and taken to the vans that drew up to take them away.

The youngsters were gathered and Julie took them to sit in the disabled cars parked well out of the way. The door was shut but they only had six of the seven youngsters. Rowena was still missing. Dan was worried; where was she and where was Stephanie?

There were two cars left in the car park, a limousine and another dark-coloured car. They waited a while. Why was nothing else happening?

****

Rowena waited almost an hour before she was taken downstairs to the large sitting-room, where Lucian Avery was waiting. Flora and Karen were also there, each with a bag at their side.

"Ah, my lovely niece has come to join us," Lucian kissed her on the cheek. Rowena felt sick but resisted pulling away. She had seen what he was like when angry and didn't want to start him off again. Where was Stephanie? Had he killed her? And what was going to happen to her? She was loath to go with him. Surely Lucy had seen her message? She noticed the two women had their fingers crossed behind their backs – what could that mean?

Jake rushed into the room. "Boss!"

"Jake, be calm. What's the matter?"

"I've tried to contact some of the others to find out how far they've got and I can't raise any of them."

"What? They are supposed to keep in touch. We must leave soon and need to know they're getting through! What are they playing at? Get Butch and see if you can catch them up! Keep me posted. Be quick now!"

Jake left the room at a run. A few minutes later, Jake appeared outside the French doors, staggering against them.

"He's bleeding!" cried Flora, and rushed to open the doors and he fell in.

"Cops!" He gasped and fell down. Moments later, a man appeared at the open French window. Lucian pointed his gun. The two women lunged, and one stuck something into his side and the other swung a fist at his neck just as he pulled the trigger. He staggered and collapsed to the floor.

The man who Lucian had intended to shoot, came in, followed by two other men in dark clothing, guns pointing.

"Police!" shouted Grant. "Stay right there, ladies."

He bent down and examined Lucian on the floor. "Hmm, I think he needs an ambulance. Good work, ladies, you saved my life and for that I thank you. Unfortunately, you still have to come with me. Gentlemen, would you escort these two ladies out?"

The two army men went off with Flora and Karen. Grant strode over to Rowena.

"Are you Rowena Thompson?"

"Yes. I thought you were never coming. I'm so happy to see you. But I don't know what's going to happen to me now that all my family are gone."

He leaned towards her and whispered. "Your family are alive and safe."

"They are?"

Smiling, he nodded and then laughed out loud when she squealed and threw her arms around him. He lifted her off her feet and then set her down, offering her his arm, and they walked out of the room into the darkness. She skipped happily along beside him until they got to the car park, where they met another man.

"This is Rowena, Sir," said Grant. "Rowena, this is my boss, DI Cooke."

"Thank you for rescuing me. I was so afraid Lucy wouldn't get my message."

"She did, and we acted at once. I think we have everyone."

"What about Stephanie? She's still in there, I think, but he might have killed her," said Rowena, anxiously.

"The guys are searching the building. They'll find her if she's there. But we need to get you kids home."

"An ambulance is needed, Sir. There's an injured man in the house," said Grant.

"We have a couple of ambulances standing by. I'll call them."

A voice shouted, "Hey! There's a severely injured woman in here. Get an ambulance, quick!"

They rushed into the building and along a corridor, which was familiar to Rowena. Although she was behind them, she gained the room moments after and gasped. Stephanie was crumpled unconscious in a corner, practically naked, her clothes torn into rags, her face pale between the purple bruises, one eye swollen and bleeding. Blood seeped from underneath her. Rowena watched, crying, as Dan snatched the cover off the bed and covered her up.

"Get the paramedics here, on the double!"

****

Dan and Grant were the last to leave after he men had combed the house. and made sure it was all clear. They shook hands with the armed squad and thanked them, also Inspector Williams and his men.

Julie Coombs went in the ambulance with Stephanie and Dan sent Johnson and Tanner with Lucian Avery.

The Welsh Inspector said he would thank the farmer and his wife and let them know it was all over.

It was a very tired couple of detectives who carefully traversed the winding roads back to Hereford but they were well satisfied with the night's work.

Chapter 40

Alex Townsend was sleeping fitfully, unsettled and worried about Stephanie. When his phone rang he came to with a jump and peered at the clock. One o'clock in the morning.

"Hello? You have Stephanie? Oh, thank God." He sank into the bed, his hand shaking.

'We are sending a car to bring you to the hospital, Sir. Someone will be with you shortly.'

"Thank you."

When the car arrived, he was ready and came out immediately.

"I'm Police Constable Conrad, sir, and this is WPC Jones. I must warn you that your wife is in a bad way and is in Intensive Care. We want you to be prepared."

Alex's heart did a thump. Although deeply frightened he couldn't wait to see her. The car sped through the darkness, its blue light flashing. They reached the hospital in record time and hastened through the corridors to ICU. A police officer helped him put on a white gown and he was admitted.

In spite of the warning, he was shocked at the sight of her. He gasped in dismay as he took in her cut and bruised face, her shorn hair, her stillness and all the tubes attached to her.

"Oh, my darling, what did they do to you?" Tears flowed as he gazed at the still face. Not a flicker came from her; the only sound in the room the quiet bleeping of the monitors.

Someone came in. It was hard to tell who it might be, as he/she wore a white gown, hat and mask.

"Mr Townsend? I'm Doctor Roberts. May I speak with you, please?"

He joined her outside the room.

"I'm afraid your wife is in a seriously bad way. We don't know the full extent of her injuries yet but she certainly has a broken wrist, some crushed ribs, a couple of broken fingers and multiple stab wounds although they are mostly surface.

"She's been severely tortured, beaten, and sexually assaulted. In fact, I've never seen anything like it and am extremely surprised she is still alive. I have to warn you that she may not survive, but we will do everything in our power to make sure she does. You can't hold her hand because both hands are injured but if you can find somewhere you can make contact, perhaps an upper arm, please do so. And talk to her. We're going to operate and theatre is being prepared now."

The words brought more tears. The doctor put her hand on his shoulder and then indicated for him to go in. He kissed the bruised and cut lips.

"I love you, Steph. You are my life, please don't leave me. I don't care what happened in your past before we met, it's now that's important. Please fight it. You're a strong woman, don't give in now, I beg you,"

He stroked the shorn head, feeling the short tufts of hair and the bald spots too. His heart as though it would burst with love and compassion for her. What terrible monster did this to his sweet love? Alex wanted to kill him, whoever he was. He hoped that the police had him and that he would spend the rest of his life in prison and be beaten up by his fellow prisoners.

'I'm sorry it's not a very charitable thought, God, but I'm just so, so angry about what the man or men have done to my Steph. Please punish him and please forgive me for my bad thoughts,' he prayed.

He sat down next to Stephanie and put his hand on her shoulder as the rest of her arm was encased in a splint. Her other hand was bound too. The rest of her he couldn't see.

He didn't have long with her before they came to take her to the operating theatre. He went to sit out in a waiting area. It was a long wait. He dozed fitfully, uncomfortable but his body was desperate to sleep. She was in theatre four hours. He came too as they wheeled her back to her place. He went back in to sit with her and to pray that she would pull through and wake up.

****

In spite of being tired when they returned to police headquarters, the job was not over. The youngsters had to be seen by the police doctor, who gave each of them the all clear. They were to return in the morning to give their statements. Sarah was able to go home with her dad, Mick. Every mother had been notified, under relayed instructions from Dan and officers had been dispatched to bring the mums to collect their offspring. The only one who wasn't there was Wiggy. Gloria shrugged, it was likely that her mother was probably already in an alcoholic haze. Rowena would join her family in the morning.

"I think we'll leave it there, Grant," said Dan. "All the prisoners are safely tucked up in cells. I'll take these two girls home for the night. Linda will look after them. I'm bushed, and I'm sure everyone else is."

Just then the phone rang. "Cooke. Ah, hello Julie. Right, thank you. You get yourself home now. " He put the phone down. "Lucian Avery died in the ambulance. Mrs Townsend is in ICU and her husband is with her. That's definitely all we can do for now. Come on, you girls. Let's get you home so we can all get some rest."

Linda greeted the girls with a hug. They'd each been given a drink at headquarters, so they said they would just like to sleep, please!

"Do you mind sleeping in the same bed because we only have the one? Or one of you can sleep on the settee, it's quite comfortable."

Linda lent them each a t-shirt as nightclothes and left them to share the bed.

They fell asleep holding hands, having become firm friends during their imprisonment and now they could sleep peacefully without fear. It felt good.

Chapter 42

"I'll take you girls to the station to give us your statements, then I'll take you home first, Gloria, and then take Rowena to her family."

"Let the girls have their breakfast, dear." Linda said as they sat down to eat. It was a happy meal, the girls so relieved it was all over and they were going home.

Statements all done, the girls set off in the car with Dan and Grant. Rowena stayed in the car with Grant while Dan took Gloria in. She hoped Gloria and her mum were having a happy reunion.

Dan came out after about ten minutes and they set off on the drive to Shropshire.

"So, how did Ruby react when you took Gloria in?"

Dan shrugged. "You know Ruby, Grant. She threw her arms around Gloria and they hugged and she cried a bit, then she asked her how long would she have to wait for her breakfast!"

The men laughed and Rowena smiled. She and Gloria had talked a lot and Gloria had told her about her life with her mum. Being philosophical, she had simply said, 'I'm used to it. She needs me.'

In the way that kids have, Rowena accepted Gloria's lifestyle and dismissed it from her mind as she watched the countryside scenery speed by. They drove for about an hour until they came to some large, solid gates. Grant spoke into an intercom and the gates slid open. They drove up the drive to a large house, where two figures were standing in the doorway.

"Mum! Mum! Harry!" she bounced up and down, eager to get out. The minute Grant pulled to a stop, she flew out the door and into her mother's arms and Harry put his arms round them both and they stood, laughing and crying.

****

Dan and Grant followed at a more leisurely pace and shook hands with Margaret and Dave Blackwood, who were standing behind the group.

"Good to see you again, Inspector Cooke and Sergeant Grant," said Dave. "Come on in."

"Thanks. We can't stay long, we have interviews to conduct back at headquarters. But we wanted to bring this girl to you personally for a couple of reasons. One, she'd been told her family were dead, and two, we thought it would be good to see you and your lovely wife again."

"You'll stay long enough for a cup of tea?" said Margaret.

"Oh yes indeed. And how is the invalid?"

"He's doing well. Come and see him."

George was in a downstairs room that had been converted into a bedroom. Dan was glad to see the man sitting up in bed, looking bright.

"Mr. Thompson, I'm so glad to see you looking so much better." Dan walked up to his bed.

"I am indeed. I'm being well looked after here. I'll soon be up and about."

"Dad!" Rowena rushed over and threw her arms around his neck.

"Oh, Rowee, Oh, I'm so glad to see you! You okay – did they hurt you?"

"No, Dad, they didn't hurt any of us. They fed us nice food and everything except we were kept locked up."

"All the kids are rescued?"

"Yes, everyone is safe."

"And, and Sally?"

"Well, we found her too. She is alive but very poorly, I'm afraid."

"He's evil. I always hated and feared him, even though he was my step-brother. I hope you got him, Mr Cooke?"

"He's dead, George. He was killed during the rescue."

"I'm glad. God forgive me, I'm so glad! He can't hurt anyone else now. He's done terrible things."

"I'm sure we'll find out about it all. Oh, thank you, Mrs Blackwood, much appreciated."

Margaret had come in with a tray laden with mugs of tea.

"I feel for poor Sally," continued George. "She had such an awful life with him. In the end she faked her death and escaped. I helped her by putting on a blonde wig and her glasses and hat and driving her car and sending it over the cliff. Some time afterwards I left Lucian's employ and made my own way in life. I met Netta and we got married. We were fine until Harry's accident. If that hadn't happened, Lucian would never have found out where Sally was. Everything is my fault."

"No. It was an accident. Don't spend your life berating yourself over it. In some ways, it's good that it's happened, because now he's gone."

****

"I am going to interview the two women. Flora first. Set it up, please, Grant. Then I'll see Karen."

"Right away."

Dan walked into interview room one where Flora sat nervously at the table. Grant took up position by the door.

She was clearly frightened, her hand shook as she picked up her cup of coffee.

"Don't be frightened. I just want you to tell me about the events that brought you to this area. Can you do that?"

She nodded.

"For the tape, please." Dan said, gently.

"Yes," she said. One day a couple o' weeks ago, the Boss tol' me an' Karen that we 'ad ter get ready cos we were goin' on a journey and were ter 'elp him wiv a job. We 'ad no idea what it would be or where we was goin'. Jake and Butcher drove us with The Boss to that place in Wales.

"It were a big place and most of it was derelict but some parts had been made liveable. Some guys were already there and 'ad fixed up the kitchen and put bedrooms in it.

When the kids started to arrive, Karen and I were upset. We were told not ter ask questions but ter feed 'em and look after 'em. We were given masks we 'ad ter wear so they wouldn't see our faces and told not to speak ter them at all."

"Didn't you question it? Didn't you try to get them to free the children?"

"Ya don' question The Boss, Sir, 'E's a sadistic monster. And Jake and Butcher are the same. Ya don' step out o' line wiv them."

She rolled up a sleeve to show a long, purple bruise on her arm. "This is what Jake did ter me jus' because I argued wiv him."

"For the tape, Mrs Smith is showing me a large bruise on her arm."

"He's dead, ain't 'e? Jake, I mean."

"Yes, I'm afraid so. I'm sorry."

"I'm not! I'm glad. 'E were a brute, I 'ated bein' married ter 'im. The Boss made me marry 'im. Mind you, it didn't stop 'im doin' what 'e wanted ter me. Jake didn't try to stop 'im. 'E din't care. I don't fink 'e wanted ter be married ter me, no more'n I wanted ter be married ter 'im."

Dan nodded slowly, his sympathy for this woman accelerating.

"So, you looked after the youngsters but were not allowed to speak to them?"

"Tha's right. I often wanted ter speak ter 'em, you know, try ter comfort 'em. But I weren't allowed, Jake and Butch was with us all the time when we went ter take 'em food."

"We?"

"Yeah, me an' Karen. 'Er's married to Butch, poor fing. 'E's even worse'n Jake. 'E ent dead, is 'e?"

"No."

"More's the pity. Wish they'd bof got shot. Karen would 'ave bin 'appy about that."

"He's likely to go away for a long time."

"Good. Me 'an Karen, we can tell yer all sorts about 'im and about all the illegal fings the Boss 'ad 'is sticky fingers in."

"Thank you, we may well get around to that, although I'm sure Scotland Yard will be most interested. Now, let's get back to the happenings at the old school. So, you and Karen fed the young captives and washed their things and so on?"

"Yeah, we did that."

"Were you told anything about them?"

"Not really. Although Jake tol' me one night that The Boss weren't keepin' 'em, they were goin' ter be released. That was why we 'ad ter wear the masks, so's they wouldn't be able ter identify us. We was orlright wi' that, we was 'appy they were goin' ter be released."

"When did you start being suspicious that they weren't going to be let go after all?"

"We dint really. Not til that last evenin' when we was told ter feed the kids an' git 'em ready ter take 'em back ter London. Thas wen me an' Karen started getting' worried and tryin' ter work out what ter do. We was also upset about Sally. What the Boss did ter 'er was terrible, jus' terrible. Karen was made ter cut all 'er 'air orf an' then we could 'ear Sally's screams when that sadistic monster was doin' terrible fings ter her. I wished I could stop 'im but I nu I'd be beaten meself, mebbe kilt. I wos terrible afraid."

Tears rolled down Flora's cheeks and she tried to wipe them away with her sleeve. Grant brought over some tissues and she nodded her thanks. Dan waited a few moments to let her settle.

"You mentioned that you were upset about Sally. Did you know her before?"

"I nu 'er years ago wen I wos a kid. Me an' Karen both nu 'er. Sally was kind to us kids. She wos kind ter our mums too. They was bof pros, workin' fer The Boss. He'd tek them when they wos teenagers, no older than them kids we was lookin' after. They 'ad me an' Karen while they wos workin' fer 'im. Then, when we was about those kids' age, 'e took us too, then made us work fer 'im. 'E made sure that none of us got away wif his hired heavies, then 'e made me marry Jake and Karen to marry Butcher. We 'ad no say in it. Sally did what she could fer all of us, but she weren't no better off than us. 'E treated 'er so badly, I'm not surprised she got brave an' ran away. We was very sad wen we 'eard she'd died, but we fort that she wos better orf dead. We fought she must 'ave fort the same, that she'd be 'appier dead. Then, last year some time, 'e found out she weren't dead at all. So, 'e 'atched this plot ter get at 'er an' punish 'er, although me an' Karen dint know that until Jake told us the ovver day. I got upset and tha's wen Jake give me that bruise."

"So, all this was a plan just to get back at Sally?"

"Yeah, tha's right."

"Why the kidnapped teenagers?"

"Well, tha's how 'e gets 'em – you know, the pros that 'as ter work fer 'im. 'E likes 'em young and 'e 'as customers 'as likes 'em young an' some likes boys. 'E took Sally wen she was young like them. He wanted ter frighten 'er good afore 'e took 'er."

Dan felt sick. He was sorry that Lucian Avery was dead. For a mad moment, he would have liked to give the man a very slow, very painful death. Getting stabbed and brained with a heavy weight from a set of scales was too good and too quick for such an evil b*******. May the man burn in hell for eternity and that wasn't long enough in his opinion. He came back to the job in hand and cleared his throat.

"What about the other girl? Rowena Thompson?"

"Well, she was different ter the ovvers. When she wos brought in, she was locked in a room near Sally's. She wasn't wiv the kids."

"But she wasn't treated badly?"

"No, we fed 'er jus' the same as the others. But me an' Karen wos worried about 'er. We nu who she was, see."

"How did you know?"

"Well, Jake an' Butch allus talked about fings in front of me and Karen. They said The Boss intended ter keep Rowena cos she wos Jimmy's kid and 'e'd keep 'er ter punish Jimmy fer 'elping Sally."

"So Lucian Avery knew that Jimmy had helped Sally to escape?"

"Yeah. I dunno how 'e nu, 'e must 'ave worked it out."

"So, Rowena was going to be kept but the others were to be set free?"

"Yeah, the plan was they was goin' ter be dumped somewhere. But then the plan changed. We wos told the Boss 'ad changed 'is mind and all the kids were being taken ter London. Jake and Butcher was laughin' an' bein' crude about what would 'appen ter 'em wen we got back. It made me sick. I 'ated wot 'appened ter me an' so did Karen. We wanted ter save the kids."

"So, what did you do?"

"When the men weren't around, we checked the batteries of the phones belonging ter the kids. We found one that 'ad some charge left so we put it in a plastic bag and put it under the pile of sandwiches. We'd bin told we dint 'ave ter wear the masks no more cos the kids were goin' wi' us. We were told ter tell the kids ter eat up cos they were bein' moved out later that night. We wrote down where we was on a slip o' paper and put it under the phone. We 'oped 'ooever the phone belonged to would find someone ter send a message to. It were all we could do and if we'd bin found out, we'd've bin beaten. But we 'ad ter try, to save the kids. We dint know if Sally was still alive but at least we 'oped ter save the young ones. We dint want them ter 'ave the kind o' life we 'ad."

"You were very brave. So, what happened later?"

"Well, we dint know why, but before we left the kitchen fer the last time, I stuck a kitchen knife up me sleeve and Karen took a weight from the old-fashioned scales that we found in the old pantry. I dunno why we did really, but we jus' felt we needed to. Then, when we was in the lounge and Jake came, shot, and that other man appeared in the doorway, Lucian was goin' ter shoot 'im. So, me and Karen acted. We dint speak or nuffink, it were strange, we just moved forward an' I stuck me knife in 'im and Karen 'it 'im round the 'ead. We kilt 'im, dint we? We'll go ter prison, won't we?"

Tears ran down her cheeks once more. "I don' mind fer meself but I 'as a kid and I don' want 'im left down there on 'is own. I loves 'im, even though 'is favver was scum."

"I'm pretty sure you won't go to prison, Flora. I know you killed Avery, but you saved my sergeant there and your bravery also saved those youngsters – and hopefully Sally too."

Chapter 43

Harry watched as Dave Blackwood pressed the remote control and the huge doors of the massive barn slowly opened. When he saw what was inside, his eyes opened wide.

"Wow!" was all he could manage. Dave Blackwood laughed heartily.

"Welcome to my little collection, Harry."

"Not exactly *little*, Sir. There must be at least twenty cars in here and other things too, by the looks of it."

"Yes, I have vintage cycles and motor cycles. I have an old penny-farthing bicycle too."

"It's amazing. How long has it taken you to collect all of these?"

"Oh, years and years. And this is the beauty that started it all off. She was already here when I inherited the farm from my uncle. Ah, and here's another vintage resident! Hello there, Ron."

Harry turned to see an elderly man, well built with white hair and beard and a bulbous nose. His eyes were a startling blue for an old man and they sparkled with humour.

"Hello, Dave, my boy. Who's this then?"

"This is Harry. He and his family are staying with us for a while. Harry, this is Lord Smethwick, or Ron to us. He lives on the estate and helps me with my collection."

Harry shook hands with Ron. "Gosh, I've never met a real Lord before. How do you do, Sir?"

"Oh, do call me Ron, lad. The old 'Lord' thing is just something I'm stuck with. Inherited the title from my father, you know. Had to give up the old pile though, gave it to the National Trust. I live in a wonderful cottage belonging to Dave here. Much better for me. I love being here, don't you know? I see you've come to look at the collection."

"Yes, Sir. It's wonderful. Dave was just telling me about this beautiful Model T that started the collection. It's so shiny and the leather seats look so perfect and polished. Have you restored it?"

"Well, I have done some work on it, yes. But it was in pretty good shape when I discovered it. It has an interesting story. I'm going to leave you now with Ron as I have some farm paperwork I must do. He'll tell you all about the car and the others, won't you, Ron?"

"Of course, dear boy, I'd be delighted. Nothing I like better than to tell people about the cars, especially that one."

"There you go then, Harry, you're in good hands. Don't let him bore you though, he can go on a bit. When you've had enough, just tell him."

Harry smiled at Dave's wink and Ron's exaggerated look of indignation. They watched Dave walk away with a raised hand of farewell, then turned back to the barn.

Ron ran his hand lovingly across the bonnet of the Model T.

"Would you like to sit inside?"

"Oh, yes please."

Ron opened the driver's door. "Come and sit behind the wheel."

Harry's smile was wide as he climbed into the driver's seat. He stroked the steering wheel carefully with one finger and examined the dashboard that was made of shining wood. Ron sat in the passenger seat beside him.

"It looks different to modern cars, doesn't it?"

"Yes. Not many dials and buttons and no radio."

"That's right. Now, would you like to hear the story about this car? It's quite interesting and goes right back to when my father owned it when it was brand new in 1932."

"Your father owned the car? How did it come to be on the farm? Did he sell it?"

"No, he didn't sell it. It disappeared, along with his chauffer."

"Oh really? The chauffer stole it? What happened?"

Ron proceeded to tell the story of the car and its driver. Harry listened, enthralled, as the elderly lord told him everything that had happened the previous year and the old murder that DI Cooke and DS Grant had investigated and how he himself had ended up coming to live on the Castle Farm estate. (See 'By the Gate,' River View book 2)

At the end of the story, Harry whistled. "Phew! That's really cool! I have a little bit to add to that, Sir – erm, Ron. When I had my accident, Lucy let my parents and sister live in the bungalow that had belonged to Sam Williams because he died and left it to Lucy."

"Well, now, isn't that just a coincidence? So, you had an accident did you? What happened?"

Then it was Harry's turn to tell Ron all about what had happened to him and his family, ending with why they were staying with the Blackwoods.

"My, my, who would have thought such goings-on would happen around here? Nothing like this used to happen when I lived in the old hall. So, you'll be sticking around here for a while then, if your house is burned out and your dad still laid up?"

"Looks like it. Good thing I'd just about finished my therapy. Although I do my exercises every day, at least, the ones I can do. I'm very lucky, you know. Did I tell you that Linda, my therapist is DI Cooke's wife? She's been amazing. In fact, I really like everyone we've met since we left Manchester – except my Uncle Lucian, of course. He was well creepy."

Ron looked at his watch. "Goodness! It's time to eat. We've been sat in this car for ages! Time we went in, Harry, my boy. We can come out again later and you can see the rest of the collection. You can help me while you're here if you like. I keep them all clean and polished, ready for when we take them to shows. There's going to be one in a couple of weeks, so I'll need all the help I can get to be ready. You up for it, lad?"

"You bet! It'll be great!" Harry was happy to think that he would have something useful to do during his stay.

They climbed out of the Model T, and Harry watched Ron close the giant doors to the barn. He ruffled the boy's hair and they grinned at each other like mischievous schoolboys, then they made their way to the farmhouse in anticipation of Margaret's wonderful cooking.

Chapter 44

When Stephanie finally woke up, Alex was by her side. Although he'd not slept that night, he wouldn't allow himself to leave. He spent his time talking quietly to her, recalling everything he could about how they'd met and fallen in love, all about coming to live and work in Sutton-on-Wye, about Lucy and Kenny, Tom and Sheila, Madge and the village shop, in fact, anything and everything he could think of. In between he prayed, all the time making sure his hand was in contact with her somehow.

"Please come back to me, Steph. I love you and can't do without you. I need you. Please, please, come back."

About the same time as Harry was listening intently to Ron's incredible story, Stephanie stirred slightly and her eyelids flickered. Alex was immediately alert.

"Steph? Steph, my darling, are you awake?"

"Alex..." Her voice was a mere whisper. Tears trickled down her face. Alex took out his own, clean, white handkerchief and gently dabbed at her poor, injured face.

"Don't cry, my darling. You're safe. I'm here. It's all over."

"All over..." she murmured, and sank back into sleep. Alex stood up to stretch as a nurse came towards them.

"She woke up for a moment."

The nurse checked her signs and the monitors and nodded. "Yes, she's in a normal sleep now. I think you should go home and get some rest. We'll give her a sedative to help her sleep more. Sleep is healing. When she wakes up again, she'll feel much better and so will you after you've had rest."

"Thank you, I think I will." He leaned over and kissed Stephanie's forehead lightly.

As he stepped out into the corridor, having shed the white gown and hat, he saw two familiar faces.

"Ken! Lucy! What are you doing here?"

"We came to see if there was anything we can do to help. How's Stephanie?"

"She has a lot of injuries to recover from but she's going to be alright. She just woke up for a few moments. They're going to sedate her and told me that I should go home to rest for a while."

"Do you have your car?"

"Oh! No, I forgot that. The police brought me here."

"In that case, it looks like we came at the right time. Come on, we'll take you home."

****

When Alex returned to the hospital several hours later, he felt much better. He'd slept knowing Steph was in a safe place and being looked after. Lucy, bless her, had left him a cottage pie which he ate when he got up. Having had rest and food, he was ready to return to his beloved.

Upon entering ICU, he was met by a nursing sister, who put out her hand to stop him.

"Mr Townsend, I'm afraid you can't go in to your wife," she said.

"Why? Has something happened? Has she had a relapse or something?" Alex was wild-eyed with fright.

"No, no, nothing like that. It's that – I'm afraid she doesn't want to see you."

"Doesn't want to see me?" he repeated, stupefied. "Why doesn't she want to see me?"

"I'm not sure. But she's been through a very traumatic experience. I'm sure she's not thinking straight at the moment. Why don't you go home and call again in the morning?"

He ran past her, quickly moving to Stephanie's bed but she turned her head away. He stopped abruptly as Sister and a male nurse caught up with him.

"Stephanie!" he cried, as they led him away.

"Come," the Sister said, leading him to a small room with soft chairs. "Let me get you a cup of tea or coffee and we'll have a little chat."

She went to the machine that squatted on a table in the corner and brought him tea in a polystyrene cup. He took it shakily and sat holding it.

"Now, Mr Townsend, I've nursed many patients who have suffered trauma and often they can be quite irrational. Mrs Townsend is now awake properly but the last time she was fully awake, she was suffering an inhumane torture, rape and beating."

"Torture?" Alex's head jerked up.

"Yes. I'm afraid so. She's been burnt with a cigarette end and cut with a knife in various places. Not stabbed, but deliberately had a knife drawn across her skin to make her bleed. Bones, such as some fingers and her wrist were deliberately broken. She had internal bleeding from being viciously kicked, which is why we had to operate quickly when she arrived and is very lucky to be alive."

Alex put his head in his hands and wept. How could anyone do that to her? She was one of the loveliest, kindest people he'd ever met.

The nurse put a hand on his knee. "So you see, Mr Townsend, she needs time. She has a lot of healing to do, both in her body and her mind and may not feel she can tell you anything yet. Give her time. She knows you were here and we will tell her that you watched over her until she came round. If she has any other relatives, perhaps someone else could visit her until she's ready to see you? It's often the person who's closest is the most difficult to face. I must go now but take your time and think over what I've said. Don't lose heart, just bide your time. Call tomorrow, alright?"

Alex nodded as she stood up. "Thank you, Sister."

She smiled and left the room. The minute she'd gone, he went too, leaving his tea to go cold in its horrible cup.

****

Lucy entered ICU with trepidation. Alex had come straight to River View after his disastrous visit to the hospital the previous evening. He'd been distraught and she and Kenny had spent a good couple of hours calming him down and talking with him, formulating a plan. The best thing they could come up with was that Lucy should try to visit Stephanie to see if she could get to the bottom of why Steph wouldn't see him. He said he would let her know what they said when he called the ward in the morning.

He'd called that morning and pleaded with Lucy to see her as Stephanie was still adamant she wouldn't see him.

She pushed open the door to the ward and went up to the desk. The receptionist looked up and smiled.

"Hello. I'm here to see Stephanie Townsend, if I may please?"

"Are you a relative?"

"I'm her cousin." Lucy felt bad about lying but she knew if she'd said 'no, I'm her best friend' they wouldn't have allowed her to go in.

"She's along there, last bed. But she's going to be moved to another ward shortly as she's now out of danger."

"That's good news. Do I have time to see her?"

"Yes, I should think so."

Lucy made her way along to the bed, shocked at the sight of her friend's poor face but hoping it didn't show. Steph was lying with her eyes closed. Lucy touched her arm gently.

"Steph?"

The eyes opened. "Lucy. Oh, Lucy!" Tears trickled down her face and Lucy gently patted her face with a tissue.

"There now, don't cry. I had to lie about being related to you, so don't let on. I'm not going to ask you how you are, as I always think that's a silly question to someone in hospital! But they say you're out of danger now so they're moving you to an ordinary ward."

Lucy chattered on, not giving Stephanie a chance to say anything while she drew up a chair to sit near her. Then, she looked at her friend critically.

"Now then, you've frightened us all nearly to death! And you won't see poor Alex! He's beside himself. What's going on, Steph? Why won't you see him?"

Stephanie's face crumpled and the tears flowed more freely. Lucy scrabbled in her bag for more tissues. The poor woman couldn't even mop up her own tears with her hands so damaged.

"There, there, cry it out. It's okay, it's only me." Lucy held a wad of tissue so the tears soaked into it and replaced it when needed.

When the flood subsided and Lucy had mopped up, Stephanie hiccupped, "He won't want me now he knows I married him bigamously. I'll probably go to prison anyway. I can't tell him about what my life was like before I met him, married to that – that monster, Lucian Avery. It's better that he just goes away. Or rather, I'll go away when I'm out of hospital."

"And where would you go?"

"Anywhere. It doesn't matter. I've done it before, I'll do it again. Anything, rather than let that man find me again. He was going to kill me and told me he was going to break me up then throw me over the cliff where I was supposed to have been killed. He'll do it next time, I'm sure of it."

"Right. Listen to me. This is Lucy, your best friend, right? I've never lied to you. Firstly, you don't have to worry any more about Lucian Avery, he's dead."

"Dead?" Stephanie whispered, wide eyed. "How?"

"I'm not clear of the details but I gathered the two women, Flora and Karen, had something to do with it. Lucian was going to shoot Sergeant Grant but they attacked him. They saved the sergeant's life."

"Flora? I remember Flora but she was only a young girl when I knew her. And Karen too. They were both there as little girls but Karen's a bit older, I think. So it was them that brought my food?"

"I believe so. I've no doubt you'll hear the full story in time. Now, about Alex. He loves you, Stephanie, you're his world. You need to give him a chance, you at least owe him that. If he walks away, then that should be his choice, not yours. But I think you're severely underestimating him. His love is unconditional. Please say you'll see him and talk with him."

"I will. Thank you, Lucy." Stephanie twisted her face into a wan smile and Lucy stood up.

"Well, I suppose I'd better go and rescue my dad, who is looking after John. He's a real handful now – John, that is, not my dad!" Lucy giggled and Stephan managed a lop-sided grin. Lucy bent and kissed her friend's forehead. "I'll see you soon. Hurry and get well."

As Lucy started to walk away, she heard Stephanie's voice. "Lucy?"

"Yes, love?"

"Thank you."

Lucy smiled and gave a wave.

Chapter 45

As soon as Lucy left the hospital, she called Alex to tell him that Stephanie wanted to see him.

"Thank you, Lucy, thank you!" he said, joyfully. "I'll go right away. I'm so grateful to you."

"Think nothing of it, that's what friends are for," Lucy replied and rang off, then went to the car park where Kenny was waiting in the car. He wouldn't let her drive because she could go into labour any time.

She relaxed thankfully into the passenger seat.

"All done. I've called Alex and he's coming over to the hospital."

"You're a miracle worker." Kenny kissed her check lovingly.

"Let's go home, I'm exhausted and I have a pain in my back."

Concerned, Kenny immediately started the car and they were soon on their way back to the farmhouse.

"Now you can get some much needed rest."

It wasn't to be, for, an hour later, it was obvious that Lucy was in labour. The young couple now had their own drama to deal with.

****

Alex and Stephanie held hands, Alex's touch light on her fingers so as not to hurt her. He listened as she told him all about her former life, how she grew up the daughter of a prostitute, was raped at fourteen and taken over by Lucian Avery who forced her to marry him. Once married, he treated her appallingly.

At times he behaved as though she was the most precious thing to him, showering her with expensive gifts and their house was the lap of luxury. But it was a gilded cage, for in return he expected her to 'entertain' men that he wanted to persuade to partner him in some shady deal. She became expert in the art of using her body to get what Avery wanted, for if she failed he meted out sadistic punishment.

Normally a kind and gentle man, Alex wanted to put his hands around the evil man's throat and squeeze the life out of him, or beat him to death with a cricket bat or something. In a way, he was sorry the man was dead because he deserved prison, although he realised that that sort of man would likely build an empire for himself inside. No, it was better than he was dead; Lucian Avery would never again be able to hurt Stephanie or anyone else. Good riddance to bad rubbish.

When Stephanie had finished her story, Alex just sat, shaking his head slightly, tears dripping down his cheeks.

"Do you hate me now?" she eventually fearfully asked in a small voice.

His head went up.

"Hate you? My darling, how could I hate you? I love you and will always love you. But I'm hurt that you never told me all this before – before we broke the law and got married when we shouldn't have done."

"I couldn't tell you. I'm so ashamed of my past, of what I was."

"But why?"

"I was a prostitute. Oh, I was married, but that's what I was, a glorified prostitute, used by my husband for his own ends. You wouldn't have wanted me and I loved you so much, I couldn't bear for you not to want me once you knew."

"Oh Steph, how would I ever not want you? I fell in love with you the first time I saw you. I understand now why it took so long to persuade you to marry me. I thought it was because you're older than me. If you'd only told me, we could just have lived together, no one would ever have known."

She nodded and blinked slowly in recognition of the sensibleness of what he said. He carried on, "I suppose I understand really. But people who truly love each other should have no secrets, Steph. And I suppose I should call you Sally really now. In some ways, I don't really know who you are. It's going to take a while to get my head around it all, you know."

Her eyes widened in alarm. "You won't leave me, will you?"

"Of course I won't leave you. My life is nothing without you. As I'm looking at you now, you're a mess! But I love you. You're more than looks, you are my heart. I admire you for getting out of your bad situation; I'm just sorry that he found you and put you through all this. He's an evil man, I'm glad he's dead."

"I am too. When Lucy told me he'd been killed, it was like a dark malevolent cloud lifted from me and I felt light, in spite of the state I'm in. I'll probably go to prison for bigamy, you know. Are you sure you'll still want me once I'm a jailbird?"

His hand moved from her delicate fingers to her shoulder and he squeezed her gently.

"Whatever happens, we'll face it together. I'm not letting you go again, you can be sure of that. If you go to prison, so be it. When it's all over, we'll get married properly. How about that?"

Her eyes were bright with tears and she lifted her poor, bruised face so he could kiss her lightly, taking care not to hurt her swollen lips. "It sounds wonderful, my love."

"And then we'll go back to normal. Right now, you have to get well."

****

Lucy waited as long as she dared before she let Kenny take her to the hospital. Sheila had already taken John to sleep at their house. That was okay because he was used to it.

The evening wore on slowly, until they finally left for Hereford about twenty past nine. Rosemary Elizabeth Baxter entered the world at eleven forty-seven.

Kenny, cradling his new daughter, fell instantly in love as he gazed at the small face and watched the starfish little hand opening and closing on the waving arm. He laid her in Lucy's arms and put his arm around his wife, kissing her tenderly.

"Clever girl. Now I have two princesses. I wonder what John will think of his new sister?"

"Well, we'll find out tomorrow. I'm bushed – what a day!"

"What a day indeed. Come on, young lady, you're going in your cradle. Your mummy needs to sleep and so does your daddy."

He gathered up the baby, he kissed her tiny forehead and laid her gently in the cradle at the bedside, covering her firmly. He watched her for a moment, then reluctantly turned to kiss Lucy goodnight and took himself wearily down the corridors and out to his waiting car. Tired, he drove home carefully, elated too, and as he climbed into his bed thankfully, aware he was alone in the house, he felt at peace and fell asleep immediately. Tomorrow, he would have time to spread the good news and celebrate.

Chapter 45

Kenny brought Lucy home the following afternoon with baby Rosemary. Sheila and Tom were there waiting with little John. Sheila made Lucy sit down on the sofa and gave her a drink.

"Mummy!" John ran to Lucy and climbed onto her lap. Glad to be home, she cuddled him to her and kissed him.

"I'll have a meal ready in a jiffy," Sheila said. "Let's have a look at our new granddaughter then."

Kenny handed her the baby, who was all bundled up in a shawl.

"Oh look, Tom, isn't she beautiful?"

Tom admired the baby. "She is indeed." He hugged his daughter and kissed her. "Congratulations, love. How are you feeling?"

She smiled wanly. "Thank you, Dad. I'm okay, just tired."

He patted her shoulder. "Of course you are, love. You must rest. We'll look after you. We'll stay and help you with John and the meal, then leave you in peace."

They did indeed look after her. It meant that she had time to not only look after the baby but have time for John as well, although Sheila took on most of the care of him until Lucy felt strong enough to cope.

After three days, Lucy realised that she'd been so occupied with the baby that everything else had gone out of her mind.

"Do you know how Steph is doing?" she asked Kenny. "And what about George? I feel out of touch with everything."

"Well, I spoke to Alex earlier and he said Steph is recovering well. As to George, I haven't a clue. I don't even know where the Thompsons are. I don't know what they we'll do now after the fire."

"I don't suppose they know either. They will have lost everything. I have Rowena's number in my phone. I think I'll call her. Tell her about the baby."

As the result of the phone call to Rowena, on a Sunday afternoon, Kenny drove his family to Castle Farm because they'd been invited by Margaret and Dave Blackwood for dinner. It was Harry's sixteenth birthday. They were joined by Linda and Dan Cooke and Ron Smethwick.

It was a joyful reunion and they were pleased to meet Lord Smethwick, Dave and Margaret at last. Leaving the women to chat, the men took Kenny to see the vintage car collection.

Much fuss was made of John and the baby. Rowena cuddled Rosemary and looked at her mum.

"Isn't she sweet, Mum? Just look at her tiny hands! I've never held a baby this young before."

Netta duly admired the baby and even had a cuddle herself, her eyes going dreamy, clearly remembering when Harry and Rowena had been babies.

Margaret chuckled when she saw the look on her face.

"Oh Netta, you look like you're going all broody! You'll be having another one next!"

Netta laughed. "Not a chance! Although I don't mind having a cuddle now and then with someone else's. No, I'll wait until I have grandchildren."

"Don't look at me – I won't be having babies for a long time! There's things I want to do first."

"Very wise, dear." Margaret patted her hand. She had become fond of Harry and Rowena; it was like having grandchildren. She was still waiting for hers to come along.

"Oh well, I'll have to hope that Harry won't be so long before he provides some!"

The company chuckled because Harry arrived in the room just in time to catch the last phrase.

"I'll be providing what?" he asked, as he sat down.

"Me with grandchildren," giggled Netta.

Harry's eyes opened wider and he groaned. "You see what you've done bringing your baby here, Lucy? Mum's set to nag me now for the next few years."

"Don't worry, son, I won't. Sixteen is much too young to become a father. I'll start when you're twenty."

"Thanks Mum."

Lucy's eyes met Linda's and they grinned at each other. Harry was a case and Netta had certainly unwound a lot since she'd been here. Obviously, Margaret Blackwood was good for her.

The large company sat around the magnificent, highly polished, dining table. It easily seated the fourteen adults and John in a high chair. George joined them as he could get up for a while every day.

"Been a while since I sat at a table like this," remarked Ron. I remember my grandparents sitting one each end of the long table at Letterton, the butler kept having to walk the length of the table to serve them. Once they'd gone, my mother wouldn't have it. She would sit next to father at the same end. She said it was ridiculous and she was right. Then, when my brother and I were old enough, we'd all sit that end. Of course, it was wonderful for when we had guests, like now."

"Your mother must have been quite something. I'd have liked to know her," said Margaret. "We hardly ever use this table – or indeed this room. I think it's my favourite in the house. I sometimes come and sit in here, on one of the window seats, just to enjoy being here and maybe gloat a little over my china collection."

It was indeed a wonderful room with a dual aspect; one diamond-paned window looked out onto the back garden and the other faced the side of the house, the view from which wasn't so spectacular. The window seats had red buttoned cushions and looked very comfortable. In between the windows were cabinets, their glass doors diamond-crossed and the dark wood that matched the table was again highly polished.

The cabinets themselves were beautiful but the displays of china within were a delight. The cabinets lined all four walls in between doors or windows. Lucy thought she could well spend a lot of time in here admiring the china tea sets, coffee cups and saucers, dinner plates and serving tureens, although some were on the table.

"It's a wonderful room," said Lucy warmly. "I'm not surprised you love it, Margaret."

"Dave collects vintage vehicles and I collect china!" laughed Margaret. "It's taken me years to collect all this. I only use some though, like this dinner service we're using. Much of it is too delicate or cost me too much money to risk breaking!"

Lucy nodded. "I can understand that."

"So, what did you think of Dave's 'little collection,' as he calls it, Ken?" Margaret turned to Lucy's husband.

"It's amazing, so much to see. And it was fascinating to finally get to see the car involved in my great aunt Rosemary's murder. You've restored it beautifully, Dave," replied Kenny.

"It was what started me off on my collection," Dave replied. "Ron and I have some good times going to shows, don't we?"

"Oh, yes indeed, my boy."

"And what about Ron being a real, live Lord?" put in Rowena. Everyone laughed when Ron's bushy eyebrows lifted comically up and down.

"I should hope I am live!" he said. "But the 'Lord' thing is a 'by the way'. It's only because my father was and I was landed with it."

"Don't spoil our fun!" Rowena poked Ron gently as she was sitting next to him.

"Ah, well then, next time you all come here, I shall expect bows and curtsies!"

"How extraordinary that your investigation into that old crime has led to Netta, George, Harry and Rowena coming here for safety, Inspector Cooke."

"Oh, call me Dan! I'm thankful that it did, for it certainly solved a problem, and Dave and Margaret have been brilliant, I can't thank you enough."

"We've enjoyed it, haven't we, Dave? And Ron has loved having Harry here, working with him on the cars," said Margaret.

"We have indeed, my dear."

"You know, I don't know when I've enjoyed an investigation more. It was fascinating. Of course, we got our confession eventually but I'd pretty much worked it out already. I do enjoy my job but there are often times when I have to do something that I really don't want to do."

That caused a few moments' silence, until Lucy broke it.

"What will happen to Stephanie, do you think, Dan?"

"Well, if she has a good representative, she may well get off lightly. I'm hoping so anyway. She's lived through enough already, poor thing."

"You haven't arrested her yet then?"

"No, I want her to recover first. It's a wonder she survived you know, she had some terrible injuries."

"He was a monster," spat Rowena. "I was only around him a short while but what he did to Steph in front of me was bad enough. I hate him!"

Ron put his arm around her shoulders. "Don't fret, girlie, the bounder is dead. Let's hope he rots in Hell." She sniffled and nodded against his shoulder.

"Yes, him and Henry Smithson both," said Dan, with feeling. "There's so much bad around us, but there's more good, I feel. I'm sitting here with some pretty special people now. Alex and Stephanie are good people. I'm glad she broke away from Avery and I'm sure things will work out for her."

"What about the two women and that awful man?"

"Well, obviously they will have to stand trial for manslaughter but I think that'll be okay. It was obviously accidental, for they acted to stop him shooting my sergeant. As for Butcher, well, he's in a holding prison until his trial. He was refused bail because he's such a dangerous man.

All the men are known in London so after their trials here they'll be taken back there. Some are known as pushers, a couple are wanted arsonists; most of them will be going down for a fair while, I imagine."

"There's a lot of people involved in Lucian's businesses." George had been pretty quiet, listening to all the conversations. "I hope the police down there manage a good clean-up operation."

"I think the two women, Karen and Flora, will be invaluable there. They know pretty much everything Avery had his fingers in. Butcher was just the man who did the nasty stuff ordered by Avery, along with his mate Jake, who's dead.

I just don't understand the mentality of someone who goes to all that trouble to do a fancy set up like Lucian Avery did, putting pushers out on the streets of Hereford to sus out potential kidnap victims, even getting someone to keep Wiggy out all night so they could capture her daughter. Just so that he could put the wind up George and Stephanie and ultimately get at Stephanie, or Sarah, her real name. He actually bought that place where they were held – in your name, George."

"You're joking!" George was incredulous. "I wonder why he did that?"

"At a guess, it was if we investigated the ownership of the building, it would look bad for you. But we know that Avery was the person who bought it."

"I see. Yes, that's just the kind of crazy thing he would do. Money was no object to him, he could afford it."

"So it would seem. But the property does belong to you, George. It's all legal. You can do what you like with it."

"I don't want it!"

"You can sell it. He didn't mean to but your brother has given you a nice little nest-egg. Sell it and buy yourself a home of your own."

Lucy's heart gave a little jump as George and Netta looked at each other, their faces full of incredulous delight. She smiled, happy to see things getting better for them. She hoped it wouldn't be too long before they could settle, wherever they choose to live.

"Have you seen Gloria at all?" asked Rowena.

"Yes. We had to go round there a couple of days ago. The Welsh police contacted us to say that a burnt-out car had been found, oh, down South Wales somewhere and it had a body in it. There was enough left to get DNA and it turned out to be a man called Paul Engledow. Flora told us he frequented Avery's casino. We wondered if he was the man who kept Ruby out all night, so we took a picture of him to see if she could identify him. She did. Avery must have made him do it and then neatly got rid of him. Ruby was very upset. She said he was the only man who ever treated her really well."

"Poor Ruby. Sad, isn't it? Poor Gloria, having to live with a mother like that," commented Linda.

"Well, yes, but Gloria is very philosophical about it, takes it in her stride. She asked after you, Rowena and said she'd look for you when school started again. She goes to Whitecross too."

"Oh, school! What are we going to do about that? Rowena needs to go back to school after Easter."

George patted Netta's hand. "Don't worry, love. I'm sure things will work out."

****

It did indeed work out. After the Easter holidays, Rowena came to stay with Sheila and Tom so she could return to school.

"I would have had you at River View, Rowena," said Lucy, "but with a tiny baby in the house, I thought you should be somewhere where you stood a chance of sleeping."

"I'll come over and help you, Lucy, if you'd like?"

"That would be good. But see how you feel."

George wasn't yet fit enough to leave his nurse's eagle eye so Netta and Harry stayed on at Castle Farm a while longer.

When he was finally able to leave the farm, the family moved back into the bungalow. It would only be temporary because, once the old school was sold, Netta and George would look for a house to buy. Because they had lost everything in the fire, they were grateful to move into a house that had everything they needed in household goods.

When the time came to leave, Margaret and Netta hugged regretfully and Ron was sorry to see Harry going. He clapped the boy on the back.

"Do come and see us as often as you can. Remember, we need your help with the cars!"

Dave and Ron promised to keep in touch and let Harry know when they had a show. After that, he went with them as often as he could.

When on their Sunday dinner visit, Kenny invited Dave to bring the Model T and perhaps some of his other vintage cars to the village's Summer Fair on August Bank Holiday Monday and he agreed he would indeed come. It would be a new feature of the Summer Fair.

George was put on light duties on his return to work. He was so happy to be back amongst his beloved plants. Kenny's foreman, Joe, was given strict instructions not to let him overdo it and he took that very seriously.

Netta was happy to be back in the bungalow, for she loved it and not at all in a hurry to move somewhere else. She was happier still to be asked by Sheila to work in the Nursery shop 'because we get so busy this time of year'.

Netta and George had had a serious talk when alone at Castle Farm and George had assured her there would be no trouble from Sally if they went back to live in the village, "Could you be comfortable with that situation?" he asked her.

Having seen Sally/Stephanie with Alex, Netta decided there was no danger to her marriage. In fact, the four were destined to become good friends. Besides, Netta loved the village and wanted to stay there. Rowena remained at Sheila and Tom's. She had her own room, could be with her family as much as she wished and spent most of her time out of school with them, and much time with Gloria too, for they had become firm friends.

George had to buy another car because his old Mondeo was damaged by the fire as it stood on the drive close to the house.

An uneasy peace settled over the village, but they wouldn't be completely peaceful until the verdict was heard on what would happen to Stephanie.

Chapter 46

Justice Janice Matthews straightened her wig and her gown before walking along the corridor to the court. She was held in awe in the courts, but this was the first time she'd heard a case of bigamy, especially when the guilty party was a woman. With a reputation to keep up, she was all set to mete out the highest punishment to the perpetrator. However, she had to hear the evidence first.

When she sat down, her eyes first fell on the defendant. She saw a small woman with shorter than short dark hair and eyes that looked too big for her face. Her eyes narrowed as she took in the man sitting beside the defendant. It was John Portland, the barrister. Janice was impressed; she knew that John was one of those barristers who would only represent clients who he believed in, unlike most who only did it for the money. Oh, he didn't come cheap, but the very fact he'd taken on the case meant he believed he could achieve something. She also recognised several police officers and detectives in the court. This was more than a straight case of bigamy, whatever a straight case might be. Hmm, maybe this was going to be an interesting morning.

Janice had heard all sorts of situations in her court over the years. It wasn't often a police detective stood up to give evidence on behalf of a defendant but Dan Cooke did just that. He described the events leading up to the discovery of Sarah Avery at the old school and the state in which she'd been found.

John Portland called George Thompson, who told the court about the cruel treatment Sarah received at the hand of her husband, Lucian Avery, and his own part in helping her to escape.

Lastly, Alex Townsend was called and described how he'd persuaded Stephanie to marry him, and, although she'd been reluctant at first, she eventually agreed. He told about their life together, how happy they'd been and how he wanted it to continue.

Throughout it all, Sarah Avery stood with her head bowed, until Alex declared his love for her and how he wanted them to always be together. Despite herself, Janice felt a lump in her throat as she saw the look that passed between them.

She asked the prosecution counsel to give his concluding speech.

"Your Honour, the evidence is clear, this woman, Sarah Avery, known as Stephanie Townsend, has indeed committed bigamy. She was legally married to Lucian Avery and faked her death to escape from him. We completely understand why she did that, and I have to stress that no crime was committed there. It's not against the law to fake your own death, unless it involves an insurance fraud or a death certificate is forged. Neither is true in this case – Sarah Avery only wanted her husband to believe she was dead so he wouldn't look for her. However, she should not have married Alexander Townsend while Avery lived. I suggest that she receives a suitable penalty for her crime."

Janice was amazed to see the man give her a slow and deliberate wink. Her face registered no emotion but she gave a slight nod to show she understood.

John Portland was, as usual, magnificent.

"Your Honour, my client has freely admitted she is guilty of that which she is accused. However, I have shown, through my witnesses, that she had a wretched life with her husband, Lucian Avery. Mr George Thompson was a witness to some of that appalling treatment. I'm sure that no one in this court would ever blame Sarah for wanting out. She couldn't divorce him, for he would never let her go and indeed would rather kill her than let her divorce him. We've heard evidence about her recent experience at his hand.

The two women, Flora Smith and Karen Butcher have told us about their own lives involving the man, and what they knew of Mrs Avery's early life.

So, she ran away, helped by her brother-in-law, George. She then spent years building a new life for herself away from the sight of her wicked husband. She went to catering college and made a new career and was happy.

Then she met Alexander Townsend and true love came into her life. But she was ashamed of her previous life, of the fact she'd been little better than a prostitute and, however much she loved Mr Townsend, she couldn't bring herself to tell him about her life, and that she was still legally married. Because she could not tell him, she couldn't give him a good reason not to marry him, for it was obvious they were in love. He kept asking her and asking her. Eventually, she gave in and married him.

They have had a good life and she has been the happiest she's ever been with a man who truly loved her and together they have fulfilled her dream of having her own restaurant.

Your Honour, this is not a woman who has deliberately set out to commit a crime. In fact, she's been a victim, the victim of a truly evil and sadistic bully. Who can blame her for taking the chance of happiness? Yes, she's guilty of bigamy but she's been through so much in her life and until the recent events was living a good and blameless life. I plead for leniency."

"Thank you. This is a convenient time to take a short break. We will reconvene in fifteen minutes. Mr Portland and Mr Lloyd, would you join me in my chambers please?"

"Court arise."

****

Those fifteen minutes was the longest Stephanie had endured. What was going to happen to her? Would she end up in prison? Would Alex really wait for her?

Although she knew that Alex loved her, her insecurities whispered that he would leave her if she went to prison. She sat in her seat, head bowed, silent tears sliding unheeded down her nose. When someone put a cup of water in front of her, she barely registered it. Arms came around her and she looked up. Lucy, had made her way down to the front. Alex wasn't allowed to come near her. A police woman stood guard over her but had received a nod from Dan and stood aside to let Lucy have access to the defendant.

"It'll be alright. I have a feeling in my bones – and Aunt Bea says it'll be fine," whispered Lucy. In spite of herself, Stephanie felt a little giggle; Lucy and her Aunt Bea! But she was usually right and did so want to believe it this time.

"Thank you. It's good to have a friend like you. I don't know what we would have done without you and Kenny during all this – horrible business."

"Shh! Don't think of it. Just think about the future. I must get back to my seat, the barristers are coming back."

Stephanie looked at the two men but, try as she might, she couldn't read anything in their faces. They both had carefully neutral expressions.

"Court arise for Justice Janice Matthews."

When the judge came back in, she looked grim. Stephanie felt her heart contract in fear. She knew she was going down.

"Would the defendant please rise."

Stephanie stood up, her knees shaking.

"Mrs Sarah Avery, you are accused of bigamy. As you have pleaded guilty, I have to find you guilty." Justice Matthews looked at the accused over her glasses and Stephanie quaked in fear. "After listening to everything that has been said by the witnesses and consulting with the counsels, I now have to pronounce a penalty upon you. This is a very serious crime you have committed. Therefore, I sentence you to an open custodial sentence. That means of an indeterminate number of years."

There was an audible gasp from the room and Stephanie sat down, unable to stand. Her head spun and she thought she was going to faint. Her guard helped her to stand up again, and held her. Another guard helped keep her up. All hope died within her and she drooped. Why didn't they just take her away now?

However, the judge hadn't finished.

"You will pay two thousand pounds to the court as a fine for committing bigamy."

"Yes, Your Honour," said Stephanie meekly.

"Plus the sum of seventy five pounds," Janice went on as if she hadn't heard.

'Seventy five pounds? What is she talking about?' Stephanie muddled brain went even more fuzzy.

"However," continued Janice, "that sum is payable to the registry office to buy a marriage licence, a legal one, and you will marry Mr Alexander Townsend as soon as possible. He will then be in charge of your custodial sentence, however long that may be. That is the judgement of this court, Mrs Avery. Go away and marry your man and I expect to be invited to the wedding."

Cheers went up and Stephanie looked at the judge in amazement. Did she hear right or was it a dream induced by her faint, if she fainted? The woman in the wig was smiling, no longer looking grim and the two barristers were shaking hands and laughing. Before she could gather herself together, Alex ran to her box and wrapped his arms around her and a moment later they were crying and laughing together. The shadow had been lifted from their lives.

****

The scene in the room was one that had never been seen before in Justice Matthew's court. The happiness was palpable.

She was glad that she had changed her mind, happy to give this couple who obviously loved each other the chance to live their lives without anything hanging over them.

Janice let the room rejoice for a few minutes, then banged her gavel.

"Order in the court!"

The noise died down.

"Sarah Avery, you are free to go. Court dismissed."

"All arise."

Janice arose from her seat and returned to her chambers. Removing her wig and gown, she let herself relax in a leather armchair. She mulled over the morning's events. Okay, so she knew the woman had broken the law, but actually, what harm had she done? Perhaps she should have given her a short custodial sentence but really, she didn't want to put that small, abused woman in a place where she didn't belong, along with women who did belong in prison – it wouldn't have done any good whatsoever.

The woman gave a sigh. No one who knew Janice Matthews had any idea that she'd grown up in a home where her father regularly abused her mother and then later his daughter as she'd grown older. She had escaped but her mother had stayed until he finally wounded her so much she died. Janice had tried and tried to get her mother to leave him but she wouldn't go because she was afraid he'd come after her and beat her up.

Janice had made a life for herself well away from her family and had studied law, gained her degree and gone on to become a barrister then a judge, all with no one behind her to give her encouragement.

Janice gave another sigh. Today, she'd had to judge a woman who had been brave enough to break away from the cruelty. It was in Janice's hands to help that woman have the life she deserved. Perhaps she should have been harsher but she was glad she had taken the course she'd decided upon. There were times when it wasn't right to put people away.

Sometimes, it was right just to help someone. Today was the day. The stern woman who was Justice Matthews, the judge people were most in awe of, was glad that today, she had given in to her soft core. But it would be quite a while before she allowed them to see it again; she couldn't let them think she was a soft touch.

Chapter 48

The last Saturday in July dawned bright and clear. Lucy was up early to give Rosemary her first feed. She was almost four months old now, a happy, pretty baby whose smiles charmed everyone. It was going to be a special day, but not Rosemary's. She'd had hers already, at two months old. The family and friends had gathered to see her christened in the village church. Joseph had been full of smiles to hear the baby's name spoken by the vicar, the Reverend Trevithick. It looked like the little one was going to have the same dark hair as Joseph's sister Rosemary had; the baby already had a crown of wispy hair.

Kenny came down with John, who immediately went to his mother and kissed the baby on her cheek. She stopped sucking for a moment to give him a windy smile and went back to the serious business of feeding.

"It looks like being a fine day," Lucy remarked as she raised her face for a kiss from her husband.

"It is indeed."

"I need to get on as soon as this young lady has finished."

"It's early yet, relax and enjoy Rosie. Everything will be done. Mum will make sure of it."

"I'm sure she will. Young Rowena has been a big help too. She loves helping with the baking. Oh Kenny, I'm so glad we can do this for them."

"Me too. Then perhaps life can return to normal and we can relax and enjoy the rest of the summer – mind you, we have the Summer Fair coming up in a month's time! No rest for the wicked!" Kenny groaned.

"Go on with you, you love it!"

"I do really. I'll fix us all some breakfast."

****

The bridegroom stood at the front of the church, his best man Kenny beside him, waiting nervously for his bride to arrive.

He knew the church was full behind him. Just about everyone in the village was there and a few others besides. As he looked around, he happened to catch the eye of a stern-looking woman, whose face softened into a smile at his glance. Alex grinned nervously at Janice Matthews, he couldn't believe she'd come!

The organ started to play Pacabell's Canon and he knew she was on her way. He watched her in his mind's eye, slowly walking up the aisle on the arm of George, who was giving her away. It seemed appropriate and fitting as he was her brother-in-law and the only family she had. Rowena would be following, thrilled to be bridesmaid. Alex had yet to see how his future wife would be dressed. Today, she would be Sarah Avery but after today, she would again be Stephanie Townsend again. They had agreed that she would legally change her first name, no longer to be known as Sarah or Sally.

When she reached him, he turned and his face softened; his look full of love. Her hair, having had four months to grow, was sleek and smooth but still short. Wearing a midi length dress of rose pink, with a crown of pink roses in her hair, she looked beautiful and she returned his loving look in her smile.

The ceremony went off without a hitch and they posed for photos outside the church. Afterwards, everyone moved off to River View, where there was a large marquee on the lawn, decorated with flower arrangements and the tables all set out for the wedding feast. The garden was decked out with garlands strung between the trees and bunting across the drive.

Lucy and Sheila had outdone themselves providing the food for the reception. The guests mingled with each other happily.

Sheila had insisted that Lucy do no serving; the workers from the restaurant were happily doubling as guests and waiters. Alex was overwhelmed by it all. When he and Steph had married the first time, it had been a quick registry office ceremony followed by a meal at a local restaurant, just the two of them. He never dreamed they'd have a wedding like this.

He looked at Lucy talking with George and Rowena, who looked lovely in her white bridesmaid's dress trimmed with pink, with a coronet of pink and white on her head. When he thought back to everything that had happened over the past six months, he was incredulous. Who would ever have though that a young lad having an accident on the river a year ago would set off such an unbelievable chain of events? And who would have imagined that Steph could have had such a colourful past?

It made him cringe sometimes when he let himself think about it. How could anyone have treated such a wonderful person like her so cruelly? It went completely beyond his comprehension. Lucian Avery was certainly the devil's spawn. Steph wasn't the only one to suffer at his hand, there was Flora and Karen and who knew how many others?

He looked around the crowd and spotted them, talking with Sheila and Tom. They had suffered terrible things, but in the end had been brave and prevented Avery killing the sergeant. He was glad the courts had gone easy on them, recognising that they had been victims too. They had been given suspended sentences for their part in the kidnappings. Flora held a small boy by the hand. Alex didn't know what she would do now but he hoped she would be happy and not pick up another bad husband. Karen had told him that she was going to divorce Butcher while he was in prison and then disappear. She'd have plenty of time to do it because he would be locked away for a long time. Beside the crimes he'd committed here, he was wanted for several offences in London.

"Penny for them?" Stephanie tucked her arm through his and he looked down at her lovingly.

"Oh, I was just mulling over all the happenings and hoping Flora and Karen find good lives for themselves now they're free of Avery, Smith and Butcher."

"I was thinking about that. Karen wants to go away completely, but I was wondering how you would feel about us offering Flora work in the restaurant? She's really good with food and she needs to find an alternative home somewhere out of London so that none of the people who were around Avery will be able to get to her. She wants a better life for her lad, Alfie, and we could help her to have that. What do you think?"

"I have no problem with that, if you think it is something she'd like. Alfie would certainly have a better life here."

"Oh, thank you! I'll tell her about it now."

Alex watched her fondly as she hurried off and smiled as she talked with Flora, waving her hand in his direction. He waved at them and then turned to speak with Dan Cooke and Linda.

"Stephanie is offering Flora a job at our restaurant."

"How do you feel about that?" asked Dan.

"I'm okay with it. I can understand Steph wanting to help a girl who's suffered like she has. The little boy will have a better life here."

Dan put his hand on Alex's shoulder. "Good man. Those women need fresh starts. I admire you for being willing to help. No one would blame you if you refused."

"But our village is a place that offers people fresh starts. We have a good community here. We will all look after Flora and Alfie."

"I know you will. This is a very special place, with special people."

"Steph and I are lucky that we came here. Everyone has given us so much support. Right, I think it's time I took my bride away. Thank you for everything you've done, Mr Cooke."

"Do call me Dan while I'm off duty."

Having bade them goodbye, Alex hastened towards his wife and together they waved goodbye to everyone and went to their car, now bedecked with white ribbons and some cans and an old boot tied on the back bumper, with 'Just Married' on a card in the back window. Alex drove off and smiled indulgently as Stephanie hung out of the passenger window, waving wildly.

****

Much later, when most people had left and the debris cleared away, Lucy and Kenny sat in the farmhouse with Dan and Linda, George, Netta, Rowena and Harry. Tom, Sheila and Joseph had gone home; for Sheila was worn out and ready for a rest.

Rowena, familiar with Lucy's kitchen, helpfully made tea for everyone and they sat together companionably, watching John playing on the floor and Netta nursing the baby.

Lucy sighed. "It was a lovely day, wasn't it?"

"It was. You did them proud," remarked Linda. "Now I understand why Dan is always enthusiastic about your cooking because the food was wonderful, far superior to most wedding caterings I've attended. But I bet you're tired, Lucy."

"I am, but really, Sheila did most of the hard work. She is amazing, I hope I'm like her when I'm her age. And the waiting staff were marvellous. They were all trained by Alex and Stephanie you know and today we saw what great training they've all had."

"What a lovely setting for a wedding reception. Perhaps you should go into business holding receptions here, Lucy," Linda said.

"No way! I don't mind doing it for a special friend but I wouldn't do it as a business, it wouldn't be fair to the children. Our home would cease to be a private home and we wouldn't like that."

"No, I think you're right," said Dan. "Pity though, it would be a lovely setting for Grant's wedding reception."

"His fiancé is beautiful and so nice with it. I'm not surprised he fell for her. When are they getting married?"

"I'm not sure. I'm expecting to hear he's transferring out at any time. Then I'll have to start again with a new sergeant. Pity, because we're a good team."

"Mm, that's tough," said Kenny. "But I expect you'll deal with it when it comes, Dan. Sometimes change is good."

"Yeah, you may be right."

"So, is everything sorted now with the kidnappers?" asked George.

"Pretty much. You already know about the girls and Butcher. The girls have been very helpful as witnesses. The Met wants some of them for drug offences and other things. We are happy to pass them over! The word on the streets is that all the new pushers we were so concerned about have gone and we have witnesses who have identified them from their pictures. They will be sewn up nice and tight. A very satisfying result."

Everyone nodded in agreement.

"I must say it's good to feel safe," remarked George. "Although I moved away and changed my name, I never felt truly safe. I always felt that Avery could materialise at any time. I'm glad he's gone but I wish Stephanie hadn't had to go through what she did."

He turned to Harry. "If I try to persuade you to do something you don't want to do, son, just tell me straight. If I'd had any idea that my pig-headedness would lead us into all this, I'd have thought twice."

"Well, in some ways, it's a good thing you were pig-headed, because it brought us to Sutton-on-Wye and we're happier here than we've ever been," replied Harry. "And although it was awful, Lucian Avery and his set-up are now crushed. I'd say it was worth it."

"I think I agree with you," said Netta, surprising everyone. "Oh, and I've found a wonderful house just gone up for sale in the village. We heard yesterday that a builder is interested in buying the old school and the land off us, so hopefully, we might soon have a home of our own and become permanent residents of Sutton-on-Wye."

"Well, that is good news!" exclaimed Lucy. I'd suggest a celebration but I'm too tired to do anything else today."

"Time enough to celebrate when we hold our house-warming. Come on, kids, let's go home and leave Lucy and Kenny in peace."

Dan and Linda stood up. "Yes, we must be off too. Thank you for having us."

"Oh, you must come again! Come and enjoy the garden when it's peaceful! We can contact each other now so we can arrange the next visit."

Kenny saw everyone out and came back to Lucy who sat feeding Rosemary. He sat down next to her and put his arm around her.

"We have made some very nice friends and it's lovely having them here but I'm always at my happiest when it's just you and me and our little ones in our home. I love you."

He picked John up. "Time for bed, little man. Shall Daddy tell you a story?"

Lucy smiled as her two menfolk left the room, chatting earnestly together. No story that Kenny could tell would be half as incredulous as that which their friends had just lived through.

Epilogue
Four Months later

"Alex! Take a look at this!"

Stephanie held out a letter to Alex, which he took and read quickly.

"My word! Lucian Avery died intestate. As his next of kin, you inherit his entire estate. My goodness, it's millions! I'm married to a millionairess!"

She sat down suddenly. "I don't want it! What would I do with a gambling casino? And as for that mausoleum of a house, there's no way I want that."

"Sell them. If I know anything about you, you'll use the money to help people. You could help Flora, buy her a house, maybe send money to Karen to help her. There are all sorts of things you can do with the money. I think it's poetic justice that you should get his money. He probably has off-shore accounts that they don't know about yet. We could buy a house for ourselves and let Flora and Alfie live in the flat here. That way she wouldn't have to worry about child-care while she worked."

"I've no doubt that some has been seized by the police because of his illegal activities but there'll still be loads left. I could help some of the women he's had under his thumb."

"It's strange that Avery never had any children, not by anyone."

"He couldn't have any. He had mumps when he was twenty and it made him sterile. I was thankful, I didn't want to bear him any children and I'm sure no other woman wanted to either. I think that's why he had so many women, he had to prove his manhood, even if he couldn't father children."

Alex shook his head in incredulous wonder. He couldn't understand the man, never would.

"While I have your attention, I have something else to tell you."

"What's that then?" He took her in his arms and she looked up at him.

"Have I told you recently how much I love you?"

"Not since yesterday."

"Well, I love you. And you're going to be a daddy."

"What?"

"I said, you're going to be a daddy. I'm pregnant!"

He picked her up and twirled round while she squealed.

"Put me down, silly!"

He set her down and held her steady for a moment. Then he bent his head and kissed her.

"You're incredible, and I love you, Mrs Townsend."

If you have enjoyed this story (or if you didn't!) please leave a short review on Amazon – and tell your friends! I'd be happy to hear from you, email me on the address below. Thank you. Jeanette

Books by Jeanette Taylor Ford

The Sixpenny Tiger a poignant story of a boy abused by his stepmother
Rosa a psychological thriller
Bell of Warning a ghostly story

The Castell Glas Trilogy: A fantasy about an orphan who finds her family, the magical Welsh castle she inherits and the wicked ghostly entity bent on destroying them all.
The Hiraeth
Bronwen's Revenge
Yr Aberth (The Sacrifice)

The River View Series
Aunt Bea's Legacy (Book One) Mysterious happenings in the house Lucy inherits from her aunt.
By the Gate (Book Two) Farmer Price finds a buried skeleton, sparking off a seventy year old murder hunt.
Jealousy is Murder to be published November 2019

Mostly About Bears, a small book of short stories and poems

For Children:
Robin's Ring a fantasy tale
Robin's Dragon more adventures with Robin and Oliver and a new friend
Robin…Who? To be published 2020

About the Author

Jeanette Taylor Ford is a retired Teaching Assistant. She grew up in Cromer, Norfolk and moved to Hereford with her parents when she was seventeen. Her love of writing began when she was a child of only nine or ten. When young her ambition was to be a journalist but life took her in another direction and her life's work has been with children – firstly as a nursery assistant in a children's home, and later in education. In between she raised her own six children and she now has eight grandchildren and two beautiful great-grandchildren.

Jeanette took up writing again in 2010; she reasoned that she would need something to do with retirement looming, although as a member of the Church of Jesus Christ of Latter Day Saints she is kept busy. She lives with her husband Tony, a retired teacher and headmaster, in Derbyshire, England.

Join her emailing list on **jeanetteford51@hotmail.co.uk**
Or follow her on **https://www.facebook.com/Jeanette-Taylor-Ford-My-Words-My-Way-699235100160365/**
Or her blog: jeanetteford51.wordpress.com

Printed in Great Britain
by Amazon

24015413R00158